The Healing Field

A Young Psychiatrist's Battle With
His Anorexic Patient, Her Hunger
Strike Against God and Their Journey
Through the Dark Night of the Soul

Howard E. Richmond, MD

"The Doctor is effective only when he himself is affected."
—*Carl Gustav Jung*

Published by Mind Expander Press

This book is not intended as a substitute for treatment of psychological or emotional conditions that may require evaluation and care from a physician or appropriate mental health professional. The intent of the author is that the book be a source of inspiration and support for one's quest for physical, mental, and spiritual wellbeing.

ISBN: 1497475716
ISBN 13: 9781497475717
Library of Congress Control Number: 2014908866
CreateSpace Independent Publishing Platform
North Charleston, South Carolina

Dedicated to those on the journey
through fear and judgment
toward love and compassion.

Praise for *The Healing Field*

The Healing Field is more than a novel. It is a beautifully crafted and gorgeously delivered composition based on a real-life story. It thoughtfully reveals the bold and unabashed narratives of a psychiatrist and his patient amid their strengths and struggles, personal and conjoint experiences, and raw texture of authentic humanness. Narrating with a mellifluous and metaphorical voice, Howard Richmond offers readers a unique opportunity—inviting them to enter the private emotional residence of an unconventional treatment room. The book is respectfully and entertainingly written. Readers are permitted to peer into the personal world of a devoted physician and the complex challenges he shares from the confidential file folder of one woman who experiences a courageous awakening.

 —Wendy T. Behary, LCSW, author of *Disarming the Narcissist: Surviving and Thriving with the Self-Absorbed*

The Healing Field is a riveting novel about the healing journey of doctor and patient—a universal story of how the power of love can conquer fear and make you want to live. Howard Richmond is the rare physician who knowingly crosses unconventional terrain, with creativity and empathy, in pursuit of saving his patient from self-destruction.

 —Bill O'Hanlon, featured Oprah guest and author of *Do One Thing Different*

Dr. Howard Richmond has an extraordinary ability to share his wisdom and experience with his patients. He helps them with clarity, love, humor and great devotion. I've observed him lecture, teach and inspire his colleagues and the community for over two decades. In *The Healing Field*, we can clearly see how Dr. Richmond is able to support, guide and empower. It is a must read for anyone who is interested in seeing what the power of the human spirit can do in the midst of terrible emotional trauma. Kudos to both teachers: Lori and Dr. Howard.

—Daniel Vicario, M.D., ABIHM Medical Oncology and Integrative Oncology Medical Director, U.C. San Diego Cancer Center Director, Integrative Oncology Program San Diego Cancer Research Institute

Dr. Howard Richmond takes us on a healing journey through a complex web of human emotions, replacing fear, anger, shame and hate, with love, hope, courage and strength. His compassion and endurance combined with humor, intelligently sweep us into a world where the impossible not only becomes possible but real.

—Nina C. Payne, Author of *Moments in Time*

Howard Richmond's book, *The Healing Field*, is a story for all of us. Dr. Richmond offers us a clue to spontaneous medical remissions and how they can occur in a single moment of surrender and trust.

—Paul Brenner, MD, PhD, author of *Buddha in the Waiting Room* and *Seeing Your Life Through New Eyes*

Sometimes a story comes along that has universal power. In the case of *The Healing Field,* it is a story that forever changed two people's lives—and because they chose to share it, it has the power to change ours.

  —Krista Roybal, MD, Founder and Medical Director of True Life Center for Wellbeing

Contents

Dear Reader,

I wrote *The Healing Field* only at the urgent call of my patient, whom I call Lori in this novelized version of our story. "You have to write about this," she implored. "You have to write about the miracles, because it can help someone else."

It never crossed my mind to share such a deeply personal and intimate journey of one of my patients. Confidentiality, after all, is a foundation of the doctor-patient relationship. Yet on a deeper level, a voice inside me knew she was right. If she had the courage to bare her soul, and if our journey together could inspire others or affect them positively, then I was all in.

The Healing Field needed more than a dozen years of cultivation before it was ready to bloom. While names have been changed and some minor characters and events have been fictionalized to maintain privacy, the novel reflects the essence of what unfolded between my patient (the aforementioned Lori) and me (Henry Kaplan in the book).

Howard E. Richmond, MD
San Diego, California

PROLOGUE

Bullets for Jesus

March 23, 1976

LORI BLACKWOOD JOHNSON finished preparing sandwiches at her parents' home in rural southern California. Tuna fish, tomato, and avocado, sliced to perfection. She barely noticed Jimmy Swaggart preaching in the living room on AM radio: "Don't listen to the hedonists," he spouted. "God doesn't want you to be a homosexual."

Her blue eyes peered out the kitchen window toward the graying sky. Other things were weighing heavily on her mind. "The Lord rained upon Sodom and Gomorrah fire and brimstone," Swaggart proclaimed, nearly sobbing. A beam of sunshine broke through the clouds without warning, highlighting vegetation on the distant hills.

In four days, Lori would be turning twenty-one. She had married hastily nine months earlier. Lori's son was almost a year old now, napping in her old bedroom. It had been a shotgun wedding. That was the murmur from the congregants. *I feel so overwhelmed,* she thought. *How did my life become so confusing?* Lori didn't feel prepared for being a wife or a mom. But what worried her most was the fact that her sister Linda, who was four years older than Lori, had become so terribly depressed and withdrawn. Linda was spending more time alone in the bedroom each day, blinds shut tight, darkness consuming her light.

Lori's soft shoulders sank heavily from guilt. Linda had become increasingly withdrawn ever since Lori gave birth. *That's because I was able to keep my baby,* Lori reminded herself. *Linda's baby was born out of wedlock.* Lori flashed back five years to the time Linda got pregnant and told their father.

Linda was nineteen, Lori fifteen. Getting pregnant outside the bonds of marriage was a serious offense in the watchful eyes of their community and church. Lori's parents called an emergency family meeting and summoned the unwed members of their flock to the master bedroom. Lori, Linda, sixteen-year-old James, and twenty-one-year-old Gail gathered at their doorway. The oldest daughter, Theresa, was married and on a religious mission with her husband in Southeast Asia.

"Line up single file," Mr. Blackwood barked.

Like the Von Trapp family, the four siblings rapidly assembled in birth order—Gail first and Lori last, with James and Linda sandwiched in the middle. Mom, tight-lipped and quietly agitated, stood next to her husband at the end of their twin beds with their old-fashioned box springs and rounded spruce headboards. Lori's tongue furtively flicked the top of her palate, a revival of the nervous habit she thought had faded long ago.

"Forward, march!" Jeremiah Blackwood commanded with the authority vested in him by virtue of his position. Dads knew best, the patriarchal tribe assured most assertively and absolutely. One by one, the frightened children entered their parents' sterile bedroom. Linda, usually so sweet, pretty, and dainty—like an award-winning Japanese orchid—hung her head particularly low. All three girls had their eyes glued to their feet. James, knowing the heat was off him, breathed easier than his sisters.

Their father began with a familiar quote. "Every man is tempted when he is drawn away of his own lust and enticed."

Lori wished she could hold and comfort her dear sister, whose pain felt like her own. She longed to reach past James with her outstretched arms and say, "Let me embrace you, sweet Linda, and remind you I am by your side and love you dearly." But she dared not risk such an effusive gesture. The fear of her father's wrath and rejection kept her own anger buried deep in a vault of trepidation and sadness.

"Then when lust hath conceived," Father continued solemnly, "it bringeth forth sin; and sin, when it is finished, bringeth forth death."

Lori's mother swallowed in wretched discomfort. She had just made a significant tithing at church, and now there was hell to pay.

"Lori!" the elder Blackwood snapped. "Which verse?"

James smirked with silent jealousy. Everyone knew Lori was a whiz on chapter and verse.

"James, chapter one, verses fourteen and fifteen," Lori muttered blankly to her ankles.

"Your sister has committed the evil act of fornication," their father proclaimed, "and has become pregnant." He paused to examine his other two daughters, as if searching for impurities. "And because of selfish gratification of her own pleasure, she has inflicted deep pain onto your mother and me."

Jeremiah L. Blackwood was a proud deacon and treasurer of the church that Lori's maternal grandfather, a minister, had founded. Lori's paternal grandmother had also been of the cloth. The whole family tapestry was woven in religious fibers. Now Father would have to resign.

No one dared breathe. Lori felt the burn of his stern gaze, but she also felt the silent despair she knew her sister was suppressing. Unable to stay silent any longer, she blurted out, "What about the baby?" She was trembling at the knees.

Her father ignored the outburst. "Since there is so much immorality, each man should have his own wife and each woman her own husband."

First Corinthians 7:2, Lori remembered. Her eyelids twitched. *What about the baby?* she screamed inside.

Father pointed to Linda's flat belly. "The child will be placed in a Christian home." He glanced at his wife, who stood by expressionless. "And your mother and I have decided it's best that Linda go away while she shows evidence of her egregious sin."

Lori gasped. Linda muffled a sob. Gail didn't know what to do. James sneezed, drawing attention he did not want.

"Young man," his father said, "where will you find the following: 'The sexually immoral will not inherit the kingdom of God'?"

"Uh…uh…" James scratched his head. "John, chapter one, verse fourteen?"

Lori's body contracted further, as a flood of grief strained to be released. *Please don't ask me,* she thought, struggling to push back her tears.

"Wrong!" his father said. "You will memorize the whole verse by tomorrow night." He turned his head toward Lori. "Which is it?"

"First Corinthians, chapter six, verse sixteen," she mumbled through her clenched teeth.

"Correct. Now then." He swept his gaze from Gail to Lori. "About face!"

They turned around in unison.

When her belly began to bulge, Linda was sent to a Christian home in Los Angeles under a cloud of shame. Lori was left to grieve in silence, counting the months, weeks, and days till her sister would return, knowing how Linda's heart would be gutted when the baby was taken away from her. As soon as the obstetrician cut the umbilical cord, a middle-aged nurse, mask covering her face, whisked the newborn away to a young married couple waiting in the next room with adoption papers in hand. Linda had tried to scream, "No! She's mine! Give her to me! She's mine!" But no words came out.

A flurry of rain pattered on the clay roof interrupting Lori's thoughts.

"Satan loves those who lust after the pleasures of the body," Jimmy Swaggart cried out from the radio.

She lurched around and reached for the off button. Flustered, she turned her attention back to lunch, a welcome distraction. *I pray that Linda is going to eat today,* she thought, counting the plates, making sure there was food for everyone.

A loud pop reverberated at the opposite end of the house and sent a jolt of lightning up Lori's spine. She recoiled in anguish, assuming it was Father shooting a rabbit from the porch outside the master bedroom. Lori and Linda cringed when he fired at the furry creatures.

"Damn critters are eating the cantaloupes and watermelons again," he'd yell, reloading his Winchester .22 caliber single-shot rifle.

"Please don't shoot them," they'd beg to no avail. Their words fell on deaf ears. Eventually they gave up and tried to be far away whenever their father got out his rifle.

But this shot sounded too close to be outside, and Lori's mind bolted forward to the present. She looked out the side window, where she saw her father and her husband, Kevin, hurriedly leaving the fruit garden at the far end of the expansive backyard. Dad wasn't shooting rabbits. Lori's heart skipped a beat.

"Linda!" she called out.

There was no answer.

She took a quick breath. Her mind started to race. She shouted, "Linda! Answer me! Linda, please!" The silence only made her voice reverberate throughout the house. Lori sprinted down the long hall toward the sound of the shot. In the doorway of her parents' bedroom, she came to a sudden halt, as if her body had slammed into a wall. Her mind reeled at the horrific scene before her.

1

Broken Spirit

August 1994

"HOW CAN I help?" His voice was warm, yet tenuous.

Lori stared at her worn-out tennis shoes, commanding her feet to stay planted on the ground. She was tall, thin, and frail, and she was getting ready to die. Her knees were pressed against each other, feet turned inward, toes touching.

"Thank you for seeing me," she choked out with a half-smile. Her face wreaked sadness.

Henry Kaplan, MD, thirty-six years old and two years out of his psychiatry residency training, eyed the anxious woman leaning forward in her seat. He was trained to fix broken minds. Before him sat a broken spirit. "I'm covering for Dr. Rosen," he said, unsure of what he could do. He adjusted his tie automatically. "I take it Dr. Rosen spoke to you about seeing me while she's on vacation?"

Susan Rosen, MD, Lori's psychiatrist, told Henry that Lori was a thirty-nine-year-old married woman, very depressed, and in terrible pain since her failed back fusion surgery three years earlier. Dr. Rosen had been treating Lori twice a week for almost seven months. There was something about a sister who killed herself in the distant past, Henry recalled.

Lori felt his gaze just as a lightning bolt of pain shot down her sciatic nerve. She tried not to grimace. *Why does he keep looking at me?*

He couldn't help but notice her blue eyes, glistening with pain. "How can I support you?" he said, a touch softer this time, with an extra dose of persistence. A strand of her shoulder-length sandy-blond hair floated down to the pale green carpet.

She glanced in his direction and noticed his clean-cut brown hair and olive complexion, then she clumsily jerked her head downward. "I...I don't think you can," Lori whispered to his shoes, shaking her head. "My back hurts so much I have to die."

Henry's mind started racing with the suggestion of suicide. He wanted to know if it was old or new, active or passive, and tried to recall if Susan mentioned anything about her level of risk. There was so much more he needed to know about Lori. He wished Susan had spent more time with him exchanging information about her.

All of a sudden Lori's hands rose to the sides of her face as if being pulled by a powerful magnet. Her thumbs and forefingers began tugging and scratching methodically at her earlobes, like two mice nibbling on pieces of cheese.

Henry's thoughts slowed down a bit as his eyes focused on her ears, which were red, raw, and swollen. "Can I ask what you're doing?" he inquired politely, as he squirmed in his seat, hoping she didn't pick up on his body language.

"I can't stop picking them," she complained, her voice hollow. "I do this all day long." She pulled her shoulders up close to her neck, bracing against the burning pain.

Henry hadn't witnessed this before. Most patients with compulsive behaviors, especially self-harming ones, performed their rituals in private. Lori appeared to be incapable of controlling hers. He wanted to snatch her wrists and handcuff them to her chair. "What if you put your hands under your thighs?" he suggested, his soft tone masking his unease.

Lori lifted her eyes from her feet to Dr. Kaplan's cushiony black leather chair. "I don't know if I can, but I'll try." She spit the words out, like broken teeth, then struggled to tuck her hands neatly under her thighs. Resisting the urge to pick her ears had become an exhausting, futile, and demoralizing battle. *He doesn't have the slightest clue how hard this is.*

"Lori?" Henry waited until she gave him eye contact. "Are you presently feeling suicidal?" He didn't want to have to put another patient in the hospital if he could avoid it. "Do you have any thoughts of hurting yourself?"

Lori clamped her knees together. "I'm in so much pain," she said, slowly and deliberately. "I wish I was dead." Her hands squirmed under her thighs. "But I would never kill myself." She paused, then she muttered to Dr. Kaplan the words she had repeated to herself countless times. "I wouldn't want anyone to have to clean up the mess."

"What do you mean, clean up the mess?"

Lori didn't hear him. Her left hand escaped from behind her knee and shot up to her ear. "I can't do this anymore," she moaned, her nails digging into the raw skin of her earlobe.

Henry felt his body tense. He nodded toward her left ear. "Why don't you try again," he suggested gently.

Lori, engaged in a tug of war, struggled to place her left hand back under her thigh. *I should've never come here today,* she yelled silently to herself. *He must think I'm so stupid!*

Henry reached for the medical chart on the desk behind him and rifled through it. Lori was on three different psychiatric medications—two tranquilizers and one antidepressant. She was also on two pain-killers. He saw that Dr. Rosen had tried her on something for her compulsive ear picking months ago, which only gave her side effects. Henry noticed Lori had not been on one of the antidepressants only recently approved by the FDA to treat obsessive compulsive disorder. He knew Susan would trust him to change any of Lori's meds if necessary.

He looked up at her, searching for her full attention. "Lori, I'm glad you're not planning on killing yourself." He inched forward in his chair. "And I can see that you are in a tremendous amount of pain." He scanned her face, registering a quiver in her upper lip. "I think there's something we can do that might provide you some relief." He hoped he could deliver.

Lori drew in a deep breath and held it.

"Lori." Henry sought eye contact.

Finally, she let her breath out, then she met his eye.

"I want you to consider a new medication to see if it will help you to stop picking your ears." He noticed her eyes becoming misty. "Would you be open to that?"

"You want me to take more pills?" Lori vacillated between fear of something new and hope that whatever he suggested might alleviate her bottomless despair. "What's this one called?"

"Prozac." Henry noticed her knee bouncing rapidly up and down. "Well, it's not really new. I'm sure you've heard of it. It's been available for anxiety and depression in the United States for about five years and in Europe for the last fifteen. But what's new is that at higher doses, Prozac has been found to significantly reduce compulsive behaviors, like yours." He waited for her to digest the information. "What do you say we try it?" He held onto his inhalation longer than usual. To his surprise, Lori nodded yes.

Henry gave her instructions on how to take it and what side effects to watch out for. Then he wrote her a prescription. He asked her to call him in case things got worse.

"Don't worry," Henry said, trying to reassure her. "Dr. Rosen will be back to see you next week." He wished her well, naïvely thinking he was done with her.

* * *

The summer sun set with a reddish-orange hue as Henry eased his Nissan Maxima out of the parking lot. His lower back was in a knot, and deep down he knew it wasn't because of his patient load. The massage he'd scheduled for eight days out couldn't come soon enough. He noted the irony that his last appointment, Lori, had chronic and severe back pain, and he now was quite aware of how his back was throbbing.

Henry had been having muscle spasms for several weeks, coinciding with the increasing tension between his wife and him. Gabriella and he were spending more evenings in silence, both nursing their own wounds. Henry struggled to understand how things had changed so much in the two and a half years since they were married, and he tried not to get stuck in blaming her for all their marital problems. During their wonderful courtship and the first months of marriage, life had seemed so magnificent. He could easily resurrect the spark he felt the night they met. It was on a Saturday during the last year of his psychiatric residency, at a party given by a fellow psychiatrist-in-training. He had been introduced to Gabriella by a mutual friend.

"Nice to meet you," she said, smiling politely and extending a smooth-skinned hand. "I'm Gabriella."

"What a beautiful name." His large fingers and wide palm slid easily over hers, and he squeezed gently and nodded charmingly, as if she were royalty. Inquisitively, he gazed into her eyes, which were brown and almond-shaped just like his. Then he scanned her physical presence. Gabriella's straight-cut black hair was parted on the side and draped over her neck like silk. Her sensual hourglass figure and olive-skinned Mediterranean look intrigued him.

"My friends call me Gabi."

Henry smiled. "So, Gabi, I hear you're studying to become a psychologist," he said, eyebrows lifting in curiosity.

"I'm in a graduate program here in San Diego," she said confidently. "I'm in my intern year."

Henry began to ask many questions, firing them at her as if he was shooting hoops at the foul line of a basketball court. "How much longer till you complete the program? What is your area of interest? Where are you originally from?" He realized her eyebrows were furrowed, and she had taken a tiny step away from him.

"What is this, twenty questions?" She laughed nervously.

"I'm just curious," he said, retreating and holding his palms up in peace.

She ran her fingers through her hair and then began to question him. "What about you? Are you a real doctor, or are you still in training? And don't psychiatrists just give out drugs?" she challenged, hands on her hips, squeezing them with her fingertips.

Henry chuckled. "I'm in my fourth and final—thank God—year of residency." He noticed how smooth her forearms looked. "And even though the University is more biologically oriented, I know how important it is to find out what makes people tick." A twinkle appeared in his eye. "What makes you tick?"

She shrugged her shoulders, ignoring his flirtatious attempt to change the subject. "I didn't think you guys did anything but give out drugs. Isn't that why the drug companies do so well?"

He could see she was holding onto her bias as if she were in a fencing match. "You're right," he conceded graciously, putting down his sword. "Many psychiatrists just prescribe medication. It's an economic thing. Insurance companies pay us more to prescribe meds and spend less time with patients. But still, these 'drugs'—which is what I prefer to call 'medications'—can be life-saving."

"You sure are picky with your words." She laughed, dropping her guard just a trifle.

Henry felt they were in an English class for a moment rather than at a social engagement. "Words are important." He nodded. "They can be quite powerful."

Gabriella's eyes narrowed, and she looked deeply into his. "I'm not sure what to make of you," she said. "You're so intense. Are you always this way?"

He paused. "Let's find out," he said, shifting gears. "Why don't we meet again, another time, a different place?"

She gazed at him a few long seconds. Then her expression softened. "Okay, it's a date."

Soon Henry began an idyllic romantic courtship with the lovely Gabriella. The first month, he spent every day he could with her. The world around him had taken on a soft, warm, rose-colored glow, and the delicate scent of jasmine seemed to perfume the very air he breathed. Then, on a weekend getaway, to his amazement and delight, he uncharacteristically threw caution to the wind and proposed to her.

"Yes," she'd said, giggling happily. "Yes, I'll marry you."

Gabi and Henry's new life together developed like a well-rehearsed tango. Their admiration and love for one another made for a magical dance, or so it seemed. She was nurturing and attentive like his mom. He was strong and confident like her dad.

Their family and friends (the tribe) nodded their heads in approval. "What a perfect match," people hummed. "Psychologist and psychiatrist. Prince and Princess Charming. Both Jews, no less." They had even grown up living abroad, sharing similar experiences. Gabriella and Henry seemed to have so much in common.

But something was missing. And that sentiment had been growing stronger in the past year as they argued more and more. She wanted kids. Something told him to wait. He wasn't ready. His chest felt heavy; there was something missing from his life, and he didn't know what it was. One Sunday, he spotted a newspaper article about an eight-week workshop in stand-up comedy and noticed his heart pounding at the prospect of performing a comedy show in front of an audience. Ignoring the fear dragon that urged him to run and hide from the prospect of humiliation and rejection, he enrolled, challenging himself to break loose from the rules and labels the tribe expected him to abide by.

Each week, he got ten minutes to stand up on stage with a microphone in front of his classmates in a darkened comedy club in preparation for the performance on graduation night. Sometimes those ten minutes were terrifying and felt like an eternity. But more recently, he'd begun hitting the humor bull's-eye and getting more laughs from his classmates. It was just the medicine he needed to release the accumulating tension from his professional and private life.

Henry veered off the freeway onto his exit and felt a shooting pain down the right side of his lower back. "Damn it!" he said out loud. More back pain could put him out of work temporarily. He had too much on his plate. His father's lung cancer, once in full remission, had returned, and he would have to undergo chemotherapy. Henry's marriage, more often than not strained, was no longer a safe haven. As he turned into the driveway of their home, he clicked on the garage door opener, squeezed the brakes, and let out a huge sigh.

* * *

"Can I talk to you for a moment?" Dr. Susan Rosen stood at the doorway of Henry's office. It had been ten days since Lori's appointment with Henry.

He looked up from his pile of chart notes. "Sure, come on in." Henry motioned his colleague, thirteen years his senior, toward one of the two chairs normally reserved for his patients. He absentmindedly twirled his pen around his thumb and fingers.

"You're not going to believe this," she said cozying up in the soft, black armchair. "Lori reported to me today that she hasn't picked her ears for five days. The higher dose of Prozac seems to have hit the mark."

"Wow! That's…uh…great to hear, Susan." Henry wasn't sure how much credit he deserved. He straightened up in his chair. "I'm delighted she's doing better."

"And another thing." Susan lifted both eyebrows. "She asked me if you would be her doctor."

Henry's pen slipped from his fingers and tumbled to the floor. His eyes darted to it then back to Susan. "What did you tell her?" He studied the lines at the sides of her hazel eyes.

"Of course I told her that was up to you." Susan cleared her throat. "And that you might not be available. I realize you have a full caseload."

Henry blinked several times. His mind pulled him in opposite directions. He knew Lori would be extremely tough, if not impossible, to treat. She appeared to be a psychiatric train wreck: suicidal thoughts, anxiety, depression, obsessive compulsive disorder, chronic pain. He knew he should have said, "No, thank you; I'm overwhelmed. My plate of extremely challenging patients is quite full, and there's no way I can take on another. My marriage seems to be on the rocks. My dad is battling lung cancer. And on top of everything else, I've got a comedy gig in three weeks, and I don't know what the hell I'm doing. I think I'll pass on your offer." But he was supposed to help. He wasn't trained to say no.

"Um, sure. Okay. I'll treat her." Henry heard the words shoot out of his mouth.

Susan lifted herself out of the chair. "That's great. I'll call her and let her know."

He had no idea Lori was about to shatter the box he lived in and the world of psychiatry as he knew it.

2

Back Fired

March 27, 1955

LORI WAS BORN on a hot and arid Southern California midafternoon, a good four hours after Sunday service. Her mother, Margaret Blackwood, had attended church that very morning, "swollen with the Lord's Glory," as Lori would describe it. She returned to worship one week later to give thanks for her newest bearer of the cross.

"What a blessing," the pastor announced from the pulpit, "that we have such an exemplary role model amongst us. Margaret is with us this God-given morning after giving birth to a five-pound, eleven-ounce little girl, her fifth child, just seven short days ago."

The tribe heaved a collective sigh of admiration and relief, shaking their heads in disbelief. Margaret was known to all as the selfless mom who tended the children's church nursery.

"Mrs. Blackwood." The powerful man motioned to her. "Please rise before your brethren."

Sitting in the third row, Margaret glanced nervously to the left and then to the right. Her face flushed. She couldn't escape the attention. Slowly at first, then with mouse-like agility, she rose from her seat, lifted by the applause of the congregants. Her smile was weak and sheepish.

As soon as she was up, she dropped back down again, mortified by all the attention. She tried to dissolve into the safety of the wooden pew. "Praise is dangerous," she remembered being told by her minister-grandfather, a man who spent many years in the pulpit sharing his devotion to the teachings.

* * *

From the cradle on, Lori accompanied her family on their frequent pilgrimages to church meetings. Three times a week, and sometimes four, they gathered with their community in pews with kneelers while the pastor bellowed at them from his platform. He would shake a big black book in his hand and raise his voice to the heavens. "There's power in the Word," he'd thunder. "Follow the Word, and you will be forgiven for your bad feelings and bad thoughts."

The tribe always kneeled, prayed, and sobbed.

As Lori grew older, she still did not understand the Word, though the boisterous man in the pulpit ranted and raved about it over and over again.

"The Blood of Jesus was shed to save you sinners," the man would shout. "Who amongst you is ready to repent?"

At that, most of the people rose to their feet in the circus-like, tent-sized room, sobbing in a cacophony of brimming, bursting, and weeping gutturalizations. Those who cried out most fervently received the coveted prize—a visit from an assistant to the vociferous leader, who placed his hands on their shoulders and said a special prayer to wash away the invisible filth of their sins.

When she was in that room, Lori always felt smaller than her little-girl size, and the man up there on that platform, the pulpit, made her feel stupid and dirty. She felt like she was never good enough, that she must be behaving badly. Otherwise, why would he be shouting?

"Christ died that you might be saved," the man roared, beads of sweat dripping from his forehead. The worshippers flocked forward to kneel before him as Lori shrank smaller and smaller in the straight-backed pew, like Alice in Wonderland falling down the rabbit hole. The meeting ended when the preacher's booming voice invited everyone to leave their dollars in the decorative baskets that were passed from hand to hand. The organ swelled with uplifting sounds that vibrated all around her, and those who had felt the Word danced rapturously in the aisles, waving their hands in the air.

Something was wrong in those meetings, Lori knew deep within, though no one else seemed to notice. She felt so insignificant. And so very alone.

* * *

Fall 1959

A sleepy preschool-aged Lori waited for her siblings to step off the orange bus they had ridden to school earlier that morning. Her tiny mouth yawned as she headed to the couch to slip quietly into a summer nap. Lying on her stomach, one of Lori's little hands was hanging down and the other was motionless, pressed between the couch and her pink-striped shorts.

When Lori's mom came upon this innocent scene, she rushed over and shook Lori awake. "Get your hand out of there," she snapped.

Startled, Lori leapt up as if she had received an electric shock.

"No touching yourself down there," her mom said, waving her finger. "Do you understand me, young lady?"

"Yes, ma'am," Lori mumbled. Confused, she hung her head low and fought back tears. She couldn't have comprehended the sacred teaching that improper touching was considered an act of physical self-defilement and led to a downward spiral of deepening impurity and spiritual defeat.

Lori heard the rumble of the bus and the sound of her siblings' footsteps running up the gravel driveway. Her only brother, James, who was one and a half years older than her, burst into the house and saw her sitting in a corner, her eyes filled with tears.

"Slow down," Mom commanded, lines of consternation forming decisively across her forehead.

"What's wrong with Lori?" James asked as he stopped in his tracks. "Why's she crying?"

Lori's three older sisters filed in one at a time. Linda, her kindred soul, eyed Lori with as much empathy as a nine-year-old could muster.

"Your sister was touching herself down..." Mom tried to reconsider. "Down there," she said, unable to apply her vocal brakes.

The three sisters gasped in unison. James muffled a laugh. Lori tried to shut off the dull pulsing sensation inside her head.

"Will Lori have to go to church more to be saved?" James's eyes shone with a combination of innocence and mischievousness.

"We do not go to church to be saved." Mom thrust out her finger toward her son. "We go because we *are* saved."

No one said a word. Lori whimpered softly.

"Now everybody," Mom said, clapping her hands twice with vigor. "Go wash your hands and face. Now!"

In the bathroom, Lori fondled the soap an extra long time. Despite all the soapsuds and scrubbing, she continued to feel dirty, though she didn't know why.

"Don't worry, dear Lori," her sister Linda whispered, taking the soap from her. "You didn't do anything wrong." Linda gave Lori a tiny peck on her cheek. Lori's heart melted.

* * *

Spring 1962

Trumpets playing taps cracked the silence of the night. At the delicate age of seven, Lori was in the midst of a horrific nightmare. Mortified and yet still sound asleep, she shot straight up in bed. In the deepest crevice of her being, she knew something extraordinary was occurring. It was the second coming of the Savior.

"Linda?" Lori spun her head toward the empty bed on her left, where her older sister usually slept. Linda was gone.

"Mom? Dad?" Little Lori cried out, kicking the sheets off the bed and racing to her parents' room. Their bed was empty, too. It had the rumpled look that said two beings had been there moments before. But now—no one was there.

Lori ran to her brother's room. James was gone. Her heart beat like a drum as she bolted down the hall to her other two sisters' rooms. They were gone too. Lori shuddered.

"Oh, my God," she bawled. "Please don't leave me." She let out a gut-wrenching scream as full-blown panic set in. She was the one who, now and forever, was left behind. In the horror of her nightmare, a torrent of sweat gushed from her head and neck, then poured out of her ears and her eyes. She began choking on her own bodily fluids.

She awoke abruptly in a sputter of coughs and sobs. Daylight streaked through a sliding glass window at the side of her springy twin bed. She heard voices in the living room. Her dad was outside showing James where he planned to plant more avocado trees on their spacious country estate. Three feet away from Lori, Linda slept soundly.

"Everyone's still here," Lori rejoiced. Clad in an oversized cotton T-shirt, she ran out into the hallway to search for Mom, who was in her bedroom preparing to leave for church.

"Mom, Mom," Lori said, panting and wiping away her tears as a dribble of mucus collected under her nose. "I had a bad dream." Each word was followed by a gulp of air. "The Rapture had come. Everyone was taken to heaven. Except me. I was left behind!" Lori paused and waited for the hug she always hoped would come.

Her mom studied her youngest daughter for a solemn second. Hugs were not an available ritual in the family's tradition. "What in the Lord's name might you have done to dream up such nonsense?"

Lori looked down as she brought her knees together. Her tongue began sweeping her palate in nervous discomfort.

"Umm, well," she cried out. "Maybe I lost that dollar bill you gave me for the fair last week." Her eyes welled up with tears. "And...and I didn't tell you." She crossed her feet and buried her chin in her chest.

"Aha!" Her mom pointed to heaven. "The dream is teaching you that you must repent for withholding the truth. You don't want to be left behind. Because the truth always sets you free, little one." She smiled knowingly. "That way, you'll be sure to enter the Kingdom of Heaven. Tell Jesus you're sorry for not being honest."

Lori bit the inside of her bottom lip. "I'm sorry, Jesus."

"For not being honest," Margaret insisted.

Lori sniffled. "For not...being honest."

"Now go brush your teeth." Mrs. Blackwood turned Lori toward the bathroom and tapped her tiny behind.

Lori pouted and marched forward a step or two. Then she sneaked a glance over her shoulder. Her mother scurried down the hall and approached the front door. Several tears fell from Lori's big blue eyes and landed on her little bare feet.

* * *

Summer 1964

Lori and Linda had a special relationship. Linda was the sister closest in age and was so very much like Lori—soft and sensitive, with big blue eyes that said so much if you only listened. Though four years apart, they were almost like identical twins, each knowing how the other felt even before the other was aware. Theirs was a relationship that flowed effortlessly in spite of growing up in a family with unspoken high tension. Each girl admired the other's gentleness, love of animals, and appreciation of nature. Lori fondly referred to Linda as Bright Eyes because her eyes had a sparkle that opened up Lori's heart. The two sisters were always together, especially at those dreaded church meetings.

"They're so alike," their mother would say to other parishioners. Then she would chuckle and wave a hand dismissively with a peculiar tinge of embarrassment—or maybe it was jealousy.

Linda, the protector, stuck up for her younger sister. And Lori was ever so grateful. Especially the time Lori was nine, and her habit of sucking her tongue and flicking the top of her mouth got so bad that her parents finally took action. She didn't know why she did it; she just did. Maybe it was because she was too old to suck her thumb. Whatever the reason, whenever she felt nervous or afraid, she'd sweep her tongue repeatedly against her teeth, hoping no one would notice the gentle rhythmic motion of her neck.

Her parents, however, believed tongue sucking, especially by one of their children, was abnormal and just plain odd—a cracked branch on their sturdy family tree—and so they took Lori to see a specialist. Linda came along at Lori's behest. The specialist told them he could implant a tiny device on the roof of Lori's mouth so that whenever her tongue touched it, the device would cause a small shock. It was a special kind of behavior modification. Lori shuddered. Linda was appalled.

In the car on the way back from the specialist's office, Linda rustled in the back seat and cleared her throat. Her body arched in suspended anticipation. "There's no need to put something like that into Lori's mouth," she said.

Dad looked quizzically at his older daughter in the rear-view mirror, then toward his right, where Mom stared silently at the cars in front of them.

"Just let her be," Linda pleaded.

Lori held her breath. She tried to hide under the door handle. Her tongue was furiously working against the roof of her mouth. Would her parents listen to Linda? She stiffened.

Their mother returned her husband's glance. Dad took a slow breath and shook his head. "Maybe Linda's right," he agreed. "Lori doesn't need that unnatural thing put in. I imagine she'll eventually quit sucking. Let's wait and see."

Lori exhaled in relief. She put her hand on her sister's thigh and softly squeezed her lily-white skin.

* * *

January 1990

"The doctors and patients are very pleased with your work." Evette, the yuppie office manager of the multi-doctor neurology practice beamed as she handed thirty-four-year-old Lori a three-month performance review. "You are efficient and well liked, and you scored excellent in all five categories, especially filing, where you always take the initiative. No doubt you're the most meticulous front office medical assistant we've had."

Lori noticed Evette's skirt was just a little too short, and she flushed. "Thank you, Ms. Franklin." She accepted the document with a nervous sigh. *Have I really been performing well?* she wondered. *I don't know if she really means that.* She fidgeted in the swivel chair, waiting for a sign she could return to her work.

"Any comments, Lori, or concerns you would like to express?"

Lori hesitated. She'd learned long ago that her concerns and opinions did not carry any weight.

Evette sensed her apprehension. "Yes?"

Lori stiffened her toes. "Well, uh, you promised me a better chair." Her workstation had a chair that was too high for the low desk her computer sat on.

"Oh, that's right!" A grimace crossed Evette's face. "I've been meaning to order it. You should have it by the end of the month."

Lori waited and waited, but the chair never came, and it didn't occur to her to remind Evette of her promise. *Maybe I didn't really need it after all,* she concluded.

Her back began to complain, though. The daily scrunching over because of her chair put pressure on two of her lumbar discs, which eventually bulged out like balloons, creating shooting pain down the front and sides of both legs. Despite muscle relaxants, pain-killers, and torturous physical therapy sessions, the pain became unbearable. Lori searched for ways to escape the numbness, the tingling, the muscle spasms—but she found no comfort. She couldn't sit, stand, or lie down without feeling as if she were on a bed of nails.

She struggled at work, unable to maintain the perfectionist standards she was known for. Her friendly smile faded as the unwanted invaders of pain and depression conquered her space. She had to miss work to keep her medical appointments. The doctors she worked for were displeased and asked the office manager to intervene.

"The quality of your work has dropped," a tight-lipped Evette said to her one fateful Friday two months later. "I've talked it over with the doctors, and I'm sorry, but we have to let you go."

Lori was crushed. Her world collapsed. *They aren't allowed to do that,* her inner voice screamed as she emptied out her desk. *They're breaking the rules.*

In the weeks that followed, feelings of sadness, anger and betrayal accumulated in her body. She couldn't find a handle to her emotions. Her back buckled under the weight of all the heartache. The pain flowed like lava inside her, burning everything in its path. She kept returning to her doctor, but when conservative treatments proved futile, she was referred to a surgeon.

"Your lower back is unstable," the orthopedic surgeon said. Lori barely heard him. Her mind was buzzing with fear-driven thoughts of disaster. She'd never had surgery before. This was major surgery. Something major could go wrong.

The doctor pulled out an expandable pointer from his heavily starched white coat and pointed at the lower two lumbar discs on the life-sized skeleton model next to his impressive mahogany desk. "First I'll need to remove some of the material on the disc to relieve the pressure that's causing the pain. Then I'll put a metal rod and screws in your spine, along with a bone graft from your hip to fuse and stabilize it. When the bone graft heals, the rod and screws can be removed."

Lori clutched her husband Kevin's hand. It felt lifeless. *I'm so scared*, she said over and over in her head.

"Don't worry," the surgeon reassured her with a smile, flashing teeth that were a shade too white. "It's a fairly routine operation."

Lori had the surgery three weeks later. She was in the hospital fourteen days in a painful blur of immense discomfort. She left wearing a body brace that kept her spine straight and immobilized, rendering her helpless to do simple things like bathing and dressing. The brace was like a turtle shell that prevented her body from twisting, turning, or bending. Touching her knees or toes was impossible. She had to wear the body shield every waking moment. It was like living in a cage. She'd been told she'd only have to use it for a few months. But three months turned into six, and then twelve.

To make bad matters worse, she wasn't getting better. She was oh so much worse. The pain did not go away, and insomnia became a relentless, remorseless nightly stalker. She felt punished, as though her suffering were her due as the worthless, sinful person she was. The pain, the insomnia, the depression, and her disgust with who she was all swirled around her like an enormous whirlpool pulling her deep into its center, all conspiring to make Lori disappear.

"Your bones aren't fusing," the surgeon muttered from beneath a furrowed brow. "I've never seen this happen before."

Lori couldn't breathe, and everything in the room seemed to be coming at her from far away. Her doctor's voice sounded like it was traveling through an ocean as he attempted to explain that her pain and suffering were from a failed back surgery. All she heard was "failed." *This could only mean one thing*, she thought. *I failed.*

The doctor sent her on her way with a new supply of pain pills that did nothing and exercises she couldn't possibly do. The pain only continued to get worse, and it filled every corner of her life—a life that quickly fell apart.

* * *

December 1993

Lori sat cross-legged on the floor in the closet of the master bedroom. Neatly hung tennis outfits, well-ironed blouses, and a handful of skirts adorned the wall in front of her. Her husband's clothes were behind her, placed with an equal amount of deliberation.

Bloodstained tissues were strewn around the carpet near her bare feet. The closet was the only safe place where she could carry out her self-inflicted torture. Her fingers dug with fury and precision into the skin around both ears. *I'm in so much pain!* she screamed in her mind, but the pain didn't matter as much as the need to continually pluck at her innocent lobes. Her pajama top was covered in red. *Why can't I stop?* she cried out to no one.

She'd long since lost her job and felt more and more worthless with each and every passing day. She was disgusted with her back, her life, and her near complete inability to function. *What a stupid spine. I'm such a failure,* her mind repeated like a broken record.

Lori paused for a moment to examine a strand of skin clamped between her left thumb and forefinger. This one was long and thin. She let out a short sigh. Longer and thinner was somehow better. If she could get longer pieces of skin off, in a twisted way, she was a success. *I must be so awful for things to be this horrible.* Her hands rose again to her fiery ears, meticulously mining for nonexistent relief. Finding skin to peel had taken over her life.

It was almost four in the afternoon. The closet was dark and windowless. Lori hadn't left all day. *My bladder is so full.* She adjusted her tense spine. *But I can't pee yet.* Picking became more important than eating or caring for herself. *I'll have to let go with one hand,* she rationalized. Her neurological circuits were stuck on compulsive drive. Somehow, if she kept picking and peeling, the pain would end. But it never did.

And she couldn't stop. She did it every day, all day, sometimes up to eighteen punishing hours a day.

The New Year promised more misery than she felt she could bear.

She didn't know where to turn. The thought-drum of suicide increased its beat mercilessly inside her temples. Finally Lori asked her doctor for help with her depression. He referred her to a psychiatrist. The insurance company refused for months to authorize treatment—until she told them she was suicidal. That's how she eventually came to Dr. Rosen, and then to Dr. Kaplan after nearly five years of excruciating back pain, feeling helpless, hopeless, and sinking into a hole so deep that darkness engulfed the light.

3

Mystery and Misery

September 1994

HENRY DIDN'T KNOW what to expect. On the recommendation from a female colleague with back pain, he'd made an appointment with a body builder and massage therapist named Darla. She was coming to his home. He was looking forward to getting relief from the chronic pain and muscle strain he accumulated sitting hour after hour, week after week, in his office chair, absorbing patients' emotional distress and providing them the space to help unload their heavy burdens of fear, anger, and sadness.

Darla knocked on his door ten minutes late. "Well, hello there!" she declared as Henry opened the door. "I'm Darla." Her enthusiasm filled the hallway and living room like a breath of fresh air. She was tan, petite, and muscular, right around five feet tall. She set down a portable massage table and extended her right hand, still carrying an oversized gym bag in her left hand.

"Welcome, Darla," he said, stepping back to make room for her surprisingly large energetic presence. He shook her small hand and noticed it was calloused and rock hard. Her dark yet freckled skin, rounded nose, and angular jaw suggested genes of mixed origin, though it was a puzzle what those origins might be. Her eyebrows were thin, either

29

plucked or waxed. Without any fat on her body her breasts appeared disproportionately undersized through her tight-fitting purple top. Her long, tan, cotton workout pants were string-tied around her ankle-high athletic shoes. She was, without doubt, super buffed.

"Thanks for coming," he said, loosening his tie and unbuttoning his collar. After a momentary pause, he looked at her with a reflective smile. "Monique spoke highly of you."

Darla opened her gym bag and began unpacking towels and massage oil. "Monique is hip," she chuckled, her ponytail swishing as she nodded approvingly. "I love going to her home. Her husband's a real challenge, though, bless his heart." She glanced up at Henry. "He's a psychiatrist, like you." Suddenly Darla bubbled over in laughter, covering her washboard stomach with her hands as if to contain herself.

"What's so funny about that?" Henry asked.

"Well, it's just that he's so up here," she said, pointing both index fingers to her temples.

Her amusement was infectious. Henry grinned. He recalled that Monique's husband was a professor of psychiatry at the university and published papers on the effect of endogenous neurotransmitters in heroin-addicted laboratory rats.

"Yes," Henry acknowledged. "Some doctors live in their heads."

"Not all of them?" Darla asked with a wry smile. She put her hands on her hips, sizing him up from head to foot as if she were a gunslinger in a Western movie, ready to draw.

Henry shook his head confidently, like John Wayne.

"We'll see about that," she said.

The living room became quiet as she prepared the massage table, blankets, and oil. With dimmed lights, soft music, and his face down on the table, Henry slipped into a silent inner retreat as Darla worked on his overtaxed, under-relaxed muscles. His breath expanded and contracted slowly and rhythmically as he let his body go, grateful for the release of the accumulated tension. Monique was right—Darla was good.

* * *

Lori tried to ignore the burning, stinging and numbing pain of sciatica that radiated down her pelvis, left hip, left leg, and the back of her left knee. *I'm not getting any better,* she worried. This was her fourteenth visit to Dr. Kaplan in half as many weeks. Between Drs. Rosen and Kaplan, Lori had been in treatment over nine months with no relief of her emotional or physical pain. Minute by minute, all she thought about was dying. During most of her sessions she sobbed silently, trying to hold back the tears, while saying very little. She was terrified of telling Dr. Kaplan how overwhelmed she was with thoughts of suicide. *Then he'll surely want to get rid of me,* she thought.

At exactly five minutes before each appointment, she entered the waiting room and sat in the same tattered armchair. She stayed hunched over, her eyes cast downward, knees together, and feet pointed inward. She was too nervous to ever glance at a magazine and too busy trying to conceal the ugliness she felt inside and out. She never wore makeup or jewelry. Her cheeks had become sunken in the past two months as she began losing more weight. Her clothes were colorless and baggy. The frayed jeans and bland blouse—she almost always wore the same ones—resembled a prisoner's garb, part of her desperate effort to blend into the background and avoid being noticed.

Despite being in such a horrid mess and feeling like such a failure for seeing a psychiatrist, she felt a tiny bit less intimidated by Dr. Kaplan. *Today I'm going to take a chance,* she told herself nervously. Without fully realizing it, she was dislodging her massive wall of mistrust one small brick at a time.

Henry came to the waiting room and brought her into his office. He observed her excessively thin body and noticed her restless agitation as she sank into the black leather chair facing him. He planned to ask her about her weight loss, but Lori had other things on her mind.

"Can I show you something?" She glanced in his direction and swallowed. Her left knee was bouncing nervously up and down. "It's not…I mean, it won't…take very long to read."

"Sure." Henry eyed the cappuccino-colored folder she clutched in her right hand. He was grateful she had finally stopped the wretched habit of picking her ears. "Please, let me see it." He opened his hand and reached in Lori's direction.

Lori pulled out a typewritten letter and handed it to him with trepidation. It was addressed to the administrator of the hospital where she'd been treated for pain two years earlier.

Henry began reading silently. "I was an inpatient of Dr. Jonathan F. Stanley at the Pain Center in October 1992. I would like to issue a complaint about Dr. Stanley. Because of his negligence, my friend and fellow patient Tom Spinoza died." He shot a quick glance at Lori. She was fighting back tears.

* * *

October 1992

"Whatcha reading, Miss Glum-Face?" The handsome Latino came to a stop and locked his wheelchair between Lori and the newspaper she was absorbed in.

She grabbed the paper and pulled it close to her chest, peering over the top of the obituary section. "Were you, uh… did you say something to me?"

"What's your fascination with death?" Tom shot back from his wheelchair. He took off his gloves, revealing calloused palms from pushing the wheels.

"Nothing, really." She folded the newspaper neatly and smiled sheepishly. "I thought I might know someone in there," she lied, avoiding his penetrating gaze.

"Oh, really? A year ago you almost would have seen my name in there. 'Tomas Spinoza, age thirty-four, died of a bullet wound to the spine, happened to be in the wrong place at the wrong time.'"

Lori smiled involuntarily at the rhyme. "But…but you're here now?"

"Yup. I got lucky." He pulled out a photo from his shirt pocket. "God gave me a second chance. This is what I'm living for." He passed the picture to her.

She handled it like it was a fragile antique. The photo was of a little boy holding a baseball bat and wearing a joyful grin.

"He's so cute," she cooed, her eyes coming alive. "Is this your son?"

"Yup, that's Ricky," Tom proudly proclaimed. "He's gonna play third base for the LA Dodgers when he gets older."

"Wow!" Her eyes met his, and for a moment, she forgot she was in pain.

Tom had a youthful innocence that reminded her of Linda before she had become so terribly sad. He became the inspiration of the pain patients on the hospital ward, despite being paralyzed and in a wheelchair.

One night Lori was terribly disturbed at the inpatient support group Dr. Stanley facilitated to help patients cope with pain. In the middle of the evening session, Tom struggled to stay awake, and his head began to bob up and down. *Surely the doctor will see how sleepy he is and how he has too many pain patches on,* Lori thought. Earlier that afternoon, Lori noticed four narcotic patches—two on each of Tom's arms. He never had more than a total of two.

But the doctor didn't do anything. He ran the group as if nothing was wrong. At one point, Lori caught Dr. Stanley's attention and pointed to Tom, who was sitting next to her, his T-shirt soaked with perspiration.

"What is it, Lori?" the doctor said.

Lori froze. She didn't want to be the center of attention. "Tom has never been this sleepy," she mumbled. "Don't you think he has too many patches on?"

"You have to trust me with my medication orders," Dr. Stanley said.

Lori looked away, embarrassed. She couldn't believe it. She hadn't seen Tom this way in all the time he'd been there. Even his breathing was funny. She felt trapped, but who was she to argue? The pain doctor was a powerful man in a white coat. She was a lowly patient. And deep down, without realizing it, he reminded her of the powerful man in the pulpit back in church, a long, long time ago.

Lori spent most of that night staring at the ceiling. She dozed off now and then, only to be startled awake by the twitching of her legs and the terrifying sensation that she was falling. She fell back into a mild slumber. At four o'clock in the morning she awoke once again, this time by a frenzy of noises and activity out in the hall. She shot straight out of bed, ignoring her throbbing back pain, and put her ear up to the door. She heard people running to Tom's room next to hers.

The loudspeaker blared something about a Code Blue. She heard a rhythmic pounding sound. *Oh, my God. Tom's getting chest compressions. They're giving him CPR!*

Someone yelled, "Clear!" And Lori heard the jolt of the defibrillation paddles on his chest.

Lori, her ear pressed against the door like a suction cup, counted each electrical defibrillation over the next forty-five minutes in total shock. She stood frozen in time, paralyzed, traumatized, and nauseated. After a total of seven attempts at cardiac resuscitation, the noise died away. So did Tom's life.

Her heart cried out. *Dear Jesus! Tom is dead!* A horrible sense of betrayal swelled inside her. Why didn't the doctors or nurses do anything? And then guilt rocked her foundation. *Why didn't*

I speak up louder? I could have saved Tom. Oh my God! Why is this happening?

Later that morning, the nurses gathered all the patients together and told them that Tom had died in his sleep. Lori felt like her mind was going to explode. Deep down, she experienced the unbearable pain of Linda's horrible death all over again—and along with it, the guilt that she should have done something to stop it.

"Get me out of here," Lori cried out to the charge nurse.

She had been on the pain unit for eight days, and she was six days shy of her anticipated departure date. Unable to keep her any longer without her consent, Dr. Stanley discharged her against medical advice when she refused to be transferred to the psychiatric ward.

Upon arriving home, an uncontrollable fury sizzled through her entire system, like an electrical charge gone haywire. The overwhelming and boundless tension converted itself into a direct current of involuntary ear picking—a continuous, nonstop, uncontrollable, self-inflicted mutilation of her skin.

* * *

September 1994

Henry placed the letter down on the armrest of his chair. "What happened to you after Tom died?" He spoke in a soft monotone.

Lori wiped her runny nose with the fresh tissues and held onto them in her hand. "Dr. Stanley tried to transfer me from the pain unit to the mental health unit, but I refused." She swallowed. "He told me and my husband that he was concerned about how my heart would respond to the new antidepressant medication he wanted to put me on."

Henry nodded gently, signaling her to go on.

"He said I should accept the transfer—that it could possibly add thirty years to my life because of my floppy heart valve. He told me he didn't want to lose another patient." Lori sobbed and sobbed, fighting to get her words out. "It didn't make any sense," she whined. "I found out later from the insurance adjuster that Dr. Stanley had reported that I was suicidal and said nothing about medication or heart problems." Lori's body vibrated with her sense of betrayal.

"Dr. Stanley lied to you."

"Yes," Lori cried out, straining to catch her breath. "He lied to me and he killed Tom. And nobody is doing anything about it." She exhaled a long, low-pitched guttural moan.

Henry took a deep breath. He had never heard Lori so animated. Usually she was way too quiet and way too polite.

His eyes penetrated her gloom searching for an opening. "There was no way you could have saved Tom."

Lori lifted her head like it weighed a hundred pounds. "What?" she whispered, barely getting the word out. "What did you say?"

"There was no way you could have saved him." Henry repeated the words slowly and intently. Then, without thinking, he added, "You couldn't save him, just like you couldn't have saved your sister."

Lori's body convulsed in grief. "I should have saved them." She let out another wail. And another. "This is too hard. I just want it to be over." Her heart beat heavily. Her face was wet with grief.

Henry reached behind him and took several tissues from a box on his desk. He glanced at his watch and noticed the therapy hour would be over in two minutes. But she was his last patient and this was a critical moment. He handed her the tissues and waited till her breath fell into a steady rhythm before asking her the question that had been in the back of his mind for a number of weeks.

"What did you mean, clean up the mess?"

Lori squinted at him suspiciously, focusing momentarily on his brightly colored Jerry Garcia tie. "Clean up the mess? What are you talking about?"

"The first time you came to see me, when I was covering for Dr. Rosen, you said you'd never kill yourself. You said you wouldn't want anyone to have to clean up the mess."

Lori's eyes fluttered, as if she were in a trance. "It's been a long time." She shut her eyes and stopped talking.

Henry pressed his back into the chair. "What happened?" he asked softly. "Tell me. Please. It's okay. Tell me."

She took a deep breath and began speaking in a faraway voice. "My sister committed suicide. It was four days before my twenty-first birthday."

Lori's tongue swept her upper lip. "Linda used to be so full of life. She went downhill real fast after she had to give up her baby. She wouldn't go out or anything. She stayed in her room for hours and hours at a time.

"Earlier in the morning, I saw Linda in the laundry room folding towels. Lifelessly. I didn't think she could see me. All of a sudden she turned around and said, 'You're so pretty.' How strange, I thought. Her eyes glowed, but only for a moment."

Lori took a deep breath and sighed in defeat. "A couple of hours later...she shot herself...in our parents' bedroom...with our father's rifle. I ran in on her just after she did it. She was lying on the floor. Dead. But I didn't know she was dead. I believed God could raise her from the dead if I prayed hard enough."

Lori cocked her head to one side, eyes shut. "Her head had pieces missing, and she was soaked in blood." Her body shuddered with pain. "The rifle was still lying there on the carpet." She pointed to her left, toward the floor. "The blood kept expanding around Linda's head." Lori's stomach felt like it was knotting up. "I really believed God could raise her from the dead if I just kept praying." Her face contorted in pain.

"I fell to Linda's side on my knees and began to pray. Dear Lord Jesus, please bring Linda back," she pleaded, as if the suicide had just taken place, right there in Henry's office. "Linda, come back," she whispered hoarsely. "Linda, don't leave me! Bright Eyes, I love you. Jesus, dear Lord, please bring Linda back now." She sobbed, clasping her hands tightly to give her prayers more resolve.

Henry sat motionless, allowing her to recount the terrifying day that ended Linda's life and changed Lori's forever.

At last, Lori wiped away her tears. "Linda continued to lie there. Still." She blew her nose. "I could see the carpet becoming soggier and changing colors to a deep red."

"What happened next?" Henry asked softly.

* * *

March 23, 1976

Lori's father and her husband, Kevin, had rushed into the room that day, staring in disbelief at the scene before them.

Lori continued to pray feverishly, unaware of their presence. "Linda, what am I going to do without you?" she shrieked in despair. She grabbed her sister's limp body and clutched it to her chest. Blood continued to flow out of Linda's ears, soaking Lori's blouse. "Linda, don't leave me! Jesus, dear Lord, please bring Linda back now."

"She's dead," Kevin said coldly. "It's too late—let her go."

Paralyzed with grief, Lori swallowed her tears.

"Let her go!" Kevin commanded.

Obediently Lori placed Linda's body carefully on the floor. She couldn't stop staring at Linda's blue eyes, which were wide open, never again to close, squint, open, or blink.

Her father walked silently to the kitchen and dialed 9-1-1. Next to him, on the refrigerator door, was a cartoon of a woman climbing off a wooden cross. The caption proclaimed, "I ain't got time to bleed."

"There's been a shooting," Lori heard her father state calmly.

Still kneeling beside her sister's body, Lori stared at the rifle in horrid disbelief. *Where did she get the bullet?* She and Linda knew their father always kept his bullets locked in the safe. *How did she get the bullet?*

"Come on, let's get out of here," Kevin grumbled. "This gives me the creeps." He tugged on Lori's arm, but she pulled away from him. Then she was alone with Linda's body, Lori's twenty-year-old mind going in slow motion as she began reconstructing her sister's last moments. Somehow, Linda had mounted the rifle on the bureau. Then she reached forward, pulled the trigger, and the gun had fired into the right side of her head.

Lori spotted a note on top of the mirrored dresser. It was in Linda's handwriting. "I can't take it anymore," she read out loud, her voice trembling. "It's nothing that you did." Lori knew the note was meant for her parents, yet somehow she felt guilty.

Lori heard her father in the next room phoning the church where her mother volunteered every Tuesday, Thursday, and Sunday. "Come home now," he said tersely. "There's been an accident." He placed the phone back on the receiver. For a long time, no one said another word.

The doorbell rang, breaking the silence. Lori's father opened the front door. A policeman stood on the doorstep. "Coroner's on his way," the policeman said.

The words echoed in Lori's mind as if she was standing in a long tunnel. She looked down and eyed her blouse with horror, struggling to remember how dry and white it had been earlier that morning. She felt the ruffles around her collar. They were wet, warm, and stained red with Linda's blood.

"This is the quietest suicide I've ever seen," said the cop, a burly veteran with thick, leathery skin.

Lori pointed to a framed scripture hanging on the wall. It read: "The result of righteousness will be quietness and confident trust forever."

"That's why," she told the cop. "We're Christians."

The policeman stared back at her, uncomprehending.

The coroner came, did his inspection, packed up Linda's body, and left. Lori's father motioned to the kitchen. "Now, let's sit down and have lunch."

Lori couldn't eat. She was full. Full of despair. Full of terror. Full of confusion. Full of horror. Full of grief.

When Mom arrived home from church, she fetched a large sponge and two pails, one empty, the other half-full of water.

Lori followed her into the master bedroom. "Mom, what are you doing?"

Her mother was down on her knees, soaking up Linda's blood with the sponge and wringing it into the empty yellow bucket. "The carpet will stain if this isn't done right away," she explained, vigorously squeezing the sponge.

"Mom, please. Let's get somebody else to do that. Or let's just get a new carpet. Mom, for the love of God."

"No, no, it's not necessary, dear," Mom said gently. "I can do it. You go have lunch with your father, your husband, and your son." With that, she dipped the sponge into the pail of water.

4

Got Doghouse?

"HOW'S YOUR COMEDY adventure going?" Susan Rosen gathered her purse and a stack of charts to take home. She and Henry were the only two people remaining in the common area of their four-person compact office. It was nearly eight on a Friday night.

"I did okay at the graduation performance last Monday night," Henry said cheerfully. "Nobody threw tomatoes." He looked up from the copier where he'd been faxing a report to an insurance company. "People actually laughed. It was quite an experience. And I don't think it was because they were feeling sorry for me."

"Good for you!" Susan chuckled.

Henry hesitated, eyeing his colleague, and then said, "I signed up for another eight-week course. Starts the last Saturday in October."

"You're joking!" Susan swatted an imaginary fly between them. "Well, have fun, but—keep your day job."

Henry ignored her jab as he collated the documents. "No, I'm taking the comedy very seriously," he said.

"Comedy. Seriously?" Susan laughed. "That's funny Henry."

"No it's not. Being a comedian is tougher than being a psychiatrist." The image of Lori reliving Linda's suicide popped into his head. "Well, except when it comes to patients like Lori."

41

"How's she doing?" Susan slowly put her purse and charts down on the counter by the coffee pot. "I saw her briefly in the lobby last week. She doesn't look good. Is she losing a lot of weight?"

"Unfortunately, yes. Her clothes don't fit anymore. She hardly eats and has a hard time bathing or brushing her teeth—or just getting out of her pajamas." Henry frowned. "She won't even walk down the driveway to the mailbox."

"Oh my. What does she do all day?"

"Don't know. Not much. Seems like she's frozen in time—in her own mental prison of gloom, doom, and eternal self-damnation."

"What about the day program?" Susan was referring to the hospital three blocks from their office, which offered an intensive outpatient treatment program for patients needing a higher level of care.

"She won't go. Every time I bring it up, she refuses. I've told her if things get any worse, she'll have to go into the hospital."

"And that terrifies her?"

"Correct."

"That's a shame. It certainly complicates things." She paused a moment, studying his face. "Sorry, kiddo. You're really concerned, aren't you?" She thought for a moment and then asked, "She's still not picking her ears?"

"No," Henry said, shaking his head. "She stopped picking her ears."

"That's good," Susan said, nodding several times, as if to ward off any guilt she had left for passing Lori on to Dr. Kaplan. "How much does she weigh?"

Henry took a deep breath. "Before her back injury, she told me she weighed one thirty-five. Now she's much less than one twenty, but she's being vague."

"And she's how tall?"

"Five feet seven inches."

"That's bad."

Henry nodded in agreement.

Susan coughed lightly, clearing her throat. "Could she be developing an eating disorder?"

"No. I wouldn't think so." Henry's eyes widened, resisting the possibility of adding this to Lori's list of diagnoses. "If she does, that would be very uncommon. She's almost forty. And anorexia, as you well know, typically strikes teenage girls. I think she's just too depressed, obsessed, and anxious to eat."

"Let's hope it's that," Susan said. "Still, I wouldn't completely disregard the possibility of an eating disorder. You might want to look at any unmet emotional needs she had as a child."

Henry nodded mechanically. He barely heard her. He was focused on the one thing he knew for sure: eating disorders had the highest mortality rate of any mental disorder. And he recalled the medical literature didn't offer much hope for these patients. Judging by the look on Susan's face, she recognized the challenge he would be facing.

* * *

July 1963

Lori and her four older siblings sat in wooden chairs with their elbows held firmly at their sides during mealtimes. Their mother and father sat purposefully at each end of the stern, rectangular table, watching over their wayward flock. The daily activity of eating was an unspoken competitive family ritual in which the children had to perform flawlessly to avoid negative criticism.

"Don't talk with food in your mouth," Mom would say. Or, "Make sure you eat everything on your plate." Father typically said little, but he zeroed in on each violator as if he were aiming through the eyepiece of his rifle. Putting elbows on the table and chewing with your mouth open were grave violations.

Speaking out of turn, talking too loudly, not saying "please" or "thank you," or expressing negative feelings, could all get an admission ticket to the Doghouse.

The Doghouse was a large plaque fastened to the wall. Its gabled roof made it look exactly like the proverbial doghouse. Hanging under it were five dogs, one for each kid, with their names imprinted on them. Whenever one of the children broke a rule or misbehaved, he or she would get a bad mark, putting her closer to the door of the doghouse. Five minor infractions, or one big one, and you'd find yourself in the Doghouse.

The Doghouse was the family's homemade chamber of shame. Once in it, you'd get the silent treatment, ignored until Mom or Dad let you out. James earned the right to be in the Doghouse the day he turned nine years old.

"I told you to eat your broccoli and carrots son," Father repeated a second time during the evening meal.

James shook his head defiantly. "It's my birthday," he mumbled, gritting his teeth while clenching the steel fork and knife.

Father stood up and pointed. "You go to your room now!"

Little James slammed several doors as he headed down the hallway. Then he made a futile attempt to run away. At the front door, Mother seized him by his shoulders and directed him to his room. Then she marched to the kitchen and put the dog with his name on it in the Doghouse.

Lori sat frozen, helpless, and guilty by association.

* * *

That summer, eight-year-old Lori went on a road trip with her family for vacation. They stopped at an all-you-can-eat buffet, and Linda became too full to finish her chicken entrée. "I can't eat any more," she said timidly.

Wasting food was strictly against the rules, and now she was busted.

"Didn't your mother and I tell you not to take so much?" her father asked sternly, like an unbending minister fixed on saving a sinner. "Starving people could eat what you throw away. Haven't we taught you: waste not, want not?" His mouth turned down at the corners in an angry frown.

"I...I'm sorry." Linda bowed her head in despair and chewed nervously on her lips.

"The Lord giveth, and the Lord taketh away, so take sparingly." Father's voice reverberated as though broadcast through a P.A. system with the volume set too high. "Do not let this food go to waste."

"I can't eat another bite." Linda gulped with remorse. Lori swallowed shamefully, by proxy. Her foot groped underneath the table to comfort Linda with a touch.

"You are not to eat another meal until this one is finished." Her father had pronounced her sentence authoritatively, his purplish lips pursed.

Mom, shaking her head with disapproval, put the leftovers in a small Tupperware container and decisively snapped the lid shut. She vowed to put Linda in the Doghouse the moment they got home.

For three days, Linda went on a hunger strike, protesting silently with her refusal to eat a morsel of food. Then her hunger pangs broke her resolve and she ate the chicken, which by then had spoiled. Instantly, she became nauseated. That made Lori sick too, and she felt her stomach tighten with an unappeasable fear and a hidden mustard seed of anger.

* * *

October 1994

Lori's hand shook as she tried to get the key into the ignition of her black Mazda Miata. The garage was dark, except for the cracks of light at the bottom seal of the garage door. She was still exhausted from her walk an hour earlier. Her back screamed at her for abusing it, but Lori's compulsion to burn off calories made her ignore the pain feedback to her brain.

I have to fast today, she reminded herself. It was getting more difficult to keep up the self-imposed grueling pace of her daily five-mile walks. And she had imposed upon herself the rule that if she took more than eighty minutes to walk the five miles, she couldn't eat for twenty-four hours. That's the way it had to be. Otherwise the suicidal thoughts would be too intense.

Her body felt heavier all the time, and most days her hands, her legs, even her neck muscles, quavered by the time she was into the second mile of her walk. But she didn't dare miss a day, no matter how much her thighs burned, her back hurt or her heart fluttered in her chest. She absolutely had to neutralize the calories she'd eaten the evening before so she could rid herself of the disgusting mounds of flesh she saw in the mirror. Otherwise she would have to fast.

A sudden wave of dizziness overwhelmed her. She grabbed hold of the steering wheel, closed her eyes, and waited. *Breathe…one, two, three,* she told herself. When she could feel her head stop spinning, she slowly opened her eyes. She looked at her watch then turned on the ignition. *Maybe I should keep the motor running, and then I can die of carbon monoxide poisoning.* She glanced back at her watch. The leather band was fraying. *Just like my life.* She'd have to hurry, or she'd be late for her appointment with Dr. Kaplan. She hated being late.

* * *

Henry put down his mug of tea and crossed his legs. He usually drank tea during therapy sessions. He noticed Lori's fingernails, poorly manicured—by her teeth. Her breasts had shrunk a whole cup size and her buttocks were as flat as a board. Her skin, usually sallow and sun-starved, was pasty gray and flaccid, giving the distinct impression of malnutrition. Her face was solemn, cheeks sunken.

"Lori, you're losing so much weight," Henry said at the beginning of the session. "Why do you think that is?"

Lori stared at a protruding strand of carpet. *No, I'm not,* she thought, glancing in his direction. "I don't want to talk about it."

"Why not?" Henry straightened up in mild indignation.

"You won't understand." Lori seemed annoyed.

"Why don't you give me a try?" Henry took a sip of his tea, savoring its warmth and vanilla flavor.

"I don't need to eat like other people do."

"I see." Henry wrinkled his forehead. "What did you eat today?"

"Can't we talk about something else?" *I wish he would leave me alone.* Lori wriggled in her seat. *Doesn't he realize how fat I am?*

"Why won't you tell me what you ate today?" Henry turned slightly to set his mug on the desk. The clock next to the tissues declared the time: 3:12 p.m.

"I haven't had anything yet." Lori moved her feet sheepishly inward.

"How come?"

"I only eat from four-thirty to five in the afternoon," she said repentantly. *Why does he keep badgering me?* She wasn't going to confess that she'd been fasting for thirty-six hours. Lori pressed her knees together so hard they hurt.

"Have you been trying to lose weight?"

"Yes!" Lori flashed a flame of anger. "I'm so fat."

Henry felt a knot tighten in his stomach. Lori's unrelenting preoccupation with her diet, along with her obsession to be thin, cried out eating disorder. Her accompanying compulsive behaviors revolving around diet and body image masked the fact that this wasn't really about food but rather an unhealthy way of coping with deep emotional conflict. And he knew very well that without some miraculous intervention she was at serious risk of dying prematurely.

"Do you ever eat a whole bunch of food and then force yourself to throw up?" he asked quietly.

"No way! I would never do that," she said self-righteously.

"Good." She wasn't bulimic. "How about laxatives? Ever use them to lose weight?" He kept his voice even, not wanting her to feel that he was interrogating her.

"No!" Lori wrinkled her face in disgust. She thought about telling Dr. Kaplan that she took a brisk walk every single day, at least five miles, more if she thought she needed to burn more calories. And if she didn't do it right, she had to fast. But she decided this wasn't a good time to share any of this with him. *I need to lose the weight,* she thought. *He doesn't understand. There's no way he can.*

"Lori, I'm very concerned about you," he said carefully. "Everything points to your having an eating disorder, anorexia nervosa." He paused to notice her expressionless daze. "I'd like to check you into the hospital," he continued cautiously. "Today. Before this gets any worse."

"No!" Lori said, her facial muscles tightening. "I told you I'm not going into the hospital. I'm never going into the hospital again. The last time I was in the hospital, Tom died." Tears flowed down her cheeks.

Henry backed down a notch, knowing he could not hospitalize her against her will, at least not right now, and his options to treat her were very limited. She would practically have to be pointing a gun to her head, ready to pull the trigger, before he'd call 9-1-1 and have her committed involuntarily.

"Lori, okay, let's give this a month. You've been coming here almost two months, sometimes three times a week, and you're not getting any better, at least not yet. You've refused to go to the day program or the hospital. I can't continue to treat you as an outpatient if you keep getting worse."

The thought that he might abandon her sent a shock wave of fear up her spine. *You can't do this to me!* She trembled inside. *No one knows how hard this is.*

"Lori, don't you understand your control of food is the only source of power you have in your chaotic and disempowered life? And it's killing you."

Lori stared blankly at him as if he was speaking gibberish. Of course she didn't understand. She wanted to scream at him: *You're the one who doesn't understand.*

"So let's work harder together to help you find better ways of coping rather than restricting food. Is that a deal?"

"Okay," she muttered.

"Understand that if you don't improve, if you keep losing weight, I'm going to have to admit you to the hospital."

I just want to die. Lori tried to stop the tears.

"Do we have an agreement? That if you don't get better in a month, you'll allow me to treat you in the hospital?"

The need to appease him and get him off her back was greater than the guilt she felt when she responded deceitfully. "Okay," she mumbled again, head still cast downward.

"Please look at me and say yes," he said softly.

Lori's eyes twitched as she slowly and begrudgingly lifted her head and granted his request. "Yes," she said. Then she dragged her tongue back and forth across her palate.

Neither of them felt any optimism.

* * *

November 1994

The sign to the left of the intimidating hospital entrance announced, LOCKED UNIT—VISITORS PRESS BUZZER. A security camera aimed down at them.

"I can't do this, Dr. Kaplan." Lori pointed to the glass-paned double doors. A bearded male patient on the other side was having a conversation with no one in particular. Lori lowered her voice. "Do you think I'm crazy?"

"Lori, when you came to my office yesterday, you were dehydrated and dizzy," he said. "I didn't know whether to call an ambulance or drive you myself to the emergency room. You've become so depressed and suicidal. You never leave home except to come see me. You barely eat. You don't bathe. You say you just want to disappear and die."

Henry pulled out his keys and thumbed through them until he found the one marked "Do Not Duplicate." He shifted his gaze to her downcast eyes. "No. You're not crazy. You're feeling extremely anxious and overwhelmed right now. And terrified."

"Just let me go home. I'll do better." She glanced up at him like a timid animal, unsure of her captor's intentions. Then she returned her gaze to the floor.

He inhaled deeply. "Try to take a breath. Focus on what we talked about in the office. Remember, you're here to get help, and that takes a lot of courage. And, like I said yesterday, I'll be coming to see you every day you're here."

Lori swayed back and forth, scarcely breathing. *I really blew it,* she thought. *I can't be here, but now it's too late to leave. I don't know what to do. He said he couldn't treat me unless I went into the hospital.* She struggled to hold back her tears. *I'm trapped. I have to die. There's no other way out.* She stopped swaying and stared at his shoulder. "I don't belong here, Dr. Kaplan. Can I go home?"

Henry turned to face her full on, trying to ease her tension as well as his own. Getting her into the hospital was a desperate measure that took a monumental effort. Despite three months of intensive outpatient treatment with him, and some minimal initial improvement, Lori had spiraled down so rapidly and had become more disabled in the weeks since she'd relived Linda's suicide. He knew he had to do something to stop her disastrous, self-destructive trajectory. Now she threatened to sabotage their fragile treatment alliance. "You promised me you'd be admitted voluntarily to the hospital today. I told you I couldn't treat you anymore as an outpatient. You're too ill."

"I feel better now," she said, pleading.

"You look horrible," he said. Henry was determined not to get entangled in her web of denial, bargaining, and threats of leaving. "You gave me your word you'd be admitted so we could treat the depression and poor nutrition more aggressively."

Lori surrendered a sigh. "Can I go to the open unit instead?" she begged.

Henry was getting increasingly irritated. "We agreed that when you first get here you go to the locked unit. Otherwise the insurance company won't cover the hospitalization. They won't believe your condition is serious enough."

She glared at her toes.

"I need you to keep your word."

Lori dug her nails into the palms of her dry hands, furiously searching for an escape. "Maybe I should go home." She tried to smile but gritted her teeth instead. "I'm okay, Dr. Kaplan, really. Just let me go home."

Henry's gut knotted up. "Lori, I want you to trust me. Would you please just—"

A woman's voice cackled loudly from the speaker above the door. "Can I help you?"

Henry looked up at the camera. "It's me, Dr. Kaplan. We're fine." He turned back to Lori, sternly. "I can make medication adjustments much better and quicker while you're in the hospital. The staff can help monitor your progress. It's the right thing to do." His voice softened. "Please. Trust me."

She couldn't hold back her tears. "I'm sorry," she said. "I feel so stupid. I've ruined everything!" She bawled like a wounded child.

"It's okay," Henry said. He waited a moment. "Let go of your judgment." He leaned toward her. "Let it go," he whispered. He lifted the key to the lock and gently inserted it. He waited half a minute, then motioned to the other side of the locked door. "Shall we?"

Lori sniffled. "Okay. Okay. But when can I go to the open unit?" She was relentless.

"Once you've been here a little bit, settled down, and can show you're not a risk to leave or to hurt yourself, I'll transfer you." He rotated the key in the lock and pushed the door open. "Come on. Let's go in."

Lori, trembling inside and out, followed Dr. Kaplan. She felt like a hostage walking into a prison. *I must deserve this,* she thought. The feeling of being punished was oddly familiar. *I'm really in the Doghouse now.*

* * *

"I'll need to take your shoelaces, honey." Roselyn, the admitting nurse on duty, was kind but unwavering. She was a rotund, well-weathered, motherly type, and her manner made it clear that there was no use arguing with her.

"You mean I have to give you my shoes?" Lori asked. The tears welled at the edges of her eyelids.

"No, no, just take the laces out. We won't make you go wandering the halls in your socks."

Lori handed two plastic-tipped, fraying white shoestrings to Roselyn, who put them in an oversized storage bag. She rummaged through Lori's suitcase in search of anything else her new patient could use to hang herself or otherwise inflict harm. She turned back to Lori, glanced kindly at her pencil-thin midsection, and extended her hand. "Your belt, please."

Lori gazed down at her brown leather belt and fumbled with the buckle, which was caught in the second of the two extra holes she'd fashioned with an ice pick when her waistline had melted away along with the last ten pounds.

I would never hang myself, Lori thought as she passed the potential noose to Roselyn. Hanging was too violent. Disappearing through starvation was far nobler. There would be no ghastly mess to clean up.

Roselyn tucked the belt into the bag and made a note in Lori's medical chart, a large blue binder.

Lori had a sudden and overwhelming urge to pick her ears as she stared at her worn-out tennis shoes, now without laces, flopping shamefully around her feet. The tongues stuck out as if they were ridiculing her, reminding her of how, in her tennis tournament days, after a deep backcourt forehand shot, she could race to the net in no time.

"Please lie down, Lori. I need to get your pulse and blood pressure." Roselyn motioned to the examination table.

Lori mounted the table mechanically, as if she were entering a coffin designed especially for her. She closed her eyes.

Roselyn placed the middle and index finger of her right hand on Lori's carotid artery. Her eyes zeroed in on the second hand of the clock on the wall as she silently counted Lori's pulse rate.

Lori, unaware of much beyond her inner torment, lay still, waiting for the lid of her coffin to swing shut.

Roselyn made a mental note of Lori's slightly fast resting heart rate. At ninety-two, it was rapid but within the normal range. She whispered compassionately into Lori's ear, which showed no sign of the rawness and tenderness present several months earlier. "You can get up now, dear."

Lori's eyes fluttered open. She rose slowly, feeling dizzy, and sat upright on the cushioned table, her heart working overtime to pump more blood to her oxygen-depleted head.

Roselyn wrapped the blood pressure cuff around Lori's withered arm, but it didn't fit. "Poor baby," she murmured as she searched the supply drawers for a pediatric cuff.

* * *

The next morning, Lori paced back and forth in her room, counting the tiles on the floor. When the minute hand on the big clock on the wall over her bed ticked to 9:01 a.m., it echoed through the room like a door slamming shut. *He's late. What if he doesn't come?* Her heart was racing. *He has to come so he can get me out of here,* she thought. Each second that passed was more intolerable than the last.

At 9:07, Henry opened the door with a pleasant smile on his face, "How are you, Lori?"

She made a half-hearted and futile attempt to hide her anguish. "Dr. Kaplan, I don't belong here. I hate this place. I promise I'll do better at home. Can I leave today?"

"Let's take a moment to talk," he said as he settled into the chair near the window. He cleared his throat. "Why is it so crucial that you leave today, Lori?"

"I have a roommate," she began, continuing her worried march from one side of the room to the other. "She's in group right now. You didn't tell me I would have a roommate. She snored all night long! There's no way I could sleep. And they come into the room at night to check on you." Lori rubbed her runny nose, sobbing. "Please, Dr. Kaplan, get me out of here. I just want to go home."

Henry felt his spine tingle with frustration. He reminded himself to allow her to have her negative reaction. "Lori, you just got here," he said softly. "I understand that it all feels pretty strange right now. But it's important that you give it some time, and work with me."

She could hear her heart pounding in her ears. Her throat felt tight, like there was a noose around it. *He's not going to let me go. I wish I were dead.*

Henry watched her body stiffen and noticed the tears spilling down her cheeks. He tried again. "Lori, why don't you sit down," he implored gently.

She focused on the soft tone of his voice. Something about the sound of it always made her feel a little safer. She turned toward him, hesitated, then perched herself on the edge of the chair facing him. Lori glanced up and saw him leaning forward, his hands folded, waiting for her to say something. *I can't do this,* she thought. "Please let me go home."

"I'm sorry, Lori, you can't go home now. Remember, we made an agreement that you'd stay for at least seven days."

A wave of shame and worthlessness rose up from the pit of her stomach and threatened to knock the breath out of her. How could she have failed so miserably that she'd ended up here? It was hard to ignore what an awful mess she'd made of things. *I'm at this stupid mental hospital,* she kept telling herself. "Dr. Kaplan, please let me go home."

"You just got here, Lori," he said firmly as he handed her a tissue. "I know you want to go. It's scary being here. You feel out of control. Everything is unfamiliar." He quickly assessed her reaction. Her resistance wasn't wavering. "Maybe we can start again and give this a chance."

She stared at him as if he were from another planet. "Please, Dr. Kaplan. You don't understand. This is a mistake." Lori bit her lower lip from the inside. *I just want to go home and die.*

Almost instantaneously she felt the rush of warm blood mixing with her saliva.

"What is so difficult?"

"Everything," she said, sniffling.

"Like what?"

"My roommate. I can't have a roommate. I won't sleep. Not only that, I have to go to the dining room and eat with all the other patients there. Do you know how hard that is?" Lori glanced up at his eyes for a moment.

Henry scratched his cheek. "No, I don't. I don't know how hard that is." He paused. "Why don't you tell me?"

"Well, they only give you thirty minutes to eat. I can't eat all the food they give me in thirty minutes. And then this nurse sits near me after everyone else is gone, waiting for me to finish. There's no way I can eat with her watching me, waiting for me to fail." A flood of tears poured out of her swollen blue eyes. Lori gulped air as her body convulsed in spasm. "I am in so much pain," she wailed.

Henry knew he'd hit a raw nerve. He wanted to place his palm on her quivering back to soothe her. Instead he whispered, "It's okay. Let yourself cry."

Lori sucked her inner lip as if it were a pacifier. *I can't do this,* she thought. *I just want to die. I don't know what else to do.* Blood, tears, and mucus trickled down her throat, almost causing her to choke.

* * *

The next day, Henry stopped by the nurse's station to review Lori's chart before heading to her room for their appointment. His eyebrows shot up as he read that she had eaten a meager eight hundred calories in the two and a half days since her admission.

Lori was alone in her room when he knocked on the door and walked in to see her seated on the edge of her well-made bed, her eyes facing the floor, knees together, and feet turned inward. "Good morning, Lori," he said, trying to sound optimistic.

His cheerful voice bounced around inside her head like a boom box playing heavy metal with the volume turned up too high. She barely lifted her head as she addressed him. "Hello, Dr. Kaplan," she mumbled.

"How are you feeling this morning?" He eyed her cautiously.

She scanned his Rockport footwear, trying to comprehend how he could ask such a ridiculous question, wondering what she was supposed to say in response.

Henry settled into a chair next to the window and waited. And waited. When the look of confusion on her face turned to frustration, he decided to help her out. "How did you sleep last night?"

"Hardly at all," she answered. "This place gives me the creeps."

"I noticed you didn't eat much yesterday or this morning," he said casually. "You told me yesterday you feel a lot of pressure to eat and to finish on time."

"How can I eat? Everyone else finishes before I do. I can't keep up with them." Lori bowed her head.

"Eating feels like a contest you're doomed to fail, right?"

"Yes." She looked up. The tension in her shoulders dropped a notch with his validation, as if a twenty-pound weight had been removed from her neck.

"Was there ever a time when you felt comfortable or safe with food?"

Lori sat quietly for a moment, biting her lower lip. "Yes. But only for a short time. In high school. When I met Adam."

"Was Adam your boyfriend?"

"No." Lori blinked back a pool of tears. "He was a forty-two-year-old polygamist."

* * *

June 1971

Adam, a church member in good standing, was a well-built man with a wife and two teenagers. He developed an attraction for Lori when she was a pretty, blond, sixteen-year-old. One morning, in the well-manicured courtyard of the church, he approached her.

"Young lady," he said. "I see how dedicated you are to the teachings of our Lord. And I have never seen such beautiful blue eyes as yours."

Startled, Lori had looked around for her family, but she found no one close enough to run interference for her. "Uh, yes, sir, it is important to obey the Word of God and those who speak it," she stammered, unsure what she might have done to receive his attention.

Adam shared with her that he was a cabinetmaker and that he did not eat meat. He invited her to his home for a taste of his cuisine. "Perhaps you can read scripture with me at my home one Sunday afternoon." He had a warm, inviting smile that revealed a slightly crooked front tooth.

She found his offer intriguing. "Okay," she whispered with a blush.

At his home, Adam fed her whole-grain bread, assorted cheeses, nuts, honey-dipped apples, kiwi, honeydew, and other ripe fruit. He sprinkled the meal with fresh quotations from his tattered black Bible in a manner she had never heard from the pastor.

"Wow!" Lori's eyes gleamed with satisfaction at the lunch spread he'd just provided. She delighted in the fact that Adam was a vegetarian and didn't believe in killing animals for food.

He made her feel light and special. And he didn't care if she put her elbows on the table.

"A woman shall be betrothed to a man and serve him diligently," Adam said, the words dancing seductively from his lips.

A shiver ran down Lori's spine.

"A man in the castle of his kingdom shall be permitted to partake of several women in the name of the one who gave his life to all." Adam put his book down and led the unsuspecting Lori to the master bedroom.

"But what about your wife?" she wrinkled her forehead, not fully realizing what was happening.

"Do not worry, my sweet nectar," he told her, withdrawing the comforter from his king bed. "She is a believer in the fruit of polygamy, which serves the good of the orchard."

He sat Lori down on the white sheets, stroking her cheeks with the backs of his hands. "You will be doing a great service to the Master," Adam promised as his calloused fingers began probing her innocence.

Lori, who had never experienced any sexual contact, became putty in his groping hands. He laid her lily-white body down and mounted her.

When he'd completed his mission, Adam's demeanor shifted. He shot up from the bed and began dressing hurriedly. "Take the sheets," he ordered Lori, "and put them in the washing machine."

Confused, Lori stumbled to the bathroom and turned the faucet on, grabbing the nearest hand towel to wash away the dirt she felt on her body. Tears fell from her lovely blue eyes.

Weeks later, her father found a love letter Lori was planning to send Adam. She couldn't get him out of her mind and didn't know what to do. Jeremiah Blackwood confronted the guilt-ridden Lori, who immediately confessed her shameful sin.

"My daughter is now filled with uncleanliness and fornication," he wailed, pointing a finger inches away from her chest.

"Why hast thou betrayed me and fallen prey to this sinful lasciviousness?" He blamed Lori for the terrible transgression and left Adam completely off the hook.

Her father's condemnation cut deep into Lori's soul and echoed the man in the pulpit, with his thunderous denunciations. *Oh my God, I am such an evil person, such a terrible failure.* Like an axe splitting a log, the terrible tryst with Adam broke Lori into a fractured and rotten being. Her Garden of Eden was forever tainted. She had taken a bite of the forbidden fruit, and now, at sweet sixteen, she was branded with the unglamorous crown of the fornicator.

Now you're really, really dirty. You are ruined, damaged, worthless. You are destined to go for certain to hell. These brutal thoughts ran continuously through her conscious mind as well as her dreams. No matter which way she turned, she couldn't shake her rancid feelings of failure and worthlessness. She was tormented to the core of her being.

Lori began to sneak out at night in an attempt to escape her ever-present shame. Her sexual stirrings were driven in large part by the deep feelings of worthlessness she hid within. The window in her bedroom was a doorway to the wild outdoors, to which she would silently slip away undetected, waiting for a prearranged rendezvous with any of several young men who should have known better.

One challenging morning, around the time of her seventeenth birthday, Lori was so tormented by her intermittent nightly escapades and her feelings of guilt and self-hatred that she felt compelled to run away. *I just need to get out of this place to work all these feelings out.* With no money and just the clothes on her back, she hitchhiked to the beach about twenty miles away.

The first night, she tried to sleep on the cement floor of the public restroom, but it was freezing. Lori shivered and rocked on the filthy floor. When the sun came up, she brushed herself off and walked on the beach, then sat in the sand and shivered, then got up and walked some more. She repeated the cycle for several days. By the fourth day, she was so hungry that she sorted through the surf and began eating the least repulsive-looking seaweed.

The fifth night brought a glimmer of light and hope. A family on vacation, roasting marshmallows at a campfire, spotted Lori in the shadows several feet away.

"Young lady," the dad called out, cupping his hands over his mouth. "Would you like to share our fire?"

Lori froze. She wanted to run, but something told her to keep still.

"Come on over," said the dad, waving a friendly hand toward his family. His wife and young daughter held out their sticks of gooey delight. "We have extra food," he offered. The campfire crackled warmth.

Lori joined the family that loving night. They put a blanket down for her on the floor of their camper. She slept soundly for the first time in quite a while.

The next day, they drove her home and said good-bye. She received three hugs and waved to them as they left her at the end of the long, lonely, tree-lined gravel driveway.

Lori slowly approached her home's front entrance, a mahogany-stained door with a peephole. She wasn't sure what day of the week it was or who would be home. She hoped, though, she would be welcomed back, like a prodigal daughter evoking the assortment of worry, fear, admonishment, angst, and tears that any concerned parents would display.

She rang the buzzer. And waited. She bit her nails. She shuffled her feet. No one answered. She rang again. Fear chilled her spine. Finally, a woman in a uniform with an apron opened the door.

"Sí?" said the stranger in a foreign accent. "Can I help to you?"

"I...I...uh...live here," Lori said, confused. *Where is Mom?*

"Ah, yes," said the Hispanic woman. "You must to be Lori. Come in."

The newly hired housekeeper opened the door to let her in—just as Lori had a sinking urge to leave. Her parents, she was reminded, had scheduled an out-of-town vacation, and they wouldn't be back for nearly two weeks.

Lori's heart sank. *How stupid of me.* She groaned as she collapsed onto her bed. *To think they were worried about me. To think they would ever worry about me!* She sank her head into her pillow and wept like a baby.

When Lori's parents returned, they did the only thing they knew to do. They sent Lori away. They enrolled her in a strict, out-of-state Christian youth reformatory program, where lessons on righteous and moral behavior were drilled into her. In a group setting, the young penitents were called on one by one to stand before a microphone so they could confess their sins in front of everyone.

Lori sat in the back of the group, dreading to be called upon to report her evil acts. But she couldn't hide.

"Lori," a voice from the loudspeaker eventually boomed out. "It's your turn."

The shackles of shame tightened around her ankles.

* * *

Thanksgiving 1994

"What do you mean, you can't go with me to the airport tomorrow?" Gabi's voice was shrill and accusatory. It was a Friday evening, and her sister and brother-in-law were arriving from Boston in the morning to stay with them for a week through the Thanksgiving weekend.

"You know I have the comedy workshop every Saturday at one." Henry pointed the remote at the TV and shut it off. He felt like he was in the Doghouse Lori had described.

"I thought tomorrow's class was cancelled." Gabriella frowned. She stood over him, hands on hips.

"No, that's next Saturday. And besides, I have to go to the hospital in the morning to discharge my patient." Henry placed the remote on the smooth and warm walnut coffee table by his feet.

"That depressed woman who stopped picking her ears? What's her name? Lauren? Lisa? I thought you discharged her today."

"Lori." Henry rarely shared much about his patients with Gabriella, but since he was seeing her every day at the hospital, his wife knew Lori's first name and a few sketchy details. "The plan was to send her home today, but it didn't quite work out."

"Why not?" Gabi tightened her knuckles.

"She got cold feet. That's not uncommon. Patients get used to the safety and structure of the hospital, they start to get better, and then when it's time to be discharged, they get scared to go back to the same environment where they were before they ended up in the hospital." Henry rose from the off-white sectional sofa he'd been lounging on.

"How long has she been in the hospital?" Gabriella put her hands down by her sides.

"About six weeks." Henry was curious as to why Gabi had all of a sudden taken an interest in Lori.

"Six weeks? How come it's taken so long?"

"Are you kidding? She's my most difficult patient. It's real slow work. Besides the depression, she has an eating disorder. She weighed a hundred and twelve pounds on admission. She wanted to leave every day for the first week. Then she started settling in, eating and bathing regularly, and making some real progress. Now she weighs one eighteen."

"Very good, Dr. Kaplan." Gabi half-pretended to be her dissertation committee chairperson, grilling Henry on his treatment approach. In another year and a half, she'd be earning her PhD and would be a fully licensed therapist. "What's your psychodynamic formulation, Doctor?"

Henry wondered if she really wanted a straight answer. "Her compulsive behavior around food seems to have replaced the compulsion to pick her ears. These maladaptive coping mechanisms are fueled by a mountain of guilt, shame, and worthlessness, not to mention repressed anger stemming from a rigid family system and strict religious upbringing in which she was shamed if she violated the rules." Henry stopped to confirm her interest and that she was tracking his words.

"Go on." Gabi's crossed her arms over her chest.

"Basically she's trapped in a prison of her past that keeps her hostage in the present, driving her to think about suicide all the time." Henry scratched his nose. "On top of that, she has unrelenting back pain, and the medications haven't been helping."

Gabi gently clapped her hands. "You're finally talking like a psychotherapist." She smiled insincerely. "Maybe all those drugs you're giving her make her worse and give her side effects so she stays in the hospital longer," she teased.

"Thank you very much for your unsolicited support," he responded sarcastically. "By the way," Henry's eyes spoke condescension, "it's medication."

"What?"

"Medication. Not drugs." Henry headed for the kitchen.

"Oh, Mr. Perfect with his words! You can't take a little joke?" Gabi huffed up the stairs to the bedroom. "I'll go to the airport myself," she shouted. "You go see your patient and take her with you to your stupid class." She slammed the door.

Henry flung open the refrigerator, pulled out a beer, twisted the top off, and downed a quarter of the bottle with one big swig.

5

Number and Number

HENRY'S SHOULDERS ACHED as he struggled to match the steady rhythm of Darla's push-ups in the mirrored and carpeted garage of her condominium. Side by side, they pressed their bodies up and down. She breezed through the set like it was nothing, while he had to give it every ounce of determination he could muster.

"Thirty-two…thirty-three…thirty-four…and…thirty-five," Darla announced cheerfully. Then she bounced up to grab the towel from one of several weight benches.

Both Henry and Gabi had been working out with Darla at her condo for months, although each came alone on separate days. Henry looked forward to his time with Darla because his body was becoming stronger and he loved to banter with her about healing mind and body.

"Thirty-five push-ups," Henry grunted as he collapsed over his hands, his chest muscles vibrating in exhaustion. "Four months ago I could barely do eight. I never imagined I could do thirty-five."

Darla giggled like a schoolgirl.

"What's so funny?" Henry sat up and wiped his brow with a hand towel.

"That's just it," Darla said with palms and arms extended upward. "You never imagined you could do thirty-five. Then slowly, very slowly, your mind lets go of words like *can't* and *never.* You see that you can do much more than you ever imagined."

"Yes, yes, I see that very clearly." Henry tossed his towel aside. "You're good. That's exactly what I try to teach my patients. How to train their minds to let go of the beliefs that keep them stuck in their—"

"Speaking of stuck, I almost forgot to tell you," Darla said. She pointed toward the treadmill. She hit start and set the speed at 2.5 miles per hour with a 5 percent incline.

Henry, accustomed to Darla's abruptness, stepped up to the conveyor belt as the workout shifted from weight-bearing to cardio. "What's that?" He grabbed the handles of the treadmill for support.

"Joanna has totally turned a corner in her training." Darla looked at his reflection in the wall-to-wall mirror in front of them.

"Has she?" The news got his attention. Darla had referred several of her clients to him, and Joanna's case had been particularly interesting. She'd been battling obesity most of her life. When she started working with Darla, she'd made good progress at first, but then she hit a wall. When three months went by with no improvement in her fitness—even though Joanna continued to work hard at it—Darla suggested she see Henry.

"It's pretty amazing," Darla gushed as she increased the speed to 3.5 miles per hour and the incline to 10 percent. "In the last two weeks, her cardio numbers have improved, and we've been able to add more weight to almost all of her resistance exercises. And get this—she lost another five pounds."

Henry walked briskly and let his arms swing by his sides. He was impressed. The ethics of confidentiality prevented him from discussing details of Joanna's treatment with Darla, but he could certainly listen. And what he was hearing made sense in light of what he'd seen. Two weeks before, Joanna had made a significant breakthrough in their work together, with some important revelations about why her body might have been holding on to the excess weight. She realized that what she'd always brushed off as her father's annoying, intoxicated behavior when she was a preteen actually bordered on incest. It was invasive, humiliating, psychologically damaging, and a gross violation of Joanna's boundaries. That was when she'd started putting on the weight. By the time she turned sixteen, she was a hundred pounds overweight.

"Joanna told me about her father, and what he did to her when she was a kid," Darla went on. "She was really broken up when she saw it for what it was. Do you think that's why she's losing weight again?" She pressed the speed button till it registered 4.5 miles per hour. The treadmill whined pleasantly.

Henry began a light jog. "That sure makes a lot of sense," he replied. "I also think the work you've been doing with her has helped her become ready to see the painful truth." His feet hit the rubber belt with a loud rhythmic drumbeat.

Darla nodded. "I see it all the time. Physical activity makes people feel better—not just physically, but mentally and spiritually as well. It carries over in everything they do."

"Yes. And it takes a lot of courage to face the pain of emotional wounds," Henry said, panting. "You help your clients become stronger in their bodies so their minds are more able to engage in the psychological work."

"And that's when you come in and teach them how." Darla burst out in laughter as she reached over and bumped the speed up to six miles per hour. "Time to run, Doctor Henry!"

* * *

February 1995

Henry shifted into third gear and accelerated as he entered the freeway ramp on the drive to his office. The sun glared down from the eastern sky, illuminating the stop-and-go traffic below. He glanced at the digital clock on his dashboard. If this kept up, he'd be at least ten minutes late for his first patient. Then, like dominoes, every one thereafter would be ten minutes late, and he was already feeling the cumulative weight of running behind the whole day before it even started. His hands gripped the steering wheel tighter.

But he had another distraction on his mind, one that took him on stage in his continuing pursuit of comedy. Stand-up was a roller coaster ride through fear he had decided he was crazy enough to take on. Performing once, or sometimes twice a week, at a club or bar, Henry had no place to hide. Alone, he had to expose himself, risking ridicule and rejection. As budding comic, he had to be writer, editor, director, and performer all in one. Except for acting in high school plays, he was a novice in this strange new world he found exciting, intriguing, and terrifying.

He feared not only being heckled but being found out. What if other doctors—or his patients—discovered he was breaking ranks and doing stand-up comedy? They certainly wouldn't approve. Doctors were not supposed to be comedians. Sickness wasn't funny. Dr. Rosen had suggested he use a nom de plume. "That's French for pseudonym," she explained.

"Yes," Henry agreed. "I'll change my name when I go on stage. That way, it's less likely I'll be discovered." He came up with a stage name: "Henry Newman." He would become...a *new man*!

Dr. Newman worked hard to make people laugh. Dr. Kaplan worked hard too, but people seemed more likely to cry, especially Lori. Being a professional, Dr. Kaplan concealed personal details about himself. Dr. Newman, on the other hand, had to learn to reveal to his audience things that were personal—and therefore most relevant—and then, try to make it funny. He was not used to that.

Henry felt vulnerable because of Dr. Newman. But despite the vulnerability, or perhaps because of it, he continued to perform. When audiences laughed at his material, he felt satisfied and worthy.

Sometimes only a few people, most of them intoxicated, stayed to see his three- to five-minute set. When they just stared blankly, ignored him completely, or, worse yet, hurled insults at him, time slowed, and he felt shame, embarrassment, and weighed down. Yet he hung in there, challenging himself to get back up on the stage again and again. And as he continued to reinvent himself onstage, he was in fact becoming a new man, though he couldn't quite imagine just how much he was changing.

As he approached the underground parking of his office, eleven minutes late, he shifted his focus again. He had a full roster of patients to see. And his most challenging one, Lori, whom he discharged from her second hospitalization less than a week earlier, was scheduled for the end of the day. Her condition seemed to worsen every day. Lori's prognosis was severely guarded, at best. She could die from a number of complications associated with her eating disorder. He quickly parked his car and ran up the back stairs to his second floor office.

To his relief, his first scheduled appointment of the day cancelled at the last minute. "Thank you, Mrs. McCallum," he said aloud, genuinely grateful for her cancellation and the time it opened up for him to take a moment for himself. Henry let out a deep sigh. He pushed his soft leather chair away from the desk, leaned back, folded his arms behind his head, and put his feet up on the polished oak surface of an end table.

He scanned his professionally appointed office, with its two black leather swivel chairs, the austere lamp in the corner, and the numerous framed certificates and diplomas on the wall. For some reason everything now looked very drab and uninteresting. He stood up, opened the blinds that covered the window, and took a step back, basking in the warm, natural light that flooded the room. Why had he never noticed just how the beautiful cluster of evergreens outside welcomed him? He took a deep breath and let it out very slowly, a quiet wave of optimism coaxing a hint of a smile from the corners of his lips.

Henry turned to see the early morning light reflecting off the glass that covered his framed diplomas, medical degree, and licenses adorning most of one wall and part of another. He flushed with embarrassment as he remembered the day he'd hung out his shingle. The first thing he'd done was to unpack all of these from their big cardboard box. He'd dusted each one with a cloth and hung them up where all his new patients would see them.

He'd worked hard enough for them, that was true. But looking at them now, he had a vaguely disturbing sense that they signified his membership in somebody else's tribe. There was a time when he thought he needed proof of his expertise to let his patients know what a good doctor he was. He realized now that those documents sometimes did more to create a barrier between himself and his patients than to reassure them. Besides, what did all those credentials mean if he hadn't learned enough to help Lori? He resolved he would rearrange his office to create a softer, gentler, more welcoming environment.

Later that evening, a few minutes past six o'clock, Lori sat down in the same chair she always sat in and squared off in front of Dr. Kaplan for her session.

Henry took a deep breath. "Good evening, Lori." He noticed that her sad, downcast blue eyes seemed more sunken than ever.

"Thanks for seeing me," Lori said politely.

"You're welcome, Lori. Have you eaten today?"

I hate when he asks me about food, Lori thought. A daily mental food inventory kept her mind abuzz as she tracked the very few calories, carbohydrates, proteins, and insignificant grams of fat she consumed. The restriction of food was literally consuming her until she looked like a starving chicken. "Yes, Dr. Kaplan, I ate today. Could we please talk about something else?"

Henry closed his eyes momentarily, took a deep breath and then let it out slowly, releasing his frustration. He worried about her. How could he help if she wouldn't even answer these simple questions? "What did you eat today?" he persisted.

Lori flinched. She shook her head. "I don't want to talk about it," she grumbled, sitting limply in her chair, staring at her feet.

"Why not, Lori?" he asked.

She shook her head defiantly. "You don't understand!" Her voice got noticeably stronger.

"What don't I understand?"

"I'm too fat," she shot back, her meekness narrowly overshadowed by her annoyance. She lifted her eyelids and glared at Dr. Kaplan for half a second, then she remorsefully returned her gaze to the floor. She shook her head again. "I'm too fat."

He glanced at her scrawny, drooping frame. She was beyond skinny. "Fat!" he said, incredulously. "You're holocaust-thin. Like a concentration camp survivor."

She pulled herself deeper into her seat in a futile effort to hide from her relentless sensation of being morbidly obese. *I wish I was dead.* Tears streamed down her hollow cheeks, no sounds coming from her mouth. Her denial was suffocating.

He'd put in so much effort for so many months, with no more than a shred of noticeable progress. She'd stopped picking mercilessly at her ears, but he honestly couldn't say he knew why. Was it the medication? Maybe. But in every other way she was as troubled as the day she first walked into his office, perhaps even more so.

"Lori," he said. "Tell me, what are you feeling right now?"

Her hunched body stiffened even more. *What does he mean, what am I feeling? What kind of question is that? What do feelings have to do with anything? I'm pathetic. A rotten failure. Nothing but bad things have happened to me and everyone around me, and it's all my fault. I don't deserve to be in this world. What difference does it make what I feel?* The tears dripped from her chin onto the frayed hem of her blouse.

"I don't know what you want me to say," she sobbed.

Henry waited for her to reach for the tissues. "Don't you realize how dangerously thin you are?"

Lori couldn't give him the answer he wanted, because she knew she wasn't thin at all. She was disgustingly, repulsively, morbidly obese. It was excruciating to sit there with him watching her, paying attention to her every move. She couldn't stand it any longer. "Dr. Kaplan," she blurted out. "You don't understand, do you? You don't have a clue—that I am so miserably fat!" She looked down at her body. Repulsed by the sight, she winced.

"What did you eat today?" Henry decided to try again.

Lori clamped her knees together. *I wish I was dead.* "I had a nonfat yogurt, three celery sticks, fourteen almonds, and one slice of diet bread with diet margarine and diet jam," she said.

"That's all?" Henry was shocked at her menu.

"I told you, I don't require much food." Lori strained to sound convincing, but she was weak from lack of nutrition. "Three hundred and fifty calories a day is all I need."

"Oh, Lori." Henry shook his head. "What are you trying to do?"

She shook her head. *He really doesn't understand.*

Henry sighed. "This isn't working. How much do you weigh now?"

"Please, can we talk about something else? I'm fine, really."

"No, we can't. How much do you weigh?" he repeated with more intensity.

"One hundred and three pounds."

"Oh, geez!"

"If I can get below a hundred pounds, then I'll eat more," she insisted.

"No, no, no. Three weeks ago you said, 'If I get below a hundred and ten pounds, then I'll eat more.' Remember? Then last week you said, 'If I get below a hundred and five pounds I'll eat more.' Now it's below a hundred. Then what? Ninety-five? Ninety?"

"But really, Dr. Kaplan. I know that if I can get below a hundred pounds I'll feel better. And then I can start eating more."

"Look," he said, letting her feel his deep concern—and frustration. "We've negotiated the numbers again and again. You've promised and promised and then have gone back on your promises and then promised again. Each time, you decide on a magic number you want to see on the scale and tell me you'll start eating when you get there. But each time the number is lower than the previous one, and still it's never good enough. What number will it take? You're trying to make your pain get numb. And then number. It's not working." He knew the futility of playing this number game with her. It accomplished nothing except to keep her talking, however reluctantly.

Lori closed her eyes. "I'll feel better when I have only two digits," she insisted breathlessly.

Henry bristled. "Lori, that's just a trick your mind is playing on you. It's like the minus points your mom and dad gave you to put you in the Doghouse when you were a kid. You never give yourself any points on the plus side. No matter how much you deprive yourself of food, or how much you exercise, it's never good enough. There are no positive points in this game. You're like a donkey with a carrot dangling in front of your nose. You'll never be able to feel good enough or worthy enough, no matter how low your weight gets. That's not the way to find yourself. You need to feed yourself, take care of yourself, and let me help you find the way to see that you have value in this world."

Henry sat back in his chair and softened the intensity of his words. "Forget about losing any more weight. You're going to need to go to the hospital again," he said, doing his best to keep the tone of his voice caring and compassionate. What he said about the hospital wasn't an idle threat to get her to comply. There was the ever increasing probability that if Lori kept on her present course, she would literally starve herself to death. "You're not making it on your own."

Lori dug her fingers into her palms. "I'm not going back." She was determined not to let him get inside the thin veil of control she had so carefully arranged around her body. Nevertheless, like a radio broadcast, her mind started to blare: *If you'd have been a better person, if you'd have performed better, then bad things wouldn't keep happening to you.*

"You could die if you don't eat more," Henry said, his jaws clenched. His entire body strained against the intensity of her combativeness. He'd consulted with his associates and searched the medical libraries, but all he'd gotten for his efforts was further confirmation of how difficult this condition could be and how dangerous.

"I'd rather die than eat," she fired back. The pain in her back made every movement a reminder of her utter failure as a human being, her body the receptacle of her shame and guilt.

Henry sighed, frustrated to new depths. His determined but futile efforts to impress upon her how her behavior threatened her very well-being seemed to have little impact on her. He wondered if it somehow contributed to her self-inflicted downward spiral. But he had to impress upon her that he could not stand by and watch helplessly as she continued in this way. Lori's growing weakness reminded him of a stubborn bull in a bullfight—worn out and ready to drop before the last plunge of the matador's sword. But ironically, Lori executed both roles—bull and bullfighter—with eerie skill and chilling mastery. As sacrificial bull, she received piercing psychological wounds throughout her body and mind, and as skillful matador, Lori got to deliver the penetrating emotional cuts to herself, mercilessly.

"Lori, are you trying to get me to dump you?" He was determined to test her fierce and partly unconscious resistance to being helped.

Agitated and supremely uncomfortable, she fidgeted in her chair as she considered his words. Though she was highly opposed to being hospitalized one more time, she still needed her relationship with him—ending it would be more terrifying than continuing. And though she craved his acceptance, she couldn't internalize it; she felt too unworthy. She was still waiting for him to tell her what a failure she was.

"No," she exclaimed quickly. "No."

"Then why do you keep sabotaging your treatment?"

Lori felt like a failure all over again. Her psychological fullness and heaviness drove her to eat less and less. She didn't really understand why, but it made her feel a little less out of control. And it made her too weak to fully remember the horror she experienced the day her sister died.

* * *

"Your mom's calling." Gabriella passed the telephone to him that evening.

Henry checked the caller ID.

"Hi, Mom." He cleared his throat. "How's Dad doing?"

"Terrible. He tries to put on a good face, but he hates what's happening to him." Ruth Kaplan, Henry's mother, exuded anxiety. "He's tired all the time. His clothes are getting baggier. He doesn't eat much." She barely managed to stifle a sob. "I don't know what to do."

"There's not much you can do, Mom. When I talked to his doctor last week, other than nutritional supplements, he said they could put a feeding tube down his nose or directly into his stomach."

"You know your father will have none of that," Ruth said.

"I know he won't. But the doctor said it's premature for something that invasive anyway. He'd have to lose more weight."

Ruth sighed.

Henry put the headset on and clipped the phone to his belt. "Can I talk to him?"

Henry heard his mom yell down the hallway toward the master bedroom. "Joe, your son wants to talk to you."

Joseph Aaron Kaplan picked up the receiver by his nightstand and slowly brought it up to his ear. He brushed aside the tube that delivered oxygen to his nostrils. "I got it."

Ruth hung up.

Joe coughed and then took a moment to catch his breath. Breathing had never been so difficult as now, with part of his lung removed and the cancer back again. "How's my son, the head doctor?"

"I'm fine." Henry walked into the family room, away from Gabriella. "Mom says you're not eating."

"I have no appetite."

"What about what your doctor's—?"

"I'll be goddamned if I'm letting them put a tube down my nose." His father rarely cursed.

"Of course not. I was going to talk to you about the liquid supplements."

"They taste horrible."

"Dad, you're so weak. Won't you give it another try?"

Joe inhaled as if a hundred-pound weight was on his chest. "Remember I told you about your grandfather...who you never met? He was in a wheelchair when I married your mother. He died of Parkinson's."

"Yes. I've seen him on the tape you made."

Joe whispered hoarsely, "I made a vow...to never allow myself to live like that."

"What do you mean?" Henry adjusted his headset.

"I promised myself I'd rather die...than lose my independence."

"Well, right now let's focus on how you can get food in your body so you'll feel better and have more energy." Henry tried to sound convincing.

"When the time comes, I want you to help me go quickly." He wheezed as he exhaled. "Do you understand?"

Henry's shoulders stiffened. "Sure, Dad," he said, feeling his neuro-circuits going on overwhelm with the realization that his father was planning suicide and asking him to help. Holy shit!

* * *

Darla pointed to the floor. It was Saturday morning, ten-thirty. "Rest period's over. Time for sit-ups." Henry lumbered over to the padding on Darla's garage floor.

"What's up?" she asked. She handed Henry a ten-pound weight to hold on his chest, then held down his ankles. "You're moving like a turtle today."

Henry grasped the weight with both hands and lifted his back and neck ten inches above the blue mat. "I'm exhausted." He tightened his abdominal muscles and lay back down.

"One," she counted, applying pressure to his ankles. "It feels like something or somebody is keeping you down. Two."

Henry paused halfway through the sit-up. "Why do you say that?"

"Keep going. Three. I'm going to make your quads burn."

Henry didn't want to talk about his father. "I have a very stubborn patient who seems stuck in a bottomless ditch of despair."

"Everyone can get better," she said, straddling his legs.

"I'm not so sure," Henry countered, lifting again. He thought of Lori tiptoeing around the cliff's edge of life and death. Darla had probably never dealt with anyone threatening suicide. She wouldn't understand what it was like to carry that kind of burden.

"Seven. Don't stop. Eight," she said. "Everyone can get better." Darla repeated her mantra, her grip on his feet more forceful as she spoke.

"My patient wants to die so badly. That's all she thinks about."

"What's your point? Thirteen. Breathe. Fourteen. Don't bend your neck. Fifteen."

"Give me a moment," Henry grunted as he struggled with his nineteenth sit-up. Sweat inched its way across his chest, dampening his T-shirt.

"Six more," Darla said, squatting gracefully at his feet.

Henry concentrated on his form and his breath until he reached twenty-five. Then he put the weight aside and sprawled back on the mat. Darla released her grip and sat down cross-legged, waiting for him to catch his breath.

"I'll call her Sonya," he said, panting. "My patient. She wants to die. She's been seeing me five or six months. She has the strongest death wish I have ever come across. Earlier this month, I had to hospitalize her for the third time. She keeps getting worse and worse. She's on the slow-but-sure train of self-destruction. She's terrified of living and talks about dying all the time. It's draining."

Henry sat up, facing Darla. "She keeps telling me she wants to die and constantly pleads with me to make it okay."

"And?"

"Sometimes I wonder if she'd be better off dead."

Darla didn't flinch.

"I mean, she's so miserable. I can't imagine being in so much pain." His chest and abdomen ached from the physical exertion. Darla worked him hard.

"Perhaps my fighting to get her better is futile."

Darla's forehead wrinkled as he spoke.

"What if I'm interfering with the only thing that will end her misery?" He shrugged. His hands fell open, as if he were waiting for the answer to fall into them.

Darla listened closely. She had gotten much better at listening.

"What if I'm just prolonging her suffering?" He looked into Darla's eyes, drinking in her concerned attention. It felt good to be able to say what he was really thinking—and not get an argument in return. He felt a flash of longing for the days when he could talk with Gabriella that way.

Darla rubbed her chin with the back of her index finger. Several moments passed.

He wondered why she was still silent.

In a single move she sprang to her feet. "Nope," she said firmly, as if he had twenty-five more sit-ups to do and was try-ing to weasel out of it. "She needs you. She really, really needs you, even if she can't show it." She bent over and extended her hand to help him stand up.

He grasped her forearm as she gripped his wrist. Her arm was like a sturdy branch on a steady tree.

"She keeps coming to see you, doesn't she?"

Henry was about to protest when Darla put her hands on his shoulders and looked straight at him, her eyes filling with a powerful story he found himself eager to hear.

"When I was young, I was teased to death." She dropped her hands from his shoulders, pulled off her headband and let her hair fall down around her neck. "I had dark skin like my father, who was adopted. We didn't know where he came from, and the kids in the neighborhood called me a mutt. When I had bad acne, they yelled out, 'Pizza Face!'"

Henry took a deep, soft breath. He felt his eyes get moist.

"I ran track," Darla said. "I ran every single day. I didn't realize how hurt and angry I was. I couldn't show any sadness. So I became tough." She wiped her mouth with her hand.

Henry wanted to put a hand on her shoulder. Instead, he gave her the space she needed.

"I became a track star. One day, after a track meet, I was headed toward school, and I heard the class bully laughing with several friends, pointing at my thighs." She paused. Her lower lip trembled slightly. "He laughed at me, pointed to my face and yelled, 'Stump Legs! Look at her. Stump Legs. They're just like tree trunks.' The other kids laughed. I was so angry and humiliated that I could have choked him. I ran away, went home, and hid in my closet all day and cried. I was so devastated." She swiped her forefingers across the corner of her eyes, wiping away tears. "I was determined never to let anyone hurt me again."

Henry took her hands and looked into her eyes. For a second she resisted. Then he felt her relax. Tears ran down her freckled cheeks. He felt a tenderness in her hands that he'd never noticed before.

"I'm okay," she said.

"I know," he said, smiling. "Darla," he whispered, then waited.

Her eyes slowly met his. She looked like a frightened little girl. Her tough shield had all but evaporated.

Henry went on, his voice barely audible. "I think you're a beautiful, sexy, graceful woman. Your spirit and energy are breathtaking, and your body is a reflection of that."

"N...no," she stammered. She pulled her hands away and brought them up to her neck. Tiny beads of perspiration glistened just below her hairline. "It's not...I'm not..."

Henry was hardly breathing. "Yes, you are," he whispered, placing his hands gently on her waist.

Darla froze. She coughed loudly, then took a deep, loud, throaty breath.

Unanswered questions hung in the air for both of them. Henry slowly removed his hands from her body and stepped back. "I'm sorry." He gazed into her eyes and detected a shadow of fear. "I didn't mean to be so forward," he said stiffly. "I so value our friendship and wouldn't want to jeopardize it in any way."

Darla's eyes softened, and the hint of a smile appeared at the corners of her mouth. "Whew!" she said. Her breathing evened out and the color returned to her cheeks. "No, I'm flattered. Really. It's okay." She wiped her hands across her face, then shook them out at her sides. "Wow! I had no idea that shit was still buried in me." She laughed. "Thanks for helping me get it out."

Henry breathed a sigh of relief. They had teetered dangerously close to a boundary he knew he could not cross. Still, he was glad she'd opened up to him, and he treasured the intimacy of their emotional connection.

"Let me know if there is anything I can do," he said.

"Thanks," she responded, then giggled. "We keep this up, we'll have to get a chaperone or something. Wait a minute. We were talking about you! When you talked about your patient, it reminded me of how I wanted to die. But in my case, I used my anger to protect myself. I redirected my feelings into my workouts so I could compete with anybody. Nobody was going to hurt me again. Your patient needs you. She needs you to be there for her." She put her hands on his shoulders and laughed, giving him a shove. "Now get outta here."

6

Out of the Box

March 1995

"GOOD AFTERNOON, LORI," Henry said. She sat in his office, depressed, silent, withdrawn, and sorrowful. Same mood, different day. Despite seeing him three times a week and finally agreeing to go to the hospital's Intensive Outpatient Program twice a week, Lori was stuck in an energy-sucking black hole. His frustration at her lack of progress was mounting. Lately she spoke very little during their fifty-minute sessions. He didn't know what to do.

Why is he still staring at me? Lori kept thinking. She was terrified to have him look at her and even more frightened to meet his gaze for more than a second. Facing him was like being in front of an angry judge in a courtroom where the whole world knew she was guilty. Though Dr. Kaplan never got mad or shouted, on some level he reminded her of the powerful man on the platform at the front of the church in her childhood.

"Good afternoon, Lori," he repeated more cheerfully, hoping to spark some sort of reaction. Henry adjusted his body in his chair. Something was different today, he sensed.

I don't know why I'm still here, she lamented. Her fingers were folded daintily on her lap. *I wish I had the courage to kill myself.* She stared vacantly at the carpet. *Then this nightmare would be over.*

"Anything you want to say?" Henry said.

"I just want it to end," Lori cried softly, enraged at herself for being such a loser.

"You're feeling overwhelmed and hopeless." Henry joined her in staring at her feet. He wished he could do something to reach her.

"Everyone would be better off if I were dead." Lori clenched her jaw and tears ran down her cheeks.

Henry began to fidget. He sniffed the air. There seemed to be a putrid odor coming from Lori's body. That was it! He sprang up and walked slowly and deliberately toward Lori, then sprawled out on his back by her feet—his head inches from her toes—and looked up into her face, mischievously. With his eyes now meeting hers, he sought to penetrate her shield of listless inertia. Maybe by doing something totally preposterous, he could break her out of her depressed mind and give them both something to work with.

The unexpected intrusion into her personal space threw Lori for a loop and she froze. *What the devil is he doing?* She had no frame of reference for his behavior. She held her breath. His intense eyes were three feet below her, looking at her in a way that was insistent—yet deeply caring.

"What are you doing down there on the floor?" She still avoided his eyes, as if looking at them might cause her to go blind.

Henry had taken a huge risk by venturing out of the safe, familiar grounds of standard professional practice into the wilderness of intuition, with nothing but his heart as his compass.

"I am down here because it's so damned difficult to reach you." After a few moments he added, "I thought it was time to try something different."

Lori resisted as long as she could. Then she dared to peer into his eyes. She couldn't believe what she saw. He's smiling?

How astonishing. He looks so silly down there! Grown man. Smiling?
Doctor. Acting like a child?

Henry watched as the hint of a smile appeared at the corners of Lori's mouth. Her pupils dilated. Suddenly, she giggled and then roared with laughter, her face breaking into the biggest smile he had ever seen. It was as if the sun had burst through a prolonged total eclipse, radiating joyous light.

"I can't believe you're on the floor!" she said, unable to contain herself. She felt lighter and more alive than she could remember.

Henry smiled widely and shrugged his shoulders. "Well, I guess it worked."

Lori continued to laugh. "I don't believe you!"

Henry began to chuckle too, and then he joined her in noisy, unrestrained belly laughs. The room resonated gloriously with the sound of one laughter shared by two human beings.

"Feel your lightness, Lori," he encouraged her between guffaws, hoping somehow the seeds of humor would stick in her dark, nettled mind.

Lori closed her eyes and tried to catch her breath as her laughter subsided. Her heart struggled to awaken from its unending gloominess and see a glimmering spark of hope. For a moment, her tiny universe expanded. There was space for her to breathe. *Ahhhh!* She inhaled new freedom.

But not for long. Soon after she left his office, the light faded, and she went dark again. Her mind spun a tighter web of sorrow, shame, and unworthiness around her being. On top of it all, she now judged herself stupid and lame for behaving like such a child. She was wracked with guilt, and her brain and body recoiled from the moment of happiness she had experienced. She felt like she was suffocating.

* * *

At the next appointment, Lori's customary cloud of gloom permeated the air. Her knees, feet, and toes were contorted in their usual posture of defeat. Her head hung low, as if waiting for an imaginary guillotine. Henry, on the other hand, was encouraged by the previous session. He had made her laugh. Maybe his venture into comedy was helping. He was tickled. Breaking through her impenetrable shame barrier was like breaking the sound barrier. He felt a surge of new hope and excitement. He decided to try boldness again.

Without words or warning, he jumped playfully out of his chair and crawled under his desk, where he scrunched himself up like a seven-year-old. His pants bunched under his knees and his tie drooped carelessly to one side as he craned his neck to see her clearly. "Do you ever feel this way?" he called out, like a child playing hide-and-seek.

Lori pushed herself up out of her chair to look around the corner of his desk, momentarily forgetting about her despair. *There he is, doing it again!* Her psychiatrist, her doctor with a necktie, looking so odd, bent up like a child, was hiding under his desk for who knows what purpose. She plopped back down in her chair and blew her nose. She had been crying, and for a moment couldn't remember why. "What are you doing over there?" she asked.

Henry loved hearing the note of wonder in her voice. "Is this how you feel—all boxed in?" he asked knowingly. "Do you sometimes get the sense you were raised with no room to move around?"

Lori stared in amazement at the desk engulfing the doctor's six-foot, folded-up frame. "Yes!" she said excitedly. "That's it! That's exactly how I feel."

Henry peeked out from under the desk, watching Lori's face as the light in her eyes became clear and expressive. Maybe she could get better. Maybe she could.

* * *

April 1995

With a large box under his left arm and braced against his hip, and two large paintings tied together in his right hand, Henry backed through the big double doors at the end of the hallway. He leaned the paintings against the wall next to his office door and fumbled with the key. Then he hauled it all through the waiting room and into his inner office. His shoulder ached from the effort, and he paused to shake it out, chiding himself for not taking the time to make two trips. But he'd wanted to have as much time as possible to complete his mini-redecorating project before Lori arrived for her appointment.

For some time, he'd felt suffocated by the austerity of his office décor. The dark paneling, the drab colors, and that god-awful wall of credentials made him feel like he was in some sanctified hall of academia or maybe the office of some stern paragon of the righteous practice of psychiatry. Henry wanted the space to feel warm, welcoming, and comforting. He wanted it to be a place where his patients would feel safe—a place for healing. But with his busy schedule, he had never seemed to find the time to do anything about it. That morning, when Gabriella headed off to the airport for a high school reunion, he took the opportunity to gather up a few of the items he'd been collecting and come in early.

The first step was to take down the dark blinds that half covered the window, allowing him to see several tall evergreens and the eucalyptus trees standing in a circle at the end of the courtyard. Just letting in a little extra light made a big difference. Next, he removed the diplomas, certificates, and professional licenses. Then he put up a large painting of a field blooming with wildflowers and another of an eagle soaring in the sky. He set a small statue of a Buddha sitting in serene meditation on the table next to the couch and placed a gurgling waterfall in the corner near the door. Lastly, he arranged an assortment of plants on his desk and around the room. When he stopped to look around and assess the results, he liked the way it looked—and he liked the way it felt even more. A new paint job and the place would be completely transformed. But this was a good start.

* * *

In Dr. Kaplan's waiting room, Lori examined one of his business cards and noticed his full name and title once again, Henry E. Kaplan, MD. She stared at his name. *I wonder what the E stands for.* Countless times, she had thought about that. She didn't know why it was important. She stared at his middle initial as if it could reveal some hidden truth. She wanted to know. But she was terrified to ask him. *That's against the rules,* she reasoned. *I'm not supposed to ask such a personal question. That could mean big trouble.*

He glanced at his watch, took the empty box and scraps of newspaper outside to the trash bin, and headed to the waiting room, where Lori sat on the blue chair by the door, right on time as always. She was wrapped in a gray sweater, looking like a mummy ready to be laid to rest. The powerful work they'd done a month ago to develop trust with humor and levity had been a major breakthrough. But that didn't last long nor change the fact that she was still deep in the throes of anorexia, dangerously close to fatal consequences.

"Good morning, Lori. Come on in."

"Thanks for seeing me." She waited for him to go first into the office, her eyes on the carpet. Once inside, she stopped, sensing a change. She lifted her head and turned toward the window.

"Wow," she said, breathing audibly.

Henry watched her scan the room, then observed her discovering the waterfall. He saw her tense shoulders soften a bit. He was very pleased with himself.

Lori turned to Dr. Kaplan, met his glance and nodded. "I really like it."

She noticed the billowing eucalyptus tree outside the window in her peripheral vision. But the beating of her heart quickened and distracted her as she suddenly thought about breaking the rule to ask him the question about his middle initial.

"How are you feeling today?" Henry asked, searching her face for clues.

Lori shifted her gaze to the floor then sputtered, "Dr. Kaplan, can I ask you a question?" She winced, anticipating rejection or punishment.

"Sure," he replied.

"What does the *E* stand for? You know—your middle initial?" She looked up at him for any signs that she'd blown it.

Henry paused and shifted his eyes to the window to his right. He wondered why in the world, after all this time, she wanted to know his middle name, which was Eric. He glanced back at her and then the corners of his mouth turned slightly upward. "Eucalyptus," he said mischievously.

"What?"

"Eucalyptus. Henry Eucalyptus Kaplan." He tried to keep a straight face.

Lori laughed long and hard, a release that began at the tip of her toes and propelled her body forward with glee. "You're fun," she said, fluttering light as a butterfly.

Henry smiled. Today was going to be a good day.

7

Definition of Insanity

May 1995

ON THE FRIDAY before Memorial Day weekend, Henry was deeply disturbed as he assessed Lori's condition. His attempts at humor and lightness could not offset the depth of her darkness. The hospital was a revolving door he had to fight her to go through again and again. And the results were the same each time. But he didn't know what else to do.

Lori dragged herself into his office, looking haggard and worn, utterly cadaverous. Her face sank hauntingly into her bones, and only a faint spark of her essence flickered in the hollow gaze of her eyes. Her matted hair was greasy, stringy, and thinning. Fine, soft hair like that on a newborn baby had begun to appear on her cheeks, around her mouth, and on her chin—a sign of severe malnutrition. Her thin skin was mottled and bruised, and she wore extra layers of shabby and ill-fitting clothing to offset the cold-sensitive, chilling reality she barely existed in.

Henry had planned a long weekend getaway with Gabriella, but it was apparent Lori would probably not make it through the weekend if he didn't intervene. She needed immediate hospitalization. His mini-vacation would have to be sacrificed.

"Lori, you have to go to the hospital," he said, firmly and uncompromisingly.

Lori bowed her head in shame. She rubbed the bones protruding from her left shoulder. It was hard work just to keep her head upright and her face pointing in Dr. Kaplan's direction. There seemed to be a thick fog inside her brain as she willed herself to lift her eyes toward him. She heard her voice as though it was far, far away. "Please, Dr. Kaplan. I'm too fat right now. When I get a better, lower number on the scale, I'll be okay."

Henry shook his head wearily as he absorbed her words. His stomach tightened. He understood the intensity of his own frustration was minuscule compared to Lori's desperation, but he nonetheless wanted to scream. Questions flooded his consciousness. Did his sense of frustration mean he was too attached to her getting well? According to conventional protocol, this kind of attachment could cloud one's judgment. Seeing Lori sitting before him in a stupor of near lifelessness, he wondered if he could be part of the problem. Did he care too much? She was one of the most demanding and challenging patients he had ever had. He wondered why he was so deeply invested in seeing her get better. Was Darla wrong? Was it Lori's fate to die like her sister Linda? What if she didn't make it? Would that mean that he too was a failure? He didn't believe that was the case. After all, as her physician, wasn't he supposed to care?

As he looked at Lori, he could not help but ponder. Since the brain could not always distinguish between emotional and physical pain, what about its ability to distinguish emotional or physical pain from spiritual distress, or matters concerning a person's perceived absence or presence of God in their lives? Could an unhealthy relationship with the God of one's upbringing cause or contribute to a disease? Was it possible that Lori's self-induced starvation, on the deepest and most spiritually clear level imaginable, was a declaration that, "If this is how God is, I do not want to live in this world, and I am going on a hunger strike till I die or something changes."

Henry took a deep breath in an effort to release the compression he felt around his chest. He recalled a quote from one of Freud's early collaborators, Carl Jung, who said, "The doctor is effective only when he himself is affected." This was certainly affecting him. His nose wrinkled in revulsion. Lori smelled like spoiled food, and the odor was filling the room. Clearly, she hadn't bathed in weeks. The stench caused his insides to churn, and he felt he might be sick.

"Lori," he said. "Let's go for a walk. Come on." He stood up, signaling her to follow him. They walked through the corridor and down the stairs to the underground parking lot on the way to the outdoor fountains. Feeling as though she was being taken out to the woodshed to be punished, she halted by the side of a shiny blue Mercedes.

Henry turned and faced her. He put one hand on the hood of the car and began his inquiry. "What is it that's underneath your stubborn wish to rot away in a stinking mound of skin and bones? This isn't just about your fear of food. Something else is going on." He paused and softened his tone. "Lori, why don't we form a true partnership in healing?"

She blinked her eyes in a futile attempt to process his words.

He continued. "Let's form a healing partnership in which there is trust and safety and honesty. What do you say? Let me treat you in the hospital, where you'll be taken good care of."

Lori heard the garage gate creak open and felt a moment of reprieve. She squinted into the stream of natural light that brightened the parking area and fixed her gaze on the sleek car that pulled into the parking place a few spaces away. She felt Dr.

Kaplan gazing relentlessly at her. "Leave me alone," she muttered under her breath as she stared at a crack in the pavement.

He waited while a woman with a stethoscope around her neck got out of her Lexus and summoned the elevator.

"What did you say?" he demanded in a stage whisper.

"Leave me alone," Lori repeated. She backed away two steps toward an exit sign.

"Leave you alone?" Henry parroted. "Why do you want me to leave you alone?" He knew he was invading her shame-shell of protection.

Lori shook her head. "Some things can't be spoken," she whispered.

Her words reached in and grabbed something in his gut. "What can't be spoken?" He moved a step closer to her. "The truth must be spoken," he said, deliberately using a religious tool from her childhood indoctrination. "The truth has to be spoken so you can be free."

Lori felt like she was going to throw up.

"What are you concealing from me?" He bored into her resistance.

She clutched her stomach and dropped to one knee.

"Tell me." Henry said, relentless. "What...are...you...hiding?"

Lori slumped to all fours.

"I was raped," she squeaked. Then she crumpled to the ground and began sobbing uncontrollably.

* * *

"Here we go again!" Gabriella's voice shook with disappointment and resentment. "This is insane."

"I'm really sorry," said Henry. He kicked off his shoes and tossed his car keys into the basket on the small table by the front door.

"You're canceling our Memorial Day plans? I don't believe it." They had reservations for a four-day retreat at Yosemite National Park. She'd already packed and made arrangements for a dog sitter, and now he was going to sabotage their get-away—again. "We're supposed to drive out tomorrow morning." She turned off the stove with a snap. "We've been planning this for months."

"I'm sorry, hon. I feel really badly." Henry bit his inner cheek. "You know I don't have any hospital backup." He wanted to console his wife, but he knew it was a lose-lose proposition.

"It's that patient of yours, isn't it? What's her name?"

"Lori. Yes. Plus a busy schedule of others. She's not my only patient, Gabriella."

Gabriella frowned, as if she didn't believe him. "She's going back in the hospital, again? This weekend?"

"I think so." Henry began setting the table. "She needs to. You understand the liability of things like this. I'm afraid she's dying. But legally she's not at the point where I can force her to go in against her will. We had a huge breakthrough today, so I think she might agree to it." He set out two forks, one next to each plate, and turned to face his wife. "Lori agreed to meet me at the office, though. Tomorrow."

"On Saturday?" Gabriella's eyes widened in disbelief. "Jesus Christ! This is just great." She gave the stir-fry one last toss and then slammed the spatula down on the counter. "You're always working," she complained, her face filled with disappointment and hurt. "We never go on vacations." She tracked her husband as he grabbed a can of soda from the fridge. "You take care of everyone but me," she said. "I feel neglected."

Henry hoisted himself up onto the kitchen counter and popped open the tab of his soft drink. A hiss of carbonated air filled the otherwise silent moment.

"I love you. I thought you loved me too," she whispered, her tone tinged with a mixture of hope and fear.

Henry sighed, knowing he wasn't putting her, or the marriage, first—clearly a violation of their vows. He was supposed to protect and defend his wife and his marriage. The trouble was, he was having more and more trouble figuring out how to preserve his individuality and professional responsibilities while honoring his obligation to preserve the marriage at all costs. Their perfect world wasn't so perfect any more. The emotional distance between him and Gabriella continued to increase, blocking the flow of spiritual nourishment he craved to share with her. Feeling bound and sometimes gagged by the confines of matrimony, Henry wanted to loosen the knots so that he could expand and grow.

He stared intently at his soda and then shifted his gaze to his wife, who stood guarding the stove.

"Say something," she said, her eyes glistening with anger and hurt. "I don't want to keep on doing this shit again and again."

Though he knew he should console her, he felt drained, exhausted, and in need of comfort himself. "I'm tired," Henry groaned, taking a long slow drink of soda in quiet resignation.

"I can't stand you. You're not the man I thought you were," Gabriella shrieked, storming out of the brightly lit kitchen, enraged at her husband's nonresponsiveness.

He slithered down the counter and slumped to the tile floor. A door slammed in the distance. He wanted to cry, but his tears would not cooperate. Something was broken, his mind told him, but deep from somewhere inside, he heard a voice say: "There's nothing to fix or solve, just an opportunity to evolve."

8

Holy Skirt

May 1995

THE NEXT MORNING at 9:55, Lori swerved her Miata back to her own lane, tires squealing, narrowly missing the white Ford Explorer speeding toward her in the oncoming lane. She paid no attention to the driver angrily honking his horn, giving her the finger and cursing as he passed. She glanced down at the brown paper bag on the passenger seat.

She had stayed up all night writing a suicide letter to Dr. Kaplan. In three and a half minutes yesterday afternoon, in the garage at Dr. Kaplan's office, her world had collapsed. She had told him something she'd sworn she could never, ever tell another soul. Now it was done. He knew. He would never look at her again. She could never, ever face him again. Her shame and ugliness were out there in the world. All she could think about was dying.

What kept her from killing herself was his offer to see her on his day off. That unbelievable promise on his part was enough to give herself permission to rip up the letter at three in the morning. *I can't believe he's coming in on Saturday, just to see me,* she thought as she struggled to concentrate on controlling her erratic driving. Her mind would not shut off. She was so overwhelmed.

The rape had happened nearly a decade ago, when she was still married to Kevin. Lori had been working three jobs. She was a full-time office manager for the city's recreation center, and in her spare time taught tennis lessons and kept score for the city's softball league. Kevin was out of the country on an evangelical mission for their church.

Lori drove into the empty parking lot of Dr. Kaplan's office and parked closest to the front door. She eyed the blue handicapped parking spaces as she headed toward the front door. *I would never get a handicap sticker,* she thought with pride, though her back begged to differ.

She took the stairs to the second floor, clutching the brown paper bag in her right hand as she walked down the long hallway through the double doors that would take her into Henry's waiting room. She knocked on the door.

"It's open," Henry called.

Lori stumbled uneasily into the waiting room. "Thank you for seeing me."

"Hi, Lori. I'm glad you're here." He motioned her inside. "Would you like some water?"

Lori hesitated. She always politely refused. Today she accepted. "Yes, please."

He drew a cup of water for her from the water cooler and carried it into his office. She followed him tentatively, wondering if she might be walking into a trap that she herself had created. As she sat down, she noticed he'd turned on the tiny decorative fountain on his bookshelf. The bubbling water somehow made her feel less dirty.

Lori knew she must tell him the story of what happened despite the immense fear she had that he would be disgusted with her inexcusable behavior and fire her as a patient. *My life depends on this.* She didn't know how she was going to find the strength to say what she was going to say.

She put her brown bag on the floor and took a deep breath. "Dr. Kaplan?"

"Yes, Lori?" Henry raised his left brow.

"Can I ask...do you mind if...you can...would you turn around and not look at me?"

"Of course, Lori." He resisted the therapist's standard response: why do you ask? He was encouraged by her boldness to ask for what she needed. He turned around, facing his desk and the wall beyond it.

Lori breathed a tremendous sigh of relief. "Thank you." She took a tiny sip of water and then put the cup down. She resisted an urge to flick her palate with her tongue, then began telling the back of Henry's chair what had happened to her nine years earlier.

"I was confused because this man who worked at the rec center would stop by my office and say nice things to me," she began. "He was black and much younger than me. His name was David. Everyone called him Davey. I guess I was attracted to him, or maybe it was the attention he gave me. He kept asking me to go to a park. He seemed to be kind, and he was very persistent." Lori sat hunched over with her knees pressed together and feet touching one another.

Henry listened carefully, grateful and somewhat surprised that Lori spoke with such clarity, without dissolving into a pool of tears.

"One day I said okay. I guess I didn't know how to say no. It was after work, just starting to get dark, and we went to one of the ballparks near the office. No one was there. Davey got out of the car and opened my door. He said he wanted to go for a walk. I followed him, like I was supposed to." Lori winced. "I don't know what I was thinking. He led me to a grassy area behind the bleachers. Then, before I knew it..."

Her voice trailed off, and Henry wondered if she'd go on. Then he heard her take a deep breath.

"He attacked me, Dr. Kaplan," Lori whispered. "He threw me to the ground, face down. I remember the size of the blades of grass. I froze. The next thing I knew, he was on top of me. I didn't understand what was happening. He pushed up my skirt, ripped down my underwear, and penetrated me from behind."

Waves of fear and revulsion coursed through Lori's body as she remembered the searing pain. She let the sobs come. "I thought that, well, somehow I must have asked for this. I felt so dirty. Then all of a sudden, he stopped. He got up and left me laying there on the grass. I felt warm fluids oozing down the back of my legs." Lori shuddered. "His semen. As soon as I got home, I just showered and showered and showered, trying to get rid of that dirty feeling."

Tears ran down her cheeks. Fearful that Dr. Kaplan would be disgusted with her for what had happened, she paused. Then, slowly, she let herself look in his direction. She was relieved to see that he was still there, his back turned to her, just as she'd asked.

"Kevin came back from overseas," she said. "And I remember repenting to him, asking for his forgiveness about being raped, and he got aroused. I couldn't believe it. Here I was thinking I was so dirty, and all he wanted was to have sex with me."

Henry couldn't see her face flush with disgust.

"And then he threw me out of the house. He gathered all my belongings—my jewelry, my clothes, my tennis rackets—and tossed them onto the lawn, yelling at me. He just kept shouting, 'You're no good. You're trash!' He even cut my tennis outfits into pieces and waved them in my face." The memory tore at her insides, but this time she refused to let herself cry. Her anger and sense of betrayal were even bigger than the pain, and they seemed to actually soothe the old shame-infested wound. "And to humiliate me even more, the next day he yelled at the top of his lungs at my mom, 'She got a black guy to fuck her ass.' My mom didn't even know what that meant." Lori shook her head.

Henry listened compassionately.

"That's when I decided I needed to divorce him," she said with determination. "Even though no one in our family believed in divorce." She sobbed heavily at the painful memory, still fresh, as if it had happened only yesterday.

Henry was deeply moved by the trust Lori had shown in recounting this horrible incident to him. This was an essential step forward in healing the life-draining wounds that had been festering in Lori for so long. "Can I turn around?" he asked gently.

"Yes," she whispered.

"I'm so sorry that this happened to you," Henry said, facing her again.

His voice trembled slightly, not with anger or condemnation but with sincere concern and care. No one had ever validated the pain of her experience until now. He understood.

A part of Henry wanted to reach out and grasp her hand, but he didn't. He knew that gesture could be confusing and might be misinterpreted.

She sighed, slowly looked up at him, and the tears continued to flow. She had never imagined that anyone could possibly hear that story and not find her completely and utterly disgusting. *How can he be that way? How can he even look at me?* She gratefully held his gaze for a moment. "Dr. Kaplan?" She eyed the brown shopping bag on the floor as if it was pornography. "Would you do me a favor?" Her body tensed.

"Sure, Lori." He leaned forward attentively. "What is it?"

She pulled a piece of clothing from the bag. "I kept this," she said, opening up a neatly folded tan cotton skirt. "I'm not sure why, but I stored it up high in my closet, hidden away all these years." She refolded the skirt cautiously and handed it to him. "It's the skirt I was wearing when Davey raped me."

Henry reached out, took the skirt from her and placed it on his lap. After several breaths, he asked, "What would you like me to do with this?" His mind flashed on an idea, but he waited for Lori to answer first.

"I'm not sure," she said with a shrug. "I thought you'd know."

"I think I do, Lori. No." He paused. "I know I do."

"Thank you," she mouthed.

Henry turned around and opened a desk drawer behind him. He took out a box of matches and lit a single wooden stick. He brought the yellow-orange flame to a vanilla scented candle perched on the end table next to his chair. The wick hungrily accepted the glowing heat. He blew out the match and held the candle up between Lori and him.

Lori held her breath. Her eyes tracked his every move.

He unfolded the skirt carefully and zeroed in to an area near its back seam. He glanced at Lori. "May I?"

Her face flushed with hope. She nodded affirmatively, giving him a resounding green light.

He carefully spread a portion of the skirt over the burning candle. The fire began to smolder in the threads of shame, which had become woven into the fabric of Lori's being for more than ten years—until now.

"With the grace of God," he said, "let this fire burn off any and all residual shame from your sexual trauma in the park so many years ago." He gently placed the candle back on its ivory holder.

Lori, crying with relief, nodded as she mouthed once again, "Thank you."

Henry smiled, openheartedly.

Suddenly, a high-pitched siren pierced the healing ceremony. The smoke detector went off.

Henry jumped up and opened the window. He grabbed a folder and began fanning the smoke detector.

Lori burst out laughing. The alarm stopped abruptly. "That was funny!" she roared, clutching her sides.

For a moment, the tension evaporated.

"Dr. Kaplan?" She looked at him straight into his deep brown eyes, tears welling up in hers. I can't believe I'm going to say this."

"What Lori?"

"I think I need more help. I think I may need to go into the hospital." Lori's tears flowed rivers of fear, shame, and relief, all at once.

9

Comedy and Tragedy

September 1995

"WHATEVER HAPPENED TO Lori?" Susan Rosen stood at the open door of Henry's office. Most days he rarely saw Susan, even though her office was right next door. This evening, however, they'd both finished seeing patients around the same time.

"I guess I haven't had a chance to tell you. I've been so busy." Henry laid his pen down and swiveled away from his desk to face her. "Lori has been at a women's treatment center in Arizona for the last month."

"Really?" Susan invited herself in and sat down. "How did you ever manage that?"

Henry rocked back in his chair. "It was hell." The back of his forefinger swept his nose subconsciously. "Remember the doctor you suggested I send Lori to see for a second opinion?"

She crossed her legs and adjusted the hem of her skirt. "Dr. Jameson. Frank Jameson. Yes, I remember. Did anything come of that?"

"After Lori's last hospitalization, in June, I finally convinced the insurance company to authorize the consultation."

"So she went to see him?"

"Yes. Three times." Henry shuffled through a stack of medical records on his desk. "Want to hear his conclusions?"

Susan nodded and cleared her throat.

Henry thumbed through a binder of papers in her chart. "Here it is. July 8. He says: 'My findings, in summary, are that Ms. Johnson is suffering from an extremely severe psychiatric condition. I would say that the chances of outpatient treatment being successful are less than fifty-fifty. The back injury and subsequent surgery and pain led to decompensation of her fragile personality equilibrium, leading to severe symptoms, including chronic pain, anorexia, a severe anaclitic depression, and an extreme state of helplessness. Such patients have a high risk of death from either suicide or complications of malnutrition and starvation.'" Henry glanced up to see Susan's reaction.

"Oh, my," she said. "That's very disheartening. What else did he say?"

"That she needs to be in a specialized eating disorder treatment program. And get this: 'Treatment,' he says, 'in the best of circumstances, will be lengthy and extremely arduous. In fact, statistically, the possibility of her dying as a result of her psychiatric condition is alarmingly high.' That's just what I wanted to hear." Henry sighed, with a dose of self-pity and sarcasm.

"Sorry, kiddo," she said. "That's a very grim outlook."

Kiddo. He cringed a little whenever she addressed him that way. Though he knew she meant it as a term of endearment, and even empathy; nonetheless, the word could trigger for Henry a feeling of being a bit belittled by his older colleague. He put the letter back into Lori's chart. "I had to fight both Lori and the insurance company to get them to agree on the program in Arizona," he said.

"And they went for it?" Susan's eyes widened in amazement.

"Yes, but it was quite a battle. I had her sign a contract I insisted she write, that read, 'I promise I will seek treatment in a hospital as an inpatient for eating disorders if I weigh below ninety pounds, and I will agree I need help and might be anorexic.'"

"*Might* be anorexic?" Susan looked incredulous.

"That's right. That's how steeped in denial she's been. It's a miracle she went. She backed out twice. To get her to finally go, I promised her I'd write her back every time she wrote me."

Susan gave him a thumbs-up. "Good for you."

"I had to. Otherwise I'm sure she wouldn't have gone."

"How many times has she written?"

"Many." Henry leafed back to the correspondence section of her chart. "Check out her first letter. 'Dear Dr. Kaplan, I hate this place. I am very angry that I came here. I'm so scared. It's a big trick. As soon as I got here, they signed me out and rushed me to the emergency room at a hospital an hour away. My blood pressure was 70/30 lying down and they couldn't find a pulse standing up. I had severe dehydration, and they said I almost died. I wish I did. They gave me IV fluids for four hours and then put a feeding tube in me. It hurts my nose and throat, and I hate it. They said the tube may be in for several weeks. My agoraphobia is severe now. I am so scared of every-one and full of anxiety. I spent all day crying today and almost left. I'm sorry I have nothing good to say. I am very upset and angry I can't leave. I want to starve myself to death very badly.'"

"When was that written?" Susan asked.

"When she first got there," Henry said. "Almost a month ago. That's when she weighed eighty-six pounds. She's back up to ninety-five now."

Susan sat up in her chair. "Wow! That's dangerous. She could've easily died from cardiac arrest. How long is she going to stay?"

Henry frowned. "Good question. Depends on who calls it quits first—Lori or the insurance company. It's costing them over thirty grand a month, and Lori threatens to leave every day."

"Tough situation. Let's hope it can help her." Susan rose from her seat. "Well, at least you're getting a break from her and all that intensive one-on-one work."

"Thanks, *kiddo*," Henry said, surprising himself with the sharp edge in his voice. "That's what Lori is accusing me of... trying to get rid of her."

* * *

October 1995

Lori sat in the lobby Monday at four for her first appointment back in Dr. Kaplan's office since her dreadful sixty-day stay at the eating disorder treatment center. *I'm so fat,* Lori told herself over and over again. She glanced at her watch. *I wonder if he's going to continue to treat me.* Her mind continued spinning its incessant worry wheel. She knew he had a steady stream of other patients. Maybe he would just be too busy to see her. *And he must know I left against medical advice. Some doctors wouldn't see patients who did that.* She could hardly sit still.

"Hi, Lori. Come on in." Henry greeted her with all the enthusiasm he could muster as he led her inside his office. "Good to see you." He secretly wished she would have stayed another sixty days at the treatment center.

"Thank you for seeing me, Dr. Kaplan," she forced herself to say. Lori sniffled several times and then peered up at him. "Thank you for all your letters."

"You're welcome." He handed her some tissues. "I've been curious as to why you left the program despite everyone on your treatment team advising against it?" He tried his best not to sound judgmental.

Lori slumped in her chair anxiously, feeling her heart pounding. "I had such a hard time at that place," she whined breathlessly.

"I know. You made that very clear in your letters."

"The psychiatrist they had me see was an old man who discounted my back pain. He said I was addicted to the Darvocet, even though I only take two a day. I asked him if he'd call you, and he said no." She choked on her tears. "I finally couldn't take it anymore."

Henry noticed her cheeks were pink and not sunken in for the first time since they met. "Well, you look much better than when I saw you last."

Lori cringed. "It was a Christian-oriented place, and they had us hold hands all the time and pray. I had to wash my hands constantly to get rid of all these germs around me. That was so hard."

Henry flinched. He hadn't realized the program was faith-based. Somewhere in the midst of the complexities and confusion of getting a referral set up for her, that detail had escaped him. Given Lori's history, the influences of the Christian treatment center could have easily opened wounds from her past. "I'm so sorry you had such a hard time."

"I'm just so happy to see you," she sobbed.

"Well, now that we're here, let's see how we can move forward." He had arranged for her to see a nutritionist twice a month, attend the day program twice a week, and see him three days a week. "I'm confident that if we work together and become a good team, we can get you better and out of the pain you've been stuck in."

"Dr. Kaplan?"

"Yes?"

"I really, really had a hard time there. They forced me to eat three meals a day and eat three snacks in between," she said. "They weighed me every day. And they searched me after each meal to make sure I wasn't hiding food in my clothing."

Henry sat still, feeling helpless. "What are you feeling right now?"

"I'm so fat," Lori said, crying.

Henry took a deep and breath blew it out noisily. "Lori, fat isn't a feeling."

"I came to the program wearing size one jeans and now I have to wear size three. I'm so fat."

Oh shit! Henry closed his eyes and took a deep breath. Then, swiftly, as if propelled by an invisible force, he opened his eyes, scooted his chair away and pulled out one of his prescription pads he kept in his desk drawer. He got out his pen and tore off a blank prescription. He put her name at the top, dated it, and wrote a sentence three times in capital letters:

FOOD IS NOT FAILURE

FOOD IS NOT FAILURE

FOOD IS NOT FAILURE

He handed the prescription to Lori.

She stared quizzically at the words, then glanced at him. He was eyeing her as if she were an alien learning the ways of a new culture. She quickly averted her eyes and peered back at the piece of paper. Lori was unaccustomed to getting a prescription for anything other than pills. She folded it twice into a perfect square and tucked it carefully into the pocket of her sweater as if it were an undeserved message from a special angel. She fingered it nervously in her pocket, anxious for a chance to be alone so she could study it more carefully.

* * *

December 1995

"It's true folks; I am a psychiatrist and a comedian." Henry eyed the sparse, mostly intoxicated crowd as he pulled the microphone from its stand on the well-lit stage. "The Comic Shrink." No laughs. One groan. Henry felt his mouth instantaneously go dry. "During the day I treat the mentally ill." He licked his lips. "And at night, I entertain you."

A pigtailed brunette in the front row, who was drinking a margarita with a straw, yelped with a high-pitched laugh.

It was Sunday night at the Comedy Store in La Jolla, California. Most of the two-drink minimum crowd had already left. Gabriella shifted uncomfortably in her chair at the back of the room, wondering why she was subjecting herself to the foul-mouthed environment of the comedy club. Even though her husband's material was squeaky clean, she had to endure the other comics, who spewed off-color material peppered with generous portions of profanity. But she wanted to be a supportive wife, she reminded herself. Still, she would have rather been at home, curled up in bed watching a good romantic comedy.

"I don't just give out medications." Henry extended his forearm. "I take them!" Two people laughed in unison. Several others joined in. "One for you, two for me!" Henry pointed two fingers to his chest. A drunk, tattooed, twenty-something male in the third row shouted, "Give me all your Ritalin—now!"

"I really went to medical school," Henry went on as he spotted the inebriated heckler through the bright lights. "I needed something to fall back on."

The brunette in front giggled loudly.

"Because it's tougher being a comedian. In my practice, people come to see me, they cry, and they pay me." He paused. "In comedy, I come here, you cry, no pay!"

A chorus of laughter reverberated through the dark room. Gabi smiled, momentarily distracted from the stench of stale beer.

10

For Better or Worse

LORI WAS IN Florida at her second specialized eating disorder inpatient treatment facility. She had been in and out of the hospital five more times since coming back from the Arizona program; nevertheless, she kept getting worse. Henry continued to do comedy, and he seemed to be getting better. He and Gabriella had started seeing a marriage counselor... and they were doing worse. Darla was still training both of them, and they were both getting better in that department. Henry's father was undergoing radiation therapy, and he was getting worse.

And like a drug addiction, the anorexia continued to enslave Lori. She was in a downward spiral of frequent relapses of food restriction, dangerous weight loss, distorted body image, starvation, malnutrition, osteoporosis, cognitive impairment, dizziness, and weakness. After all the treatment she had been getting, she wasn't showing any signs of progress.

Henry toyed with the unopened letter he had received from Lori earlier in the day. It was postmarked March 27, 1997. He dreaded the bad news he anticipated she would be conveying. He took a breath, plunged his letter opener into the envelope, and pulled out the neatly handwritten note:

Dear Dr. Kaplan,

Today is my birthday. I got the best birthday gift in my life today, and it's okay to cry about it. It is out of happiness and release. Dr. Kaplan, you wrote me a new prescription: "As long as you're trying to get better, I will not drop you as a patient, and I will never lose respect for you or judge you."

Henry had been sending Lori prescriptions with affirmations and words of encouragement to motivate her fragile mind to hold onto.

I've been looking at it all day long, and I can't believe how relieved I feel. I have a promise of hope. When I feel so suicidal I will repeat your promise over and over again.

Wow! This was a different, more hopeful letter. He put his feet up on the desk.

I am learning to change my thinking every day. When I read the prescription you gave me last year, "food is not failure," I put it on the table next to my food before I eat and repeat it over and over again. Then I repeat it after I eat, when I feel that horrible feeling of despair.

Henry smiled, thrilled that Lori had actually made use of his prescriptions and that they were having a positive effect.

I learned a lot about myself today at group therapy. I have evil pride because I think I don't need to eat when I watch other people eat or see TV commercials about food. I make myself in a superior position. This makes me feel safe. I use starvation as a cop out when things don't go my way. Or in a passive-aggressive manner, like believing I don't have to eat today because no one in my family called me on my birthday. It shouldn't be an issue about food.

Henry put the letter down and then drew in a deep breath of cautious optimism.

* * *

May 1997

"You have to come now," Ruth Kaplan demanded nervously, the panic in her voice ringing inside his head so that the thousands of miles between them evaporated. "Your father doesn't want to live any more. He's stopped eating."

"Don't worry, Mom. I'll get a ticket this evening," Henry assured her.

Fortunately, Lori was still tucked away at the inpatient unit in Florida, and he didn't have to arrange coverage for his out-of-town family emergency.

On the redeye to the east coast, Henry thought about his father. Joe Kaplan was a self-reliant and confident man who had the respect of everyone who knew him. When he was first diagnosed with lung cancer he fought a tough battle to get well. He underwent lung surgery with a positive attitude and external bravado. When the report showed no more cancer, the war seemed to be over. He waved his hand and called for a victory celebration with family and friends.

Sadly, the cancer came back a year and a half later and spread throughout his lungs and lymph nodes. He attacked this setback with as much energy as he could muster, in spite of the many rounds of chemotherapy. Joe was a warrior with a spirited focus on living in the present without giving power away to the possibility of a worse tomorrow. He never complained about getting cancer and disregarded its ill effects on him by saying, "It's better than being six feet under." He loved his wife and children. He wasn't ready to leave. He was hopeful and optimistic.

But the cancer had spread to his brain ten weeks earlier. The radiation didn't help, and he had become physically so very weak and frail that it was clear he wouldn't live much longer. He needed oxygen all the time, and much to his disdain, had to use a wheelchair, like his father did.

Two nights ago he decided there was no point in going on. When he needed help with his bowel and bladder, it was the point of no return. That evening, he and his wife, Ruth, stayed up into the early hours of the morning, cherishing their lives together as they pored over stacks of old picture albums strewn across their bed. They turned the pages of the black-and-white photographs of their initial courtship and traditional wedding, complete with long gown and tuxedo and tails. They wiped away tears as they looked again at the color pictures of the births of their three children. Images of the many graduations and ceremonial milestones that flashed before them created a slow-motion picture story of their union...now coming to an end.

"I'm not going to fight any more," he announced with a resigned determination in his weary eyes as he closed the last of the albums. "I'm tired of living like this. I hate this damned wheelchair and oxygen tank. I'm not going to eat any more."

Henry's mom buried her head in a pillow and sobbed silently. She wasn't ready to accept the end of their partnership.

Henry stretched his feet out, brushing aside the carry-on backpack he'd stowed under the seat in front of him. In a few hours, he would be landing in Miami, where his parents lived. He was grateful he was able to get an aisle seat. As the drum of the plane's engine continued to lull other passengers to sleep, Henry's mind drifted back to his first memory of death.

* * *

May 1965

Seven-year-old Henry threw the basketball to his brother, Jacob, a year older, slightly taller, and more athletic than him. Their cemented backyard was the site where he and Jacob tossed the ball or Frisbee to one another after school. Nearby, the family parrot, Izzy, stood perched on a ledge on the outside wall of their house. Izzy's cage featured a center swing on which the beautiful bird would prance and flutter his orange and green feathers.

Jacob bounced the basketball to Henry, but it slipped away from him and careened into Izzy's steel cage. Izzy and his humble home came tumbling to the ground.

"Izzy!" Henry ran to the floored cage. "He's not moving, Jacob," he shouted.

Jacob sprinted into the house to get their mom.

"Izzy's dead," Mom whispered softly as she eyed the unmoving, silent, colorful creature.

Later that evening, Henry, his mom, dad, older sister, Sarah, and Jacob went to the front yard. His father brought a shovel and dug a hole in the soft dark earth near the budding lemon tree, put Izzy in, and covered him.

"Izzy is buried now," Joe Kaplan declared to his children as he finished patting the soil with his shovel.

"And he's going to heaven," Mom quickly added with a confident smile.

At bedtime, Henry couldn't sleep. Confused about death, he sat up in bed. His blue cotton pajamas, buttoned up to the collar, seemed to be choking him.

Izzy died. Henry pondered the meaning. His breathing quickened. Dad had buried him. When Dad died, Mom would bury him. When Mom died, Sarah would bury her. When Sarah died, Jacob would bury her. When Jacob died, Henry would bury him. All of a sudden, he panicked. *Who will bury me?*

With his heart racing, little Henry thought about Izzy's lifeless body in the darkness under the dirt. But didn't Mom say Izzy was going to heaven? Where could heaven be? What happened when we died?

Henry could not imagine himself after death, just as he could not fathom his existence before birth. If he had become him only after he was born, then he was nothing before he was born. What if he would be nothing after he died? Nothing? Not a thing! He gasped for air. No more toys? No more cartoons? Never, forever and ever?

His fragile young mind spun cartwheels. In tears, he jumped from his bed and ran to his parents' bedroom.

"Who's going to bury me?" he sobbed, his lower lip quivering. "What is heaven?" he sputtered. "What happens after we die?"

"Don't worry, Henry, dear." His mother pulled back the sheets and helped her son up to her side of the bed. "Your wife will bury you. We'll all meet in heaven and be together with God."

"Where is God?" Henry tugged at her soft cottony nightgown.

"God is everywhere," she answered, combing his brown hair back with her hand.

"Where?" he asked again, wriggling his feet in the bed.

"He is invisible."

"What is heaven?"

"It's a place where we all meet." Mother propped her head up on her elbow.

"Is heaven invisible too?"

Mom laughed. "You ask a lot of questions, my sweet boy."

Henry didn't understand what was funny.

"Don't worry," his mother said. She brushed his flushed round cheek with the back of her free hand. "Everything will be okay."

Little Henry went back to bed, but he didn't sleep much that night.

* * *

May 1997

"It's time. Let's go. How are we going to do it? What about the garage and the car? Do you think that's the best way?"

Henry froze in the family room, suitcase and carry-on still in his hands. "Whoa, whoa, whoa. Wait a second, Dad." His mind was spinning. "Don't I even get a 'Hello, how are you?'"

His father's temple bulged angry veins. "I said it's time to go." The elder Kaplan huffed, barely getting enough air to his lungs, even with the help of the portable oxygen machine with the tube inserted into his nose.

"Wait," Henry implored, releasing his bags to the floor. "Let's think about this for a moment or two."

His father erupted. "You gave me your word," he yelled. "You gave me your word." His glare was like an arrow piercing deep into his son's belly.

Henry absorbed the anger, casting about for a way to buy some time. Jacob had arrived the day before. His sister, Sarah, was not coming for another day and a half. "Let's not do anything impulsive," he said hopefully. "Wait until Sarah comes. She needs to say good-bye to you. Don't you want to say good-bye to her too?"

Henry's father relented, temporarily resigned.

The next thirty-six hours were excruciating. Joe Kaplan was so weak he could hardly get out of bed without assistance. He would only drink small sips of juice. The cancer had spread to his bones, causing him such searing pain that he finally gave in to stronger pain pills, which unfortunately had little effect. The thought of saying good-bye to his daughter would calm him down for brief periods of time. Then he would get mad all over again, demanding that his son help him.

"You promised me," he would bark. But his energy would drop so precipitously that speaking became a monumental effort, like trying to swim through quicksand.

Henry considered his father's request and was troubled by it. Euthanasia—assisted suicide—was not only illegal but rife with ethical complications. Would his father be better off having his wish honored? Was helping him die really the right thing to do?

"No way," Jacob cried out passionately. "I'm not going to be a part of helping Dad die." He was in the kitchen beside their mom, who was huddled over the sink crying. Henry stood by his father seated in the family room adjoining the kitchen. The purring oxygen machine droned in the still air.

"But that's what he wants." Henry put his hand on his father's shoulder. "What about his wishes?"

"No! Count me out. I want none of it," Jacob said.

Their mom wailed, "I don't know what to do." She looked at each of the three men for guidance, one after another. Then her eyes rested on her husband, and she began to tremble. "Joe...?"

His father reached his hand up and placed it over Henry's. He needed his young son to be his spokesman.

Henry knelt down on one knee and put his mouth near his father's ear. "Dad," he whispered, "hold on, please. The doctor is ordering you a stronger pain medication and Sarah is coming tomorrow. She needs to see you."

Dad raised a weary brow. "No hospitals?"

"No, Dad. I promise."

The next day Jacob went to the doctor's office and returned with an injectable narcotic pain reliever. He handed it to his brother, the doctor.

At the fortieth hour, Sarah arrived via airport shuttle. She entered the master bedroom where her father lay, his eyes shut, the constant hum of the oxygenator interrupted by occasional hacking as he struggled to pull air into his scarred lung tissue.

His daughter ran to his side. "Dad!"

"Hello, beautiful," their father gurgled, opening his eyes halfway.

When she left the room, Henry got out the syringe.

"You're going to get some rest now, Dad."

His father opened one eye partially, as if to give a sign of thanks.

Henry swabbed his father's wasting belly with an alcohol wipe and delivered the medication. Some minutes later, his proud, strong father drifted off into a sweet sleep, his last one.

11

Mystical Moments

February 1998

HENRY PLACED HIS fingers on his carotid artery at Darla's one Saturday morning to calculate his heart rate while he pedaled the exercise bike at an RPM rate in the mid-eighties. Darla's biceps glistened in rippled perfection as she increased the resistance of the bike. He grunted as he silently counted twenty-four beats during fifteen seconds, which made his heart rate ninety-six beats per minute. Satisfied, he turned his full attention to his trainer, whom he noticed was ready to engage in conversation.

"You won't believe who I saw yesterday," she said excitedly. Her energy throttle was wide open, revving, and provocative.

"Who?" Henry asked, without missing a beat. He wiped drops of perspiration from his brow.

"I saw this woman, Mariette. She's an intuitive healer."

Henry's pedaling slowed to sixty-five RPMs. "Intuitive healer?" he inquired. "You don't mean 'psychic,' do you?"

"I knew you'd say that." Darla laughed. Her smile bared a row of straight white teeth. Her chin dimpled.

"Well?" The stationary bicycle was quiet.

"Keep pedaling," Darla commanded.

He obediently began moving his legs again.

"You could call her a psychic," she said, "But that would probably make you not go see her."

"Why should I go see her?" he said as he pedaled faster.

"To open your mind." She lowered the resistance of the bicycle as he pedaled furiously.

"My mind is open," Henry exclaimed, almost shouting. He gripped the handlebars tighter.

"We'll see," Darla said with a wink. "Now get off that bike and prepare for some real uplifting," she kidded, pointing to the bench where a barbell and two black weights waited.

She went on to describe her experience with Mariette as Henry slowly moved the weights up and down, up and down. He was aware of his reflexive fear of ridicule and rejection by medical colleagues if they knew he was engaging in a serious conversation about someone who claimed to have intuitive healing abilities. At the same time, he felt a space opening up inside that would allow him to explore, without any attachment to outcome. His triceps and pectoral muscles were nearing the point of fatigue.

"Come on," she said. "Two more."

His chest expanded to draw in more breath. He pushed his wobbling arms upward to full extension.

"Great!" she said, stepping back from the bench. "She's the real deal. She even picked up on that ACL tear I had in my senior year and had some great insight on what's kept me in relationships with controlling men. She only takes donations, and she's got a waiting list. You better hurry up and give her a call."

Henry was amused as well as curious. It probably couldn't hurt. He put down the weights, and then a flash appeared on his mental screen: Maybe Mariette could shed some light on why Lori was not healing. Or if his Dad's spirit was hanging around. Yeah, right! He took the number Darla gave him and stuffed it into his wallet.

* * *

The cobbled-together look of the small house Mariette rented on the edge of town stood out for its simplicity. When Henry decided to call, he was told it would be six weeks before he could see her—and today was the day. He rang the doorbell, not knowing what to expect, and heard a soft voice from inside call out, "Come in." He opened the wooden door, which needed a fresh coat of varnish.

The skin on Mariette's face seemed too taut. She was tall and warmly dressed. She extended her right hand, which was contracted, as if she had suffered a stroke. "I have scleroderma," she explained as she saw him studying her physical appearance.

He noticed both her hands were deformed. Scleroderma, he knew, was an autoimmune disease that caused hardening of the skin. When scleroderma affected the normally soft major organs of the body, they became like petrified wood—hard and stiff. The prognosis could be fatal.

"Please sit down." She cordially motioned to an old but comfortable corduroy couch in her small living room. She sat down across from him on a dining room chair, which had extra cushions for her back and buttocks.

He imagined she did a lot of sitting, like he did, though her chair clearly cost a fraction of what he'd spent on the one in his office.

She began telling her story. "I was dying fourteen years ago, but I didn't know it. As I got worse and worse, the doctors wouldn't look me in the eye. I felt like a leper. They spent less and less time with me. I was terrified. I got weaker and weaker, to the point where I had to be carried from the bedroom to the living room. I didn't know what was happening to me. Finally, one doctor, the only one who would look at me, said, 'There's nothing we can do. You're going to die. You have less than two months to live.'

"I was relieved," Mariette reflected, nodding her head stiffly. "I was finally being told the truth. But at the same time, I was also enraged. Why me? I wondered. God, why me? I went home. I wasn't ready to die. My daughter was six years old, and she needed me. I needed her. I was a mess." Her face showed little expression, but her eyes were glowing.

"Then a miracle happened. I was put in touch with a very special being, a man who prayed for me—and with me. I'd been told he had a special ability to help others heal. His name was Max."

Henry listened carefully to her story. Nothing thus far had popped up on his skeptic screen to indicate that she was anything other than credible. If she was getting rich off her work, it certainly wasn't reflected in her dwelling. He turned his attention back in to her story.

"Max explained to me that it wasn't really him that did the healing. It was the power of the Creator, the God force that healed. 'We all have the potential to access this force,' Max told me," she said, unwavering in her gaze.

Henry couldn't help wondering if she told everyone the same story. He shrugged it off.

"Max came to see me every day for several months," she said. "Sometimes he would stay for a short while, other times longer. He was always reassuring in his quiet way. At first when he told me I would get better, I didn't believe him, even though I wanted to so badly."

She reached toward a mug of water next to her on a coffee table. She carefully placed the handle between her thumb, which was mobile, and her other fingers, which were stiff and contracted, working as one unit. She lifted the cup and took a sip of water. Henry watched her drink and resisted a tiny urge to do something to help.

Mariette went on. "Max told me it would take me two years to get my strength back. He said I would receive gifts, which some would label as psychic, to help others heal. He said people would come to me and seek my gifts. And he described the first person who would come to my door to receive the gift."

Henry uncrossed his legs, starting to relax.

"It was just as he predicted," Mariette said. "I began to get my strength back and developed a newfound appreciation for life. The scleroderma—I could never have imagined this—was a true blessing in disguise, because it opened me up to a way of being that I never knew before. Now I am so present and appreciative of life. I never realized how anxious and busy I was before."

As she spoke, she radiated a deep inner peace Henry recognized as the power and energy of love. Then Mariette shifted in her chair and turned her attention to him. "Could you give me something of yours to hold?"

"How about this?" he said, slipping off his wristwatch passed down to him from his grandfather. He handed it to her.

Mariette grasped the object in her contracted left hand. "Is there something troubling you?" she asked gently.

"Aren't you supposed to know that?" Henry was tempted to ask. Instead he replied politely, "No, I don't think so."

"Your father is no longer here, is he?"

Next month would be a year since Henry's father's death. "No, he's not."

"Your father is very proud of you."

He wondered how she could possibly know that.

She beamed. "I see him smiling, right now." Her face lit up, the color rising in her cheeks.

"Hi, Dad," Henry said to himself, just in case his father was around. At the same time, another voice inside scolded, "What are you doing?" He recognized the critic's appearance on his mental screen. "Are you crazy?" the inner critic screamed.

"Dad's dead!" Henry observed this internal dialogue and reminded himself to let the thoughts flow unimpeded, like logs on a river.

"Your father didn't want to leave this plane," Mariette said, more as a statement than a question. "I sense he stayed on as long as he could, but he finally accepted the inevitable."

She was right. His father fought the cancer for four years.

She interrupted his thoughts again. "He didn't believe there was any existence after death, did he?"

Henry shook his head again. His father often said people lived on through the memories of others. There was no after-life mumbo jumbo in his belief system.

"He says, 'I love you,'" she said.

Yes, but didn't they all say that? Aloud, he muttered a clumsy, "Thank you."

Mariette went on to give him tidbits about his grand-mother and other deceased relatives. Although the informa-tion she provided rang true, it was relatively nonspecific and unspectacular.

Henry started to speak, but he held his tongue. Part of him wanted to know if Mariette knew about Lori, why she kept get-ting worse, what he could do to help. But he couldn't form the words. He just smiled meekly and looked toward the door. He was ready to go, anxious to get back to his office.

Sensing there was more to do, Mariette asked him, "Do you mind if we spend a few minutes looking into each other's eyes?"

Henry felt his conventional training send up a flash of resistance. He recognized the inner critic again, and with that awareness he was able to release it. Space opened up in his mind and in his heart.

"Sure," he replied, not knowing what to expect, but decid-ing to be okay with not knowing.

Mariette recited a prayer. Then they began staring into each other's eyes. Henry looked at her left eye. She chanted a long guttural sound and asked if he would join her. He followed suit. They chanted several times, continuing to stare at each other without blinking. Henry's breathing became more rhythmic and prolonged. His eyes started to water. At the same time he noticed Mariette's facial features begin to shift, as if her face were suddenly more fluid. He wondered if his eyes were playing tricks on him. He stopped wondering and went back to experiencing. Her features again shifted—swiftly, subtly, and intermittently. The shading of her face changed and then took on the appearance of a photo negative. He noticed a ring of white light surrounding her head. All of a sudden, he saw a mustard-colored light spreading out in front of, on, and around her face. Then her face began to morph from a younger to an older version, back and forth, almost simultaneously. A tingling sensation ran up and down his spine. His breathing slowed and deepened. He had no reference point anywhere in his mental software for what he was observing and experiencing. His body relaxed, and he was filled with a strong sense of inner peace.

"Oh, my God," Henry said. He had never witnessed or felt such an extraordinary and profound experience. He shared with Mariette what he had been seeing.

"You are having a mystical experience," Mariette gently informed him as they continued their locked gaze.

They both stared longer into each other's eyes. Henry continued to see Mariette's features shift in a mystifying way.

She took a deep breath and then slowly handed him his watch back.

Henry had nothing to say. He had no need to speak. He noticed something very peculiar about his watch, all three hands, the second, minute and hour—were rotating—counterclockwise! He stared at the timepiece in amazement. "Look at this Mariette!" he exclaimed, showing her the movement back in time. The watch continued its march backward for several long minutes.

Mariette smiled and shrugged her shoulders. "Sometimes we get the grace to witness these things," she explained.

Henry felt like hugging Mariette. Then he did. And when he left her humble home, he looked around, scanning the world around him in slow motion, as if he were seeing it for the very first time. He had an inner knowing, for the first conscious moment in his life: There was a God force, a Creator, something extraordinarily magnificent, something beyond the perceptions of our senses. He didn't have to think, believe, feel, question, ponder, or wonder any more. He knew! Without realizing it, he had left his mind and entered his heart. He was truly out of his mind. What a joyful feeling!

12

The Healing Battle

October 1, 1998

OVER FOUR YEARS had passed since Henry first laid eyes on Lori. Her mental and physical health plummeted to an all-time low, and her life force kept dwindling.

Henry felt like he was going toe-to-toe with her dark side, a monolithic, negative, fearful shadow energy that sucked the life force out of her and challenged his. The efforts to treat her were exhausting—so much energy expended—with no hint of sustained improvement.

Lori had fallen deeply into a self-imposed imprisonment of blame and judgment so well constructed that not even Houdini could have escaped. She was stuck, blind, divided, fragmented, separated, and suitably punished. Her weight nosedived once again until it hovered at around eighty-five. And after eleven inpatient psychiatric hospitalizations and two extended stays at eating disorder treatment programs out-of-state, there was nowhere else to turn. This was it. Henry was going to give it one last try. Once more he told her exactly what he'd told her a thousand times before, that unless she stopped starving herself she would have to be hospitalized again.

As soon as he said this, Lori leapt to her feet with her usual resistance. He could hardly stand to hear it again himself. Then he noticed that she looked at him directly, fire in her glowering eyes. She seemed to awaken for just that brief moment, no longer frail and brittle. Her meekness and submissiveness vanished in her defiance. She tapped into her power when she defended her right to the seeming absurdity of her behavior.

He waited.

Minutes passed. Neither of them backed down.

They had become intertwined in a dysfunctional healing battle. Lori, in an attempt to release overwhelming tension, tried to get Dr. Kaplan to do the one thing he would not do: repudiate, condemn, and abandon her.

Henry, on the other hand, had become trapped in the endless reruns of her bad-movie scenarios, watching her mind playing the same pointless episodes over and over again. How he wished he could direct a new script where he would be the welcome healer rather than the reproving judge—the role her subconscious mind had cast him in.

He broke the silent stalemate. "What is it that you are trying to get from me?" Henry asked with compassion, watching her to see if she could receive it.

"I don't know," she wailed. Lori sank back into the soft leather chair. The pressure inside her head mounted until she felt it was a balloon about to burst. She silently recounted each of the times she'd been admitted to the hospital, and she felt the unbearable sensations of anxiety and self-condemnation that wracked the inside of her body. *If I go in again it'll be the twelfth time. I'll be the dirty dozen,* she thought irrationally. *Everyone will know how despicable I am.* What else could they think? Her pain and suffering spread undeterred, like a tsunami radiating from an ancient, timeless quake. *I want all this to stop,* she screamed silently. *I'm in so much pain. I just can't stand it anymore! It would be better to die. I can't let Dr. Kaplan send me to the hospital.* But there he was, insisting on sending her back. He wouldn't go away. For the life of her, she could not comprehend why he didn't go away. *Everyone else eventually goes away and leaves me alone. Why does he keep coming back?*

Henry felt like he was on a train racing toward sheer disaster as he desperately tried to find the controls to avert the crash. He had to stay the course. There was no stopping, no turning back.

"You'll be safe in the hospital," he said. "For the love of God, Lori, let me treat you in the hospital." He got up and squatted down close to her so that he was looking up into her frightened blue eyes. They were lifeless. Her face sagged, her skin was pale, and her cheeks hollow.

Lori felt tears welling up in her eyes. A tremor started in her belly and moved up her burning spine and out through every limb. It frightened her to feel so out of control. She fought to keep from crying, but the sobs rose up from deep inside and wouldn't be stopped. Her iron will was starting to collapse, and she slumped into the chair in defeat.

"Okay, I'll go," she whispered.

Though the battle was temporarily over, the war would continue.

* * *

"Your room is number 173," said Wanda, the plump, hardworking, likable ward clerk. Her gray hair hung in limp waves tucked behind her ears, and her fingers were yellowed from a lifetime of too many cigarettes. She handed Lori a stack of forms to read and sign. "You can settle in after the admitting nurse does an intake."

"Are you sure I have a room all by myself?" Lori asked timidly.

"That's right." Wanda knew Lori from her many previous hospitalizations. "You got lucky this time, girl." She laughed as Lori's eyes widened in disbelief.

No roommate! Wow! She'd had to put up with having room-mates during all of her previous admissions, and she'd hated it. It took more energy just to stay alive. Roommates were like invisible mirrors. They reflected back a projected self-portrait aptly named "pathetic loser." At least for now, Lori had one less judge to remind her of her pitiful worthlessness. That was a welcome reprieve.

"Here you go," Lori mumbled as she finished untying her shoes in the examination room. She and Roselyn, the admit-ting nurse, had the routine down pat. Shoelaces and belt were removed, and then came a quick check of Lori's suitcase for any obvious instruments of self-annihilation. She was glad they could never take away the one tool she actually intended to use. They couldn't force her to eat.

13

Food Fight

October 8, 1998

THE STAFF REPORTED to Henry that Lori ate only bite-size shredded wheat, and it nearly always sat in the bowl until it turned to mush. Dr. Kaplan asked the dietician if this was correct. "Did she really only eat shredded wheat?"

"That's the only thing she checks off on the menu," the nutritionist said.

"And she only adds three drops of low-fat milk," added the day shift nurse. She held up three fingers.

Kaplan shook his head sadly.

* * *

Lori sat in the deserted fluorescent-lit dining room, struggling to eat her cereal the second Saturday of her stay. Eating required an impossible amount of effort. She felt like an elephant in the room that no one was talking about. *I know everyone knows how fat I am.* She was sure the other patients experienced her disgustingly obese body as an overflowing Dumpster, and she knew they could see what a disaster she was. *I'm such a loser! If only they knew how hard I try to obey the rules. I can eat no more than three single-serving boxes of bite-size shredded wheat a day, with water, not milk.* Her elbows were always off the table. She chewed in

135

super slow motion, and her face always pointed down toward her bowl. Once in a while she added three drops of skim milk. Just three drops. She counted each one.

Her right hand clutched her spoon tenuously, like she was holding the thorny stem of a rose. By the time she finished her third or fourth spoonful of the shredded mush, everyone else had long since left the table. The empty room watched her eat in strained silence.

Lori would always make sure she counted each nugget of shredded wheat before she put them in her bowl. *There are twenty-two to twenty-six pieces in each box,* she noted. If a box had more than twenty-two pieces, she would deduct the extra pieces from her next serving. She ordered three boxes for each meal but could never eat more than one. *I'm such a failure!* She would carry the uneaten boxes back to her room, where she hid them away in the dresser drawers.

Her father had always finished his shredded wheat. He ate it every morning for breakfast when Lori was a child.

Dr. Kaplan walked in and eased himself into a chair next to her. She glanced at him with a scowl, ashamed that she was alone and hadn't yet finished her lunch. He studied her bowl of soggy brown cereal. "I've decided not to call your food shredded wheat anymore," he announced as he turned the chair next to hers backward and slipped into it like a saddle. "From now on…it's shredded shit."

Lori's mouth dropped open. She spat out a muzzled laugh. Shit was not a proper word in her vocabulary. "No." She shushed him reflexively. That word made her feel uncomfortable. "Don't call it that."

"Well, that's what it looks like." Henry grinned slyly, pleased that his word choice got her attention. "Aren't you tired of eating this shredded shit three times a day?" He hoped the shock value might shake something loose in her.

Lori shuddered and shook her head. She tried to wipe away the disgusting imagery.

"Touché," he muttered under his breath. Henry pulled out a prescription from his pocket that he had composed earlier in the day. He placed this mystery note on the table where she was sitting, got up, and left.

Lori hurried back to her room and stared at the new scrip, which she had carefully unfolded. She struggled to comprehend the puzzling message, which read:

I'M LEARNING TO HATE MYSELF A LITTLE LESS...
I'M LEARNING TO HATE MYSELF A LITTLE LESS...
I'M LEARNING TO HATE MYSELF A LITTLE LESS...

* * *

"Lori sat with her eyes closed during process group again today," Carol, the head nurse, reported to Henry during a weekly treatment team meeting.

"Yes," said Olivia, the perky psychology intern with hair a shade too yellow. "This seems like Lori's passive-aggressive way of not participating."

"I beg to differ," Henry said, straightening up in his chair. "Lori, in her emaciated state, is struggling to concentrate, and by closing her eyes, she conserves a little more of her energy."

"Isn't this more a reason to transfer her to the medical ward?" Carol pleaded. She was worried about Lori dying on her unit. The last thing she wanted was a lawsuit for wrongful death.

"No," Henry stated. "We can't move her now in her fragile condition. She'll only get worse. It's a risk I have to take."

Carol raised her eyebrows. "Okay," she sighed, shaking her head.

"Trust me." Henry knew Lori could not tolerate a different environment with unfamiliar, "unsafe" people. Keeping her on the psychiatric ward was the only chance he saw for a potential turnaround. But his confidence was rapidly waning as each week passed with no real progress. It had occurred to him more than once that she would likely die on the ward.

Henry took a deep breath. "And, Carol, one more thing. Because numbers have too much power in Lori's mind, please ask your nurses not to weigh her or measure how much food she's eating." He lightly touched her shoulder for emphasis.

Carol glared at him. She was at least fifteen years his senior and had three times as many years in nursing practice as he had in doctoring. Her training had taught her to document those important numbers meticulously so the nurses would be safe from accusations of malpractice. But he was the doctor and captain of the mental ship.

"I hope you know what you are doing," she said.

Henry cleared his throat. "Lori will attach to any number and obsessively ruminate on it. If she knows her weight or how many calories she's eating, that's all she'll think about or talk about. Let's not make that an issue."

"Okay," said Carol. "Just make sure you write it in the chart as a doctor's order."

He nodded. A small victory for him, a bigger one for Lori.

* * *

"Thank you for coming," Lori mumbled. She moved toward the door haltingly as Dr. Kaplan entered her room. Even though he came to see her day after day, she was a little surprised that he would bother with her one more time. As she watched him move confidently across the room, she felt relieved and nervous at the same time. All morning long her mind had spun in circles. *Is he coming? When is he coming? I hope he's not coming. What if he doesn't come? Why does he keep coming?*

Her anxious anticipation made her feel like a student waiting for the principal to show her what she had already seen a thousand times: her failing grades on her report card. She couldn't exactly remember a time when Dr. Kaplan had shamed, blamed, or rejected her. But she knew he must. Everyone did, and besides, she knew it was what she deserved. *He couldn't possibly think anything but the very worst about me.* Still—he always came back. For all the world, she couldn't fathom any reason why he would.

Henry embraced her with his smile. It always amazed him how austere her room appeared, the bed so neatly made with sheets so wrinkle-free they looked as though they had been dry cleaned. The other bed in the room stood stripped, its plain gray nylon pad stretched over the bare mattress. Next to the dresser was a matching inexpensive wooden desk on which a single rose released its fragrance over several get-well cards. The walls were bare.

"Hi, Lori. How are you doing today?"

The wrinkle on her forehead softened a bit, and her shoulders dropped an inch. He dragged the brown vinyl chair from her desk to her bedside and motioned to her to join him, to sit down on her bed or on the extra chair.

"Marilyn is my nurse today, and she ignored me all morning," Lori muttered as she sat down on her springy bed. "She was too busy to talk to me."

Henry listened to the hurt and dejection in her words, knowing her energy was exhausted by her supersensitive internal rejection meter. "Did you let her know how you felt?"

"What do you mean?" Lori said indignantly. Sometimes he just made no sense at all. Her knees twitched with agitation. "She never spends any time with me. I don't want her to be my nurse anymore." She glared at her foot, tapping urgently on the floor.

"So you felt angry that she didn't spend more time with you?"

"No," Lori snapped. Her chest tightened. She wanted to curl up inside herself. *How ridiculous,* she thought. *Of course I wasn't angry.*

"Okay," Henry said. "Did you feel frustrated?"

She paused. *I guess it's okay to feel frustrated.* "Well, yes," she said.

"Did you feel resentment?"

She stopped breathing, flooded with confusion. Her right hand moved up toward her ear but stopped halfway there as she considered an alternative. Then, hoping to win him over to her argument, she proclaimed, "I don't want her to be my nurse anymore. Will you tell them not to give me her?"

Henry could see real agony in her eyes. He took a deep breath and released his own frustration as he exhaled. He fished in his wallet for a blank prescription sheet, which he kept for emergencies. He pulled the pen from his shirt pocket and wrote:

ANGER IS OKAY!

ANGER IS OKAY!

ANGER IS OKAY!

He held up the prescription for her to read.

Lori felt like she'd been shot by a stun gun. *What does that mean?* She searched her mind for an explanation. *Anger is not supposed to be okay.*

Henry waited. Then he said, "Lori, it's okay to have anger. It really is. It's an emotion that we all can have. If you don't claim your anger, it will go underground and fool you with symptoms."

"I'm so fat," she declared.

"No," countered Henry, eyeing her malnourished body. "You're soooo thin. You just feel fat," he articulated, emphasizing the word *feel* to help her understand. "Feelings aren't fact. Even though you feel fat."

"No," Lori responded, trying hard to explain it to him. "My body is special, and I don't need to eat like other people."

Henry tried hard not to express his annoyance. He knew that Lori fully trusted her distorted reality, but her bones, protruding beneath her dry skin, betrayed this distortion. Her hair protested by falling out due to lack of protein. Her sunken eyes and gaunt cheeks made her look twenty years older than she actually was.

"I'm going to start calling you Frau Lori," Henry said, casually, hoping to draw her out of her cloud of misery.

"What do you mean, 'Frau Lori'?" she asked, not really wanting to hear what he had to say.

"Look how you treat yourself: angrily—with restriction, punishment, oppression." He pointed a finger at her, drawing an imaginary line from her head to her toes. "Frau Lori," he exclaimed with a thick German accent. "You are behaving like a sadistic Nazi guard."

Lori withdrew, closing down in response to what felt like an attack. *Is he mocking me?* Deep down she knew he was right, but she didn't know what to do about it.

Henry switched back to his usual voice. "Lori, please look at yourself. You've got to see how you are harming yourself."

"You don't understand, Dr. Kaplan. I am so fat!"

Henry suddenly realized how uncomfortable he felt sitting there in Lori's room. The air was thick and heavy, like a San Francisco fog. It was dark and felt like it would never leave.

* * *

During their next several sessions, the fog settled in with such dense negativity that Henry felt like he would suffocate if he stayed in Lori's room. On Friday afternoon, as he eyed the antiseptic floor and sterile curtains, he began to sense that he was a prisoner in her world. He faced her wall of resistance and declared, "We're going for a walk." He jumped up from his chair and motioned to her to follow.

She obeyed mechanically, carried along by his surge of energy.

"We'll be back in a short while," he chirped at Wanda, the ward clerk, as they passed through the locked double doors of the hospital entrance.

They stepped outside. The sun shone mercifully against a postcard blue sky.

Lori squinted against the brightness of it all. She looked up at Dr. Kaplan. He seemed taller and stronger than he did inside, as though this bright and shiny world was exactly where he belonged. For a moment, she missed the walls of her prison and the dark shadows that made a space for her to hide. But then she looked out across the parking lot to a spot where a grassy field spread itself out, open and inviting. She breathed in the sweetness of the air.

Henry strolled toward the nearest group of satiny-barked fig trees and orange-flowered hibiscus shrubs that lined the perimeter of the hospital. Lori scurried ahead as if she were a rabbit in a race, fueled by nervous energy, burning off more calories. Henry slowed down and came to a halt.

"Lori," he called out dramatically, luring her back as if he had a carrot in his hand. "Look at the pink geraniums." He gazed deeply at them himself, inhaling the beauty before him. He could see Lori in his peripheral vision as she lingered several feet away. "Feel the sunshine on your skin," he sang out brightly, aware that she was considering entering his strange world, where beauty was something to notice, appreciate, and take real pleasure in. He tilted his own face toward the sun-sparkled air, closed his eyes, and breathed as if in meditation—hoping he could seduce her into slowing down and slipping into the sacred present.

Curious, and perhaps even a bit enchanted, Lori inched her way closer to the doctor with his eyes shut. She let her nostrils sip the fragrance of the soft pink hyssop. Mesmerized, her face drifted skyward like a vine in bloom.

From the corner of his eye, Henry saw Lori's furrowed brow soften. Her weary eyes closed, and the frown she always wore seemed to melt away. He beamed. Not only was it great to get out of that dungeon of a hospital room, but he was also inspired by the cracks in her dark force field of negativity. She could lighten up.

Lori opened her eyes. "Thanks!"

Back in her room, following their outing, Lori was like a child, hungry for more playtime. She tugged on Henry's sleeve as he readied to leave the hospital. "Can we do it again?" she begged. "Can we go for more walks?"

"Why, sure," he said, smiling with delight. "Tomorrow we'll take a field trip to the main cafeteria downstairs—that's where all the really good food is." His intention had been to provide Lori with something to look forward to the next day. But she looked ashen. He might as well have said they would be going into enemy territory with bull's-eyes printed on them. Food mortified her. But he was nearly out the door before she could protest.

* * *

The next morning at nine, when Dr. Kaplan arrived, Lori was in her room pacing back and forth between the desk and her bed. Frightened, she murmured, "I can't go."

"Why not?" As Lori backed up against her desk, crossing her legs and pressing her knees together, Henry tried to suppress his impatience. He had a full office schedule and couldn't spend all day with her. "What's wrong?" he asked, glancing at his ticking watch.

"I don't know. I just can't go. I'll eat more shredded wheat, I promise," she said. "We don't have to go."

He wasn't going to give in. The momentum from the previous day was still strong in his mind. "Oh, no," he insisted. "No, no, no, no, no. We're going. Come on." He sallied out of the room.

Lori held on tightly to the edge of her desk.

He turned and stepped back into the room. "What's the matter?" he said softly.

"I'm not hungry," Lori protested.

Henry knew that wasn't true. He was aware her "fullness" reflected an overflowing trough of shame, fear, and pain. "What could be so scary about a cafeteria?"

Lori couldn't speak.

"What on earth could you have done to make you beat yourself up like this without end?" he asked. He could feel his frustration rising. "You're acting like you murdered someone." He could not have anticipated her response.

"I did," she croaked.

"What do you mean?" he asked, watching her bottom lip quiver.

"I…I killed someone."

Uh, oh. Henry felt a flash of heat rush throughout his body. "What do you mean?" He anticipated her response. It could only mean one thing. And now she had to speak the unspeakable.

Lori's throat felt like it was clamped in a strangle hold. "About twelve years ago," she sputtered, covering her eyes with her hand as her voice dropped to a whisper, "I had, uh, I had an abortion."

He waited for her to say more, but she didn't. She couldn't. Fear and guilt engulfed her to the point of near catatonia. In her world, having an abortion was far worse than receiving a death sentence. She was raised to know that anyone who committed this unpardonable sin could expect eternal damnation, a one-way ticket to hell, and the promise of fire, brimstone, teeth gnashing, and other diabolical consequences.

She had never told anyone what she had done. She had tried to forget the uncharacteristic one-night stand she had shortly after her humiliating divorce, tried to push out of her mind the terrifying discovery that she had become pregnant. Mortified, and feeling completely trapped and alone, she had committed the unspeakable act.

Her eyes still covered, she managed to squeak out a desperate plea. "I can't talk about this to another human being. Not even you."

He thought for a moment, then spoke with a gentle ease. "Think of me as a soul, Lori, not another human being."

Ever so slightly, the vice grip on her throat began to loosen, and the pounding in her heart slowed just a bit. She spread her fingers, still pressed tightly against her face, and peeked through them. She looked at Dr. Kaplan to see if what he'd just said was for real.

He said it again. "Think of me as a soul, Lori, not another human being."

She gazed up at him, hoping this miraculous escape hatch from her dungeon of silent despair was true. "Okay," she hedged. "Can I really speak to you not as a person?" She held her breath at this possibility.

"Yes," he said calmly.

She exhaled. She painfully described the time she went on vacation by herself to Hawaii, something she had never done before. She visited missionary friends there, but stayed in a hotel by herself. One night, Lori went to the hotel bar and met a man who treated her kindly. He bought her several drinks and they ended up in bed, much to her surprise and, later, tremendous remorse and shame. When she found out she was pregnant, she considered killing herself but decided against it.

"Lori," Henry said when she'd finished. "Thank you so much for trusting me with your story."

She winced, unable to receive his compassion and still unsure if it had been wise to reveal her blasphemy.

"Listen to me. You act as if you believe that God is punishing you. Can you consider the concept of forgiveness?"

She shook her head. No. She looked at the floor again. *What the hell does he know about God or forgiveness?* She seethed with secret anger.

14

What If Love?

October 21, 1998

LORI WAS WEIGHED down by the shame of speaking about her abortion. She lay curled up on her hospital bed, grasping the blankets as if they were a parachute. *He'll be here any moment*, she thought. *Dr. Kaplan doesn't give me a day off.* She tried to hide her face as he appeared at her door.

"Let's go, Lori." His voice seemed to fill the room. He'd decided to forge ahead with their field trip and put aside talking about the past for now. "I'm hungry, and it's almost nine in the morning." He planted himself in her doorway. "Time for breakfast. Just you and me."

Like a child plagued with school phobia, Lori shivered at the suggestion of a trip to the cafeteria. Mealtime on her own, in the relative quiet of the mental health unit's dining room, was traumatic enough. The prospect of facing food in the main cafeteria, with Dr. Kaplan's confident voice shattering her crumbling defenses, was terrifying.

"Dr. Kaplan," she murmured tentatively, barely breathing, "I'm scared."

He waited three full breaths. "It's okay," he said, wanting to acknowledge that this expression of fear might actually be the beginning of a breakthrough for her. "You'll be safe with me. I'll make sure you are."

She heard his words, but was still reluctant. She scanned his energy to detect signs of danger, manipulation, or trickery. Exhausted, she released her grip and let herself be led away into the eye of her storm of fear. She was too exhausted to fight.

The brilliantly lit cafeteria was bustling with doctors, nurses, patients, and families. A food line and servers' area occupied almost half of the expansive room. In the center was a self-serve buffet of breads, fruit, and scrambled eggs. Two cashiers busily rang up purchases.

Henry took two trays, several napkins, and silverware. He got in line, ordered two platters of eggs, sunny-side up, and moved to the toasters to heat two bagels. He picked up two plastic bowls and put a scoop of mixed fruit into each one, along with a slice of cantaloupe.

Lori followed behind him, dazed. Her inner tension was rising as the bagels warmed.

"Lori, when was the last time you had a bagel?" Henry asked.

She stared inward, trying to tune out the rumble of her mental motor, which carried her back in time, revisiting painful, long-ago family meals and her father's ceaseless recriminations. She dared not share these experiences with any other human being.

Lori forced herself to look at the people sitting at the tables. Everyone seemed to be okay—and they were eating. Lori knew she wasn't okay, and she couldn't eat. She was fat. How could she eat? Especially those unfamiliar foods Dr. Kaplan was putting on her tray. They weren't safe foods. He must know that. Panic-stricken, she thought, *What is he trying to do to me?* She could only eat shredded wheat, and just trying to eat that was a huge struggle. *But that's all I deserve,* Lori heard herself think. Her back hurt. She was in constant pain. She was useless. She was a miserable failure. She was fat. In fact, she was obese.

And to make matters worse, everyone in the cafeteria was eating normally. They're all performing well. Her performance was obviously unacceptable. She was so inadequate. Her church and family had taught her that if you were a failure, you couldn't get into heaven. Her life had turned into a living nightmare.

She wanted to leave, but she felt trapped, boxed-in. There was nowhere to run, and she was too fat to hide. She felt raw, denuded. As she tried to tune out the noise inside her head, she heard Dr. Kaplan's voice coming from somewhere in another world.

"What did you say?" Her words stumbled out, disoriented. She jumped when the bagels popped up from the toaster.

"I asked you when was the last time you had a bagel?" He put some packets of butter and jelly onto their trays.

"I used to love bagels," she said with a sad fondness.

"Well, come on," he said, heading toward the tables. Henry was aware of her deep inner struggle, but did not want to empower her deeply ingrained position.

While Dr. Kaplan cheerfully carried their trays, Lori staggered along behind him, preparing to languish in humiliation as they headed toward a table in the far corner of the cafeteria. The trip from the food line to the table, though shorter than the length of her tiny room, was exhausting.

Doesn't he realize how excruciatingly difficult this is? Lori thought as she contemplated which seat to take. *Should I sit in the chair next to him? Will he think I'm being too difficult if I sit in the one across from him?* Food, and everything about eating it, represented shame and fear and guilt and worthlessness and emotional bulk—and more and more helpings of misery. *How in the name of God does he expect me to eat?* she wondered, her brain stuck on high volume. Glancing around nervously, she saw other people eating with ease, even talking in a relaxed way while they ate. *This proves I'm such a loser!* Her mind screamed its judgments at her. Inside she was hemorrhaging emotionally, but no one could see or hear her silent torment. She felt like she was being gutted from the inside out without anesthesia.

Defeated, she sat down across from Dr. Kaplan, sobbing softly, hoping no one could see her tears or the shaking of her body. Dabbing at her eyes with a napkin, she did her best to hide any evidence of her failure. Before she could stop it, a drop of mucus fell from her nose onto her bagel. The eggs on her plate stared up at her without judgment. The fruit sighed.

Though Henry was famished, he was also acutely conscious of Lori's growing anxiety in this environment, fully aware of the risks he would be taking by bringing her face to face with the demons that tormented her around food. As he prepared to take his first bite, something clicked in for him from his experiences with stand-up comedy. Comedy had the power to defuse the thoughts and feelings that people feared, allowing them to look at these fears more closely. He picked up the edge of his napkin and unfurled it theatrically, unveiling his silverware as an overly zealous magician might do. Gripping his knife and fork with over-the-top histrionics, he pierced the eggs in a delectable dance that would culminate with the warm yellow yolk slithering down the inside of his cheeks. He turned toward Lori—and stopped short, her fear-shriveled face interrupting his mouth-watering revelry. Slowly putting his utensils down, Henry embraced her warmly with his eyes as he uttered an uncharacteristic plea: "God, please help Lori eat."

Lori shuddered. *What did he say? Why was he acting like this?*

Eyes fixed on his patient, Henry peeled a piece of cantaloupe from its warty rind and chewed deliberately. As he swallowed, he let out a soft, guttural sound of satisfaction and encouragement, as if to say, "This is good. Why don't you join me?"

Lori bolted from the table and raced to the napkin dispenser, returning with several dozen brown paper napkins. She arranged them in a thick stack, with all their edges straight, as if they were a new deck of cards.

Henry ignored her compulsion and bit into his bagel.

But Lori didn't eat, not even a crumb. She couldn't eat. She was too fat. She was huge and uncomfortable. Her mind-body had not even the slightest capacity to accommodate another molecule of food.

"Hey, Lori, watch this," he said, trying to entice her. Taking care not to tease or taunt, he swooped a chunk of bagel with his fingers like a pelican diving for a fish, splashed it into the yolk of one of his eggs, and brought it to his mouth to devour.

"You're mixing food?" Lori blurted, as the yolk-soaked bagel disappeared behind his lips.

"Yes!" he said, gurgling with pleasure, mouth full, yoke dripping from his thumb and index finger. "Have some." He licked his fingers and smacked his lips with delight.

She recoiled with nervous giggles. He was talking and eating at the same time. She didn't know whether to be amused or repulsed. *Stop showing off!* she wanted to scream. But instead she muttered meekly, "I...I could never mix food."

"Why not?"

"I don't...I don't know." She shrugged her shoulders.

He knew she didn't know, of course. He also knew that combining foods repulsed her, and the sense of contamination she experienced was absolutely real in her mind. Her mind converted the energy of her shame and sense of worthlessness into a physical sensation of density. If she were to get better he would have to break the toxic grip her distortions had over her being.

Lori closed her eyes, overwhelmed. "I just can't eat. It's too hard." In her mind's eye she saw a familiar scene from her childhood. She sat huddled in a straight-backed pew between her parents and her siblings in their church, just as they did three times every week. Her eyes were clamped shut, and her knees and toes were touching. Her body was wound tightly, heart pounding so hard she was afraid others might hear it. Everyone had their eyes closed. She knew they did. Once she peeked and saw for herself. Prayers were always delivered in the dark. Prayers were pleas of forgiveness for the bad things she and others had done.

Suddenly Dr. Kaplan's prayer, "God, please help Lori eat," echoed in her ears. It was so different from all the prayers she knew. For one thing, his eyes had been open. And he didn't shout, cry out, or rise up like the powerful man in the pulpit. Lori's confusion ate away at her. She drew a deep breath and mustered the courage to ask a lifelong question, one whose mere asking could invoke shameful repudiation and accusations of disloyalty and faithlessness. Now she was faced with receiving the wrath of rejection or developing an unfamiliar sensation: *trust*. Trust had always traveled with another word: *obey*. Trust and obey. These words were knotted together in her biology and psychology. Could she trust and not feel like a subservient, lesser-than-other weakling? She crushed the blasphemous thought down with a judgmental sledgehammer. *Don't be silly*, she chided herself. Yet she couldn't help eking out a question to him. Inhaling bravado, she trembled as she asked, "Dr. Kaplan, what in heaven's name is God?"

Henry set down his cup of Earl Grey tea, wiped his mouth with a rumpled napkin, and cleared his throat. Instead of speaking, he reached into his shirt pocket, retrieved his black felt-tipped pen, then stretched out his other hand to take a brown napkin from the pile next to the platter of food that Lori hadn't touched. Without even pausing, he began writing on the napkin, stringing together long strands of words.

Lori stared on curiously.

When he was done he slid the napkin back across the table to her and smiled.

Lori looked at the words on the napkin as if they were written in Greek. She brought them up to her face for magnification. Her pupils dilated in fascination. The napkin read:

God = LOVE, total pure,
unconditional, nonjudgmental, compassionate,
loving, warmth, white light, nurturing,

soothing, comforting, cleansing,
purifying LOVE!
Energetically healing, breathtaking,
inspiring, blissful and joyful LOVE!"

Lori read the words to herself. They were enticing and exciting, yet scary. She had never ever heard anyone describe God with such love and with the absence of fear. How could this make sense? The vise around her body loosened one ratchet. She hungrily read the words again and again.

Could it be true? Could there be a God that was love? In her world, God was always watching. God was always waiting. God was watching and waiting to make sure your performance was good enough and that you followed the tribal rules. If your performance wasn't good, then you had to ask God for forgiveness. Then you had to perform better. You had better perform better, because if you didn't, things became really scary. Bad things happened to those who performed poorly. The man on the platform had always reminded Lori and the other church members of that fact. *I'm living proof of that*, Lori agreed. *I've performed badly, that's why I'm here in this hospital, no matter what's written on a stinkin' brown napkin. That's why I have a band on my right wrist with my name on it, which shows everyone that I'm a patient in the section of the hospital reserved for people who are failures.*

Her eyes tracked the writing on the napkin once more. She was confused. Is God a God of love—not a God of condemnation, punishment, and repentance?

Wanting to touch her soul, Henry opened the windows of her eyes with his gentle stare. "Lori, you deserve to eat." He waited a dozen heartbeats and repeated, "Lori, you deserve to eat."

Lori's body went into deep freeze. Did he say, "You deserve to eat"?

Just as those words were beginning to find space in her mind, he made another astounding statement: "What if, Lori— what if love?"

Perplexed, she asked, "What do you mean?"

"Lori, what if you choose love instead of fear?"

Sitting motionless amid the cacophony of dishes and the ringing of cash registers, Lori tried to digest the words he had just spoken: "you deserve to eat." And the brand new concept he introduced to her: "what if love?" *These words taste good,* she dared to think.

Cautiously, tearfully, and bravely, she uncovered her fork as if it were a harpoon waiting to spear its prey. She pierced a small piece of egg and lifted it warily. Her dehydrated mouth began to salivate. She put the egg on her tongue.

"This is yummy!" she whispered, surprised. She was crying, but for the first time in a long time she felt calm. The turbulence inside her had quieted down. She felt—was it possible?— a ray of hope shimmer in her inner being.

* * *

Lori had so many questions tumbling around in her mind the next day. She tried to keep them all sorted into neat piles, but it wasn't easy. There was one question that kept jumping out in front of all the others, demanding her attention. *What if love? What does that mean?* She grappled with this question all day long. What could that mean?

And then another question crossed her mind and wouldn't go away. This one excited and terrified her. *Dare I ask him?* Lori's eyes widened. *What if he says yes?* The thought of it made her stomach tighten. But still, she was a shade more excited than nervous. She couldn't wait till he showed up. *I'm going to ask him, I have to.* She paced up and down the hallway till she spotted him coming into the building.

"Dr. Kaplan," Lori said breathlessly as she hustled to meet him by the front door of the hospital.

"Yes, Lori? What's up?"

"Could I ask you a favor?" She swayed gently back and forth, knees bent, a sail caught in a crosswind.

"Go ahead." He nodded encouragingly.

Her knees stuck together like they'd been glued. She couldn't find her tongue. "Yesterday you said…'what if love,' right?"

"Yes, Lori, I did." Henry peered into her eyes, trying to find out where she was headed.

"What if…what if I could call you…?" Lori stammered.

"What if you could call me?" Henry asked. "What do you mean, Lori?"

"What if I called you…would you mind if I called you… Dr. H? Would that be okay?" The tribe was super strict about keeping boundaries very formal when facing authority figures like doctors, lawyers, pastors, principals, preachers, and police officers. Might she be entering a forbidden trail?

"Dr. H." Henry repeated the name. His grandfather had called him "H" as a boy. "I like the sound of that," he said. "Sure, Lori. You're welcome to call me Dr. H."

Lori beamed. "Really? It's okay?"

"Yes."

"Thank you, Dr. H." Lori sighed. "Thank you. That means so much to me."

15

Grapeshots

October 31, 1998

"I HAD A horrible nightmare last night Dr. H," Lori said quietly in session. She twirled a strand of her thinning hair like a string of worry beads, her legs hanging limply over the side of the bed. It had been ten days since their first trip to the cafeteria, and he'd been on the lookout for signs that this unconventional approach had caused a shift in Lori.

"Say more," Henry urged.

"There was this creature that was so ugly and grotesque." She frowned, pushing at her cheeks with her hands as if to imitate the horrible vision still fresh in her memory. "It was drowning in the ocean, and debris was crashing into it—like it was trash." Grasping her neck with her ghostly white fingers, she made a choking sound. She peeked at Dr. H to make sure he wasn't getting sick to his stomach the way she was.

"Please continue, Lori. Your sharing this terrifying dream with me is very helpful. Trust me. Please, go on."

"Well, the creature had a misshapen face," she said, her voice trembling. "And it was the most vile sight you could ever put your eyes on. I could hardly look at it, it was so horrible, but I did, and in my dream I yelled out, 'If you want to save it, you must feed it.'" Her stomach and chest contracted, as if she were about to have the dry heaves.

"Oh my," Henry said softly, not wanting to interrupt the flow of Lori's thoughts. He inhaled deeply, encouraging her to breathe as well. "What happened next?"

"There was someone holding this repulsive thing, trying to squeeze its tiny mouth open." Her face blanched. "I mean, it was hideous."

"Then what?"

"This person was cupping its mouth like this," she said, demonstrating with her hands. "And the person had a small dropper, you know, like the little bottles you feed birds with."

"Yes," Henry murmured.

"Well, the person was coaxing the creature to relax, to open its mouth, to release the tension in its jaw," she said, fumbling. "So it could learn how to swallow." She pulled her long sleeves down her forearms, covering her knuckles.

"You don't have to hide," he whispered. "You can feel safe right here, right now." He opened his hands, trying to shift her consciousness to be nonjudgmental.

She gulped, fixated on her ghoulish dream sequence. "All of a sudden, the creature began to take in the liquid, one drop at a time—and I woke up." Her eyes fluttered, and then she wiped them as if she had just awakened. "Then I knew I was the creature," she declared tenderly, as she slowly looked up to meet Dr. H's gaze. "And you were the person feeding me."

Henry was moved to silence by Lori's profound experience. He could feel in his bones the dream's powerful reflection of her surrender to trust and her potential willingness to learn how to care for and accept herself.

"Thank you," he whispered after a moment. "Thank you." And then, in full voice, he gently affirmed. "Yes, Lori, yes. You can feed her. She needs to be fed. And she needs to be fed love."

Lori let the sobs flow and flow without restraint. As she acknowledged and recognized the judgment and shame revealed in her dream—and accepted Dr. H's validation and understanding—she felt a huge wave of release flow through her. It was as though her tears of relief were washing away a tiny morsel of ancient grief, a loathing toward the creature she had grown to know as *self*.

"And one more thing, Lori." Dr. H paused for emphasis. "Maybe it's time to add more milk to your shredded shit."

"Oh, Dr. H." Lori stomped her foot in lighthearted annoyance. "I wish you wouldn't say that."

"I'll stop saying it when you stop adding water to it and start adding milk, okay?"

Lori stuck her tongue out at Dr. H.

* * *

The next day, Lori was sitting alone in the day room, eyes closed, clutching the prescription Henry had written: "Anger is okay!" Slowly she nodded off to sleep.

"Lori, wake up!" Henry whispered loudly.

Startled, she opened her eyes and straightened up on the corduroy loveseat. She stuffed the prescription hurriedly into her pocket.

"I'm awake," she said apologetically, as if she had been napping on the job.

"Come on, Lori," Henry urged, nodding his head toward the door. "We're going back to the cafeteria." He stood firmly in front of her, thumbs hooked in the sides of his pants pockets. His small, ever-present beeper hugged his belt with its coiled clasp.

"No, no," she protested, shaking her head and looking at her watch. "Lunch will be here in ten minutes, and I have to be on time," she said, as if she were reporting to a probation officer.

"No shredded shit today," he ordered with casual authority. "I told them to hold it."

Her jaw dropped. "I'll eat all three boxes today for lunch," she said, trying to bargain. There was no way, she was certain, that she could handle another torturous cafeteria outing.

He wasn't surprised that all signs of the progress they'd made were gone. He'd been through the cycle with her a thousand times: one step forward, ninety-nine hundredths of a step back. "Too late," he said, hoping to build on the success of their last trip, when Lori had eaten a whole egg. He knew that had been no small feat, and that it was essential to build on that momentum. Otherwise, her powerful negative resistance would sabotage the small but significant progress she'd made.

"Lori, it's time," he demanded, leaving her no room to protest. He motioned her to rise as if he were an usher assisting a patron. "We're going on another field trip. Let's go." He snapped his fingers and pointed to the door.

* * *

"Hey, watch this," Henry called out playfully to Lori. His eyes twinkled as he made his way toward the huge fruit bowl near the end of the cafeteria line. "Do you think you can do this?"

Turning cautiously, she walked a few steps toward him, unable to imagine what he might be up to. "Do what?" Lori responded meekly, apprehensive but curious. *What's he going to try to get me to eat this time? He didn't comprehend how god-awful difficult it was to eat an egg, much less a piece of fruit that was mixed with other kinds of fruit. He still doesn't understand that when different foods touch each other they're contaminated.*

He tossed a plump purple grape high in the air, startling her out of her thoughts as he threw back his head, opened his mouth wide, and waited for it to fall. A herd of people milled about. The grape came down quickly and disappeared deep within his mouth. He chewed, swallowed, and embellished his success with a raise of his eyebrows and a Cheshire cat smile.

"Ahhh. That tasted good." He wiped his mouth with the length of his finger. "It's fun to break the rules, isn't it?"

Lori's mouth dropped open. Her wide eyes sparkled. "I don't believe it," she belted out, doubling over in laughter. "You're not supposed to act like a clown." She couldn't contain herself and almost fell to the floor. "Who do you think you are?" she said, incredulous, giving him an uncharacteristic light shove of delight across his shoulder.

Henry beamed, watching her momentary break from her morose frame of mind. She needed to laugh.

And to her own amazement, she wanted to laugh. "Do it again," she demanded, snorting in delight, oblivious to the others around them. "Do it again," she shrieked, like a four-year-old clamoring for more gifts.

"Did you like that?" Henry teased, pleased to have a standing ovation for his performance—and a request for an encore. She was a better audience than any he'd encountered in the comedy clubs. "Would you pay good money to see it again?" he said playfully, his cheeks flush with merriment.

"Yes, yes." She nodded eagerly. "Do it again!"

"You bet." He gave her a thumbs-up, then announced, "Second serve." He tossed another grape even higher into the air than before. The grape made several somersaults in the air before it smacked solidly onto Henry's tongue. "Yum," he said as he smacked his lips triumphantly. He shot out in an English accent, "Advantage, nutrition for all."

"You crack me up," Lori yelled. A dam had burst wide open releasing a flood of energy. "You're outrageous!" Bent over with laughter she gulped down giggles, wiping tears from her ebullient face. "I can't," she moaned between belly laughs, nearly choking. "I can't...I can't believe you did it again, and you caught it in your mouth." She roared, momentarily forgetting where she was, who she was, or who she was with.

Henry beamed with pride. "I can't believe you," he said as he laughed, throwing her a high five. He had never seen her exude such freedom. "I can't believe how you just roared like a lioness. Lori, you radiate such light when you laugh." He pointed toward her heart with one hand, while his other hand spread lavishly over his chest.

Then Lori's laughter stopped abruptly. She fell into deep silence. Her high vanished out of nowhere. "Can we go now?"

"What just happened, Lori?" Henry turned and followed at her heels as Lori headed out the cafeteria door and paused in the hallway.

"You know, Dr. H," she whispered sadly. "When I grew up, playing with food was never okay. We would get restricted if any of us did anything to break the rules. It was so tense at the dinner table."

"That must have been difficult," Henry said. He watched her contract, like a turtle tucking its head into her shell. A tear formed in her eye, and her smile, so illuminating just a moment ago, had completely vanished.

"Please don't make me eat today," she begged. "I'm just too—"

Henry knew exactly what she was about to say. He could scarcely control his frustration. "Look, Lori, you're dangerously thin. You're not fat. The weight you're feeling is the weight of your sadness, anger, resentment, guilt, shame, and helplessness that you felt in the past." He paused, considering his next move. "Now let's go back inside."

Lori sealed her lips and crossed her arms. "No," she mumbled. "I can't." She was back in the Doghouse of yesteryear, mercilessly replaying a never-ending tape from her childhood.

Henry winced. Her words felt like the doors of a prison clanging shut.

* * *

On the next cafeteria outing, several days later, he walked with Lori. Her head was bowed as he searched for new openings to unlock the bondage of her anorexia, and she stopped in her tracks about thirty feet from the cafeteria entrance.

Henry did an about-face. "What is it?" he asked cautiously.

"Why do you always pay for me?" she inquired softly, eyeing him with curiosity.

He resisted the temptation to ask her why she wanted to know. Asking patients questions about their questions was the fallback technique for minimizing a therapist's influence and giving the patient an opportunity to say more. But he knew it could be maddening for a patient too.

"Because you deserve it," he responded. Besides, he didn't care about the money and would certainly not risk having Lori contribute, fearing her mind would find any reason to sabotage the whole outing. He continued walking.

She hurried to catch up, stumbling once before she reached him, struggling to digest what he'd just said. "I deserve it?" She stuttered, forcing her mouth to enunciate the unfamiliar words.

"Yes, Lori," he said, holding the door for her. As he handed her a tray, he was conscious of his efforts to foster an environment in which she could feel like a person rather than a mental patient with several diagnoses strung around her neck.

"Still serving eggs?" he asked the short order cook.

"Yes," she said.

"Two orders of sunny-side up eggs, please."

Lori paced awkwardly nearby.

At the self-serve section, Henry placed two bagels in the toaster and picked a large, shiny grape from the edge of the fruit dish. He tossed it high into the air. Lori giggled at his performance, and he allowed himself to be hopeful. Maybe she'd eat today.

"Dr. H, you're such a show-off!" She looked up at him with a wide grin.

"Yup." He smiled confidently as he flicked another grape square into his mouth, dazzling her again. He paused purposefully and winked at her. "Sometimes, Lori, it's good to express yourself in a silly way."

She followed him like a loyal puppy, bouncing delightfully to the checkout counter. The clerk, an older Latina, rang up their bill. Henry flashed his doctor's badge to receive his employee discount.

"That will be eight thirty-two," said the clerk. "I hope you feed her well." She smiled sweetly as she motioned her head toward Lori.

Lori tugged on his right sleeve. "Dr. H?"

He turned toward her. Several people waited behind them in line, holding their trays.

"Dr. H," she repeated with a steady gaze. "Let me pay today."

He glanced at her extended hand, in which a ten-dollar bill lay between her bony thumb and nail-bitten finger. A glint of a smile flashed in her eyes.

"Please take it," she said passionately, as if the green paper might combust if she held it any longer.

"Thank you. I so appreciate it, Lori." He nodded graciously, accepting the bill. He knew her offer was a significant shift in her willingness to accept responsibility. She was beginning to show stirrings of being a partner in her healing by making an investment far more profound than the dollar amount. The more she tended the garden in her own precious healing field, the better the probability her life would shift its trajectory to blossom rather than wilt and die.

When they sat down at their usual table, Lori took a determined breath and glanced at Dr. H. Cautiously, stiffly, she leaned over her plate, her eyes wide with apprehension. "Dr. H," she whispered, "will you help me eat today?"

"Of course I will, Lori, in whatever way I can," he replied, hopeful, curious, and alert. "Thank you for asking." He leaned forward just a tad. "Tell me what I can do."

"Will you…would you say a pray…um…a prayer for me?" she bravely asked, hardly able to meet his gaze. Her throat tightened around the word *prayer*, and notes of fear, shame, and repentance echoed as she proposed using prayer in such an inappropriate way.

Henry held out his hands, palms up, extended his fingers, and began silently composing the perfect prayer. Lori closed her eyes. Then, with her thin hands palms down she met his midway across the table. She drew in a somber and serious breath.

"We give thanks," Henry began, "for being here to honor and nourish our bodies, our minds, and our spirits with these golden eggs and crispy bagels." The ambient cafeteria noise blended in seamlessly with their next breath, taken in unison. "Please assist Lori, oh Great One and Creator of the universe." He continued with his eyes open. Lori's were tightly shut. "Lord of all that is, help her to accept this food as fuel to strengthen her body, a sacred temple." He was silent for a long moment before she opened her eyes and retrieved her hands, placing them neatly on the table beside her cooling platter of food.

"Thank you," she said, crying and smiling simultaneously, trying to assimilate this new approach to the sacred. "That was so nice," she sang out softly, pressing her hand to her heart.

"You had better take this holy wisdom into your heart," he teased her, wagging his finger across the table, shifting the somber seriousness into a lighter playfulness. "This meal is so much better than the shredded shit you've been eating. Besides, look at you." He pointed to his behind. "You need to get a butt."

Lori flashed a wide-open smile and wiped away a tear. "Okay, okay," she promised. "I'll try to eat today. It's not that I don't want to eat." She eyed her plate—food was momentarily no longer the enemy. "It's just that I've been so full," she whispered to no one in particular.

Hesitant at first, she meticulously cut a small piece of egg and brought it to her mouth. And then she took the plunge and bit into it. The yolk felt so soft and sweet. She swayed back and forth, feeling buoyant and free as the ever-painful tightness of her joints was released.

"This tastes so good!" She chewed with gusto, not caring that she was talking with her mouth full. Her eyes glowed, as if she had discovered eating for the first time.

"Yes!" Henry affirmed, mirroring her gustatory enthusiasm. "Yes, indeed. Food tastes good." He held out his arms for added emphasis. "It's okay to eat, Lori."

"Umm-hmm," she murmured. Her body's unbearable heaviness seemed to lift.

"Lori," Henry exclaimed through his mouthful of food. "It is such a joy to share this moment with you."

The corners of her lips curled in joyful sadness as tears welled up in her eyes. "Thank you," she mouthed, as a bit of yolk slithered down the corner of her lip. "Thank you."

* * *

A few days later, Lori observed Dr. H doing it again: acting outrageously. As he was leaving the unit for the evening, she stood a stone's throw away in the shadows of the day room, watching him. He sauntered up to the partition that separated the nurses' station from the patients. Lori could see the side of his face and body approaching the glass. The nurses, busily charting notes, did not seem to notice him.

By now, Henry was a familiar sight on the ward, and he knew the staff fairly well. On a whim, he decided to break the monotony of the nurses' administrative tasks. He pressed his face against the glass and twisted his nose and mouth into mashed potatoes.

I don't believe this! Lori shouted to herself, suppressing an urge to dance. The nurses looked up in unison. *Do it again,* Lori thought, recalling his hilarious grape-swallowing antics. As if on cue, Dr. H started making funny faces in the glass again. The nurses burst out laughing, shaking their heads in comic disbelief at the silly doctor and putting aside their pens for a hearty laugh.

This is amazing, Lori thought, smiling inside. *I can smile and even laugh, even though I feel compelled to die.* As the thought flitted through her mind, her neck, shoulders, trunk, and legs began to stiffen spontaneously, the feelings of tightness taking her back in time, about to be discovered committing some horrible, unforgivable sin. *You're not supposed to speak or feel,* reprimanded her inner critic. She felt the wave of emotion slipping away, frightened back into hiding, shamed into silence once again.

But maybe life doesn't have to be so serious, a happier voice countered. Maybe it could actually be fun to be alive. Lori's whole body seemed to sigh—comic relief by proxy—as her tension ebbed away.

Henry waved to the nurses, and turned back toward the elevators, but not before he noticed Lori watching him, a new softness and openness in her unfamiliar smile. "Goodnight, Lori," he said quietly.

"Goodnight Dr. H," she said. She looked down at the floor, then back again at his gentle face. *If he can change and loosen up,* she thought, *maybe I can too.*

16

Obese with Shame

November 7, 1998

"HEY, GABI, DID you see this?" Henry broke the seal at the edge of the booklet and dropped the rest of the pile of mail on the corner table. He carried the brochure into the kitchen and held it up for his wife to see. "It's the announcement for next year's Integrative Medicine Conference in San Francisco." The brochure said there would be speakers from the alternative healing and complementary medicine communities, and he saw that they touched on a wide range of subjects outside of his traditional medical training: hypnosis, meditation, guided imagery, Zen Buddhism, and Psychotherapy. The conference promised to focus on these "right brain" areas of inquiry that Henry was curious to explore.

"Yes, I saw it." His wife's voice was muffled as she reached deep into the refrigerator. She pulled out a large stalk of broccoli, and scoffed. "I don't know how we got on that mailing list."

"Probably because of those tapes I ordered last month," Henry said. "The ones on mind, body, and spirit. The therapists and doctors who created them will be presenters at the conference. Why don't we go together? What do you think? We could make it a working vacation, maybe stay on and spend an extra day or two in San Francisco." Even as he heard himself

169

say the words, he regretted them. Things had been so tense between him and Gabriella, he wasn't so sure he really wanted to spend that much time with her. And he knew that having her with him would prevent him from immersing himself in the conference. He still harbored some hope that a break in their routine might give them a chance to reclaim some small piece of common ground in their relationship. The marriage counseling seemed to be headed nowhere.

"Henry, you've got to be kidding me. Do you seriously want to spend four whole days around those people, listening to their off-the-wall notions about oneness and miracles and all that nonsense?"

"Gabi, I can't believe you won't be just a little open minded." Henry sighed. He wanted to understand how these other professionals might deal with patients like Lori. Perhaps they had understandings that conventional medicine couldn't offer about why she felt so fat yet was so dangerously thin, and maybe they'd even touch upon the effects of religious and spiritual conflicts that patients like Lori struggled with. It was certainly worth exploring. He had asked others in his profession how they would handle patients like Lori, but as often as not their responses were as frustrating as Lori herself. Sometimes, they'd just fall silent, shaking their heads and silently concurring about how stubborn and challenging such patients could be, rejecting anything and everything conventional medicine had to offer.

"Do you actually get continuing medical education credit for a conference like that?" Gabriella asked. "Go if you want to. I'm still working on my dissertation."

Gabriella's words stung, reminding him that the distance between them was growing deeper and wider. The more he strove to expand his own world, the more he felt his wife resisting and the more he felt the desire to live in a space of greater openness, exploration, and nonjudgmental curiosity. With each passing week, he lamented, it became increasingly difficult to see a pathway for them to find each other again.

Even as he chafed against Gabriella's derision of his alternative approaches to therapy, Henry was deeply gratified that his unconventional way of reaching out to Lori was opening up windows of light in her dark interior. He tried to comfort himself with the idea that since she wasn't going with him, he'd be able to relax a bit more.

That night, he stayed up late, watching the quarter moon rise over the ocean, thinking about his complicated, desperately ill patient. He felt as though he'd been on a four-year ride through an endless expanse of desert, the road heading nowhere. He felt desperate for some way to finally, convincingly, enduringly reach her and help her break through the distortions of her ego-mind.

The next morning as he drove to the hospital, an idea popped into his head, a way to try to demonstrate to Lori that her perceptions of physical weight were merely that—her perceptions, and more importantly, misperceptions. On the ward, he hurried to the nurses' station, grabbed a roll of two-inch white surgical tape, headed briskly down the hall to Lori's room, and gave the door a sharp knock.

"Lori," he said excitedly as he walked into her room. "If you were a coroner and you were to outline your body's width on the floor with this tape, show me how wide it would be." He waved the roll of tape in the air as he spoke.

"What? I...I don't understand," Lori shook her head and blinked her eyes. *What is Dr. H talking about?* The grape-tossing, funny-face-smashing doctor of a week or two ago was nowhere to be found and she didn't know what to make of it. *What does he want me to do?*

Again he explained, "If you were a coroner, and you were to outline your body's width on the floor with this tape, show me how wide your body would be." He was aware of the association this might have for her, of bringing up memories of her sister's death, but he had to risk it, and he was fairly certain she could handle that aspect of what he was about to do.

Lori stiffened. "Uh-uh, no," she said. She glanced at the tape in Dr. H's hands. Deep in her subconscious, she remembered the coroner removing her sister's body forever. But Dr. H seemed to have other things in mind.

Neither of them said a word. Henry tore off two long strips of tape. He squatted down on the floor near her feet. "Here," he said, reaching over to give her the tape. "Go on, Lori, show me how fat you are."

She looked at him like he was a lunatic. And didn't budge. For at least three minutes.

"Okay," he finally said, "I'll go first." He placed two strips of tape on the floor, about two feet apart. He lay down on the ground and fit his whole body nicely between the two strips of tape. After a few seconds he said, "Now it's your turn." He got up and tore off two more long strips of tape and held them out for her.

Lori felt backed into a corner. "Okay, okay, I'll do it!" Ever so reluctantly, she took each strip of tape from him, one by one, at the same time trying not to touch them, pinching them with her thumbs and forefingers. She knelt down on the gray industrial carpet, then slowly and very meticulously placed each strip on the floor, parallel to one another about five feet apart. Her hands were trembling. She ran her palm over each strip purposely several times to hold it in place.

Arms folded, Henry stood and watched silently as the minutes passed. When Lori finished, she inched her bowed head upward and stole a glance at him like a well-behaved prisoner as if to say, "Now what?"

He ran his fingers through his hair. "Now," he went on, "if you lie down on the floor, would you cover both strips of tape? Would you fill most of the space between them? Or would there be some distance between you and the two strips on the floor?"

Lori immediately crossed her arms, protecting her gut. She was annoyed, and her body swayed like a thin evergreen tree. *He must be a moron! Of course I would cover the tape! Doesn't he know how fat I am?*

Aloud she said, with saccharine politeness, "Obviously, my body would be touching the tape."

Henry, looming above her, nodded to the floor. "Please lie on your back and show me," he requested, extending his right hand downward. "Humor me, if you will."

Having gone this far, Lori decided to placate him with his request, though she had to work hard, because she didn't want him to see how angry she was.

Henry watched in silence as she uncrossed her arms and lay down on her back, mummy-like, between the two strips of tape, her arms held closely to her sides as they extended down toward her knees, which were squeezed together. Her feet could have been bound; there was no space between her legs. She was lying stiffly, her eyes darting nervously from left to right, her face pale and glowering. The two pieces of tape sandwiched her body like bread, with a spacious eighteen inches stretching out between her body and the tape on both sides. Several strands of brittle hair fell to the ground next to her shoulders.

Lori watched Dr. H from the corner of her eye, on the lookout for any trickery that he might try. *Why is he having me do this?*

Henry stepped beside her and carefully walked down the length of her scrawny frame in the space between her body and the tape, first on the left side, then on the right. She peered up at him, then to her left, then to her right. She was baffled. What is he doing? He continued his march up and down alongside her body, wrestling away the distorted grip the dark hand of her mind had on her, neither touching her loose-fitting clothing nor the white tape on each side.

Her head and neck twisted to follow her glance back and forth and side to side as he walked, and her mind shouted out, *No, no, no!* She tried desperately to process what was happening, but her mind felt numb, unable to put what she saw together with what she knew. It didn't make sense. *My body should be covering the tape!* When Dr. H paused momentarily at her hips as he headed toward her feet, she asked herself, *How can his feet be between me and the tape?*

Still, Dr. H continued to walk, up one side and down the other, then down one side and up the other. Lori looked left and right. *This can't be, this can't be, this can't be! Why is there so much empty space between the side of my body and the tape?* She struggled to know. She couldn't believe his shoes were plodding up and down alongside her body—without touching her or the tape. *How can this be? I take up so much space. I am so disgustingly fat. This must be a trick,* she concluded. *He's ridiculing me.*

Henry stepped aside and turned toward Lori. "Looks like you're a lot thinner than you realize," he said.

She unfroze and got up abruptly, brushing her pant legs as if to ward off invisible rug toxins. "This doesn't make sense," she said, waving away the truth with several backhanded wrist swats. She paced around the tape—dazed, confused, and feeling violated.

"Lori, I'm going to have to go in a moment," Henry said, knowing he had rocked her fragile world. He had to return to his office and see his other patients.

She stared at the floor. She wanted to say, "Fine, you can go, but what about me? What do I do with this?" But she sat sternly on the edge of her bed and said nothing.

"I'll be back tomorrow, don't you worry." He tried to console her, touching her shoulder lightly. He glanced at his watch and left, heading toward the nurses' station to get her chart and return the roll of tape.

Shortly after he sat down to write a note, he felt a tap on his shoulder. Lori's nurse was standing behind him.

"Lori wants to see you before you go," she said casually. "She's in the day room."

"Okay." Henry finished his note and went to see her.

Lori waited until he was just a few feet away. She glared at him with hot, laser-beam eyes, her body poised to harpoon a whale, and declared, "You are the stupidest doctor in the whole wide world, and I hate you very, very much."

Henry felt as if he had been punched by a willful child. "Ex…excuse me," he said, pushing down a flash of irritation. He felt a rise in his blood pressure.

"You are the stupidest doctor in the whole wide world, and I hate you very, very much," she repeated forcefully.

Henry felt the full rush of his own emotions: anger, frustration, and resentment for her ingratitude. He inhaled deeply, smiled at her insincerely, and headed toward the door. Halfway there, he stopped. He took a deep breath and felt a calming sense of knowingness. The burning flash of feelings from moments before died away as rapidly as it had arisen. The tension in his body shifted to ease.

He turned around and greeted Lori with his eyes. She was wobbly, looking like she would crumple to the ground if he blew a gust of air toward her.

"Thank you, Lori," he said softly, his heart smiling. "Thank you very much. Thank you for expressing your feelings so clearly and directly." He left the day room, leaving her standing all alone, his words lingering.

Lori was stunned and perplexed, and her body reeled. Her thin belly ached with gut-wrenching pain, as if her nerves had been severed. She couldn't believe her ears.

He must be mocking me! She hated him even more. But she was confused. He had spoken so gently. He didn't appear to be angry. Was it mockery? She couldn't tell. She had little experience, if any, of being spoken to like that, without getting hurt.

She hurried back to her room and lay back down on the floor to try to figure out why there was so much space between her body and the tape.

* * *

"Lori is obese with shame!" Henry stood proudly at Susan's open door that evening before either of them left the office.

"What are you talking about?" His colleague lowered her reading glasses as she looked up to him.

Henry went into her office, too excited to sit down. He described the tape measuring experiment he did with Lori. "She's obese with shame. It makes sense to me now. All the emotions we consider to be negative: fear, anger, sadness, worthlessness, guilt, and shame—they have gotten stuck in Lori and they cause her to feel heavy."

Susan put one ear piece of her reading glasses in her mouth and bit lightly on it, saying nothing.

"Lori experiences herself as fat. She feels heavy, as if she's wearing two hundred pounds of body armor."

Susan put down the chart she was working on. "I've never heard those three words put together before—obese with shame."

Henry inhaled with excitement. "All those emotions, they're just energy, right?"

Susan squinted as if there were too much light in the room. "Well, yes, I suppose you could say emotions have energy."

"Well, in Lori, those emotions, the energy of them, especially shame and guilt and worthlessness, have stagnated," Henry said. "And those stagnated emotions, at least with Lori, have turned into mass."

Susan stared at him dubiously. "What have you been reading?"

"All those emotions, all the trauma from her past, all those unhealed wounds—"

"Yes?" Susan lifted both eyebrows.

"Have become massive. She is obese…with shame. That's why she feels, thinks, and experiences herself to be so fat." Henry inhaled a breath of satisfaction. "She's obese with shame."

Susan tilted her head to one side. "That's an interesting way to look at it."

"Yes, I think so too. Do you know what else that means?"

"Do tell me, Inspector Clouseau." Susan humored him with a smile.

"Emotions not only hide, they don't know the calendar." Henry shrugged.

"Yes, of course," Susan nodded. "To understand the present you have to understand the past. Okay, Einstein, if she's obese with shame, how does she get skinny and shame free? What will the past tell you about that?" Susan put her reading glasses back on.

"Um…" Henry's forehead wrinkled. "I don't know. I don't have a clue." He scratched his head. "Well, actually, that's what I'm trying to figure out." He turned and started walking out of the room.

"Let me know when you find out, kiddo," Susan called out after him, chuckling to herself.

17

Weapons of Mental Destruction

November 14, 1998

L IKE A NUCLEAR winter, the hospital nighttime, for Lori, seemed to last forever. The second sleeping pill she had taken wasn't working. She tossed and turned in her bed, agonizing over her session with Dr. Kaplan earlier that afternoon. She felt so grotesquely uncomfortable and so massively full.

I blew it! I just totally and completely blew it! Lori rebuked herself. She had made a fatal and irreconcilable error. She had scathingly condemned and criticized the one person who had unfailingly tried to help her. There was no way that their relationship, now severed by her wanton words, could ever be restored. She had to die. There was no alternative.

Her mind-field had become a minefield. The hidden WMDs—weapons of mental destruction—were on auto-destruct. Her anger-arrows, levied at Dr. H, backfired and turned into guilt-grenades. The ensuing shame-shrapnel scattered, penetrating every part of her body. She could not sort through her sordid emotions. Death beckoned her as the only way out of the colossally painful and bloody mess she had obviously created.

The past twenty hours had been her worst day and night yet in the hospital. She could no longer trust her relationship with Dr. H because she had gotten angry and yelled at him. *He probably won't see me anymore. Or if he does,* she reasoned, *he'll only stop by for five minutes, like most of the other patients' doctors do.* Just thinking about it shocked her body in a convulsive wave of fear, guilt and supreme worthlessness.

She sat up in bed, faced the closed door, and thought about dying. *If only I could sleep and never wake up again, I'd be out of all this pain.* Disgusted with herself, she put on her slippers. Trying her best to ignore her searing back pain, she crept out of her room and walked slowly down the dimly lit hall to the nurses' station.

Sandy, an RN who liked the graveyard shift, was alone charting within the steel-reinforced windows and ever-fluorescent brightness. Another nurse sat in the locked unit nearby. The locked ward was a place for the more dangerously disturbed, agitated, impulsive, or impaired patients. It adjoined the open unit by two sets of locked doors and a small passageway.

Lori swore to herself she would never end up back in the locked unit as she tapped on the window to get Sandy's attention.

Sandy rose and straightened her blouse before opening the door. "You're up again," she said, glancing at the clock. "It's almost five in the morning. Still not sleeping?"

"No," Lori said, glaring at her feet. "Could I have another sleeping pill?"

Sandy put a rubber stopper under the door and motioned for her to come in. "Lori, dear," she said comfortingly. "You got your regular one at ten last night, and I gave you another at two this morning. You know Dr. Kaplan only allows you one extra pill each night."

"Okay, I'll go." Lori turned to leave, her face downcast.

"Wait a minute," the nurse said, wrinkling her forehead and pushing aside her stack of charts. "Have a seat. Tell me. What's really keeping you awake?"

"You're too busy," Lori said, pouting, protecting herself from the sharp stab of rejection always just around the corner.

Nodding toward the stack of charts, Sandy shrugged and said, "I can do this in a little while."

Lori shuffled to the chair. She tugged at the collar of her rose-pink terrycloth robe. It used to be her favorite, but now it was always falling off her shoulders and hung limply around her waist.

"What's wrong?" Sandy gently asked as she sat back down in her chair.

Lori sank down, aware of how much space she occupied, as if she were an obese person sitting in the middle seat of an overbooked airplane flight. "Everything. I'm such a loser!" She burst into tears.

Sandy handed her several tissues.

"Linda killed herself, and I could have done something to stop it." Lori sobbed like her heart had sprung a leak.

"Hey now, stop beating up on yourself," Sandy said, scooting a little closer. Lori had opened up to Sandy about Linda's suicide a week earlier. "It's not your fault," she reassured her. "Stop blaming yourself. And please blow your nose. You're going to get my charts wet."

Lori wiped her face as she breathed in staccato. "I am such a loser," she repeated, mostly to herself, careful not to reveal the depths of her despair. She knew if she revealed any thoughts of suicide, they'd get reported to Dr. H and she'd never get out of the hospital.

"Have you talked about this to Dr. Kaplan?" Sandy pressed on lightly, careful not to make her feel worse.

"I can't talk to him anymore," she muttered, her breath finally less laborious. "I told him I hate him, and now I don't know what to do." Her chest and shoulders sagged.

"I'm sure you and he can work it out," Sandy said with optimism. "He's very compassionate, you know."

Lori lifted her head. "Okay," she said, an idea hatching in her mind. "I'm feeling much better," she lied as she folded the tissues carefully and placed them in the garbage can. "Thank you for taking the time to talk to me."

Sandy looked at her quizzically. "You're welcome," she mumbled. "We can talk some more if you want." She was suspicious that something was not as it seemed.

"No, thanks. I'm all right, really." Lori rose to leave. "I can talk to Dr. Kaplan if he decides to come later today."

Sandy shrugged.

Lori returned to her room. She knew there was only one thing to do. As red-orange hues of brilliance streaked across the purple horizon outside, Lori developed an endgame plan, a way to leave the hospital so she could end her life once and for all.

Starvation wasn't working. Although restricting her food intake to almost nothing seemed like the polite and tidy way to die—there would be no mess to clean up like there had been with Linda's blood and scattered brain fragments—it was taking much too long. And besides, she reasoned, at her autopsy the coroner would weigh her body, she would be too shamefully fat, and all would know the mortifying number registered on the pathologist's scale.

She had to go home. She had secretly amassed a flotilla of pills in a small box in the back of her kitchen pantry—white ones for depression, pink ones for anxiety, yellow ones to sleep, blue ones for agitation, and football-shaped orange ones for mood swings. Once she got home, she determined, she could overdose and end her miserable and worthless existence.

I'll put on a happy face, she concluded, as she changed from her nightgown to her worn, ill-fitting Macy's jeans. *That way the nurses will report I'm okay to leave.*

She waited until Sandy left and the morning shift arrived. In her sneakers—without shoelaces—she walked briskly to the nurses' station where she spotted Kathy, an old-school day nurse, busily absorbed in reviewing the nightly reports. Lori approached the open door and raised her hand awkwardly. She smiled. "Hi."

There was no response. Lori cleared her throat.

Kathy continued reading.

Lori smiled again, baring teeth with receded gums, anorexia's fingerprint of decalcification. "Did you have a good night?"

Kathy's eyes moved up from the charts and met Lori's. "Why, yes, Lori. Why do you ask?"

She faltered. "Uh, well…I…uh…just was wondering. That's all."

Kathy scanned her scrawny body for hidden clues of concern. Finding none, she shook her head imperceptibly and then returned to her task. As if she had erroneously entered a one-way street, Lori backed up and headed toward her room.

Out of view of the staff and other patients, she began pinching her cheeks. *I'll have a healthier pink complexion,* she rationalized. *They'll be sure to notice and report it to Dr. H and he'll discharge me.*

At that moment, she totally understood why Linda had killed herself. Linda's uncompromising pain after getting pregnant out of wedlock and being treated like a sinister heathen and sacrilegious harlot was too much to bear. *I have to join Linda, that's my fate,* she thought. It was her just reward for her own unpardonable sins. She had no reason to live. Dying was the only way she could acknowledge her sister's life and death—and why Linda had no choice but to kill herself.

Lori sat in her room with her head bowed like a death row inmate awaiting execution. Her mental torment was too much to bear, and her physical body screamed out at her to end its agony. The awful limitations she had in bending, squatting, walking, and even just sitting still or lying in bed just made her emotional despair worse. She watched the clock tick and tock, mercilessly and timelessly.

She dreaded the upcoming interaction with Dr. Kaplan but felt the only choice she had was to convince him she was ready to be discharged. *I can't let him know how much I'm thinking about suicide,* she thought. *I must get him to let me go home,* she fantasized. After several hours she left her room and hovered around the nurses' station.

Henry appeared on the ward at three.

Lori greeted him as if she were president and founder of a newly formed doctor welcoming committee. "Hi, Dr. H. Thank you for coming," she said, thrusting out her hand.

He took her aging, rough-skinned hand in his and shook it. "Hello, Lori." He noticed a tint of red on her cheeks. "Did you put makeup on today?"

"Uh, no, but I feel so much better," she lied. She retracted her hand and fluffed her dirty, matted hair with her fingers as if to say, "See how hygienic I am." Then she politely said, "Please let me go home." She pretended to be whole and assertive. "I'll eat more when I'm at home."

Henry squinted at her, his spirit sighing wearily. "Are you nuts?" he said, blinking, feeling a heaviness in his chest. "If you go home, you'll die, and I can't let you do that. Look how emaciated you are. You get dizzy all the time. You barely eat four hundred miserable calories a day. Lori, I can't let you go."

"Please," she begged, stomping her foot on the floor. "I can't stay here anymore. It's too hard to sleep and follow all the rules. I'll eat when I get home."

"Lori, let's go somewhere private and talk." Henry could feel her tension. He braced himself for the inevitable battle her ego would wage against him. "Let's go to room 173."

At the sound of those numbers, Lori turned and headed toward her room. Inside, Henry stood in a corner while Lori paced.

He inhaled slowly. "You're trying to fool me into thinking you're safe to be discharged, and it's not working. You're running away from something, acting like you have to kill yourself for some crime you committed."

Lori stopped abruptly. "This isn't helping. I should go home." Her face felt hot. She eyed the door. "You don't understand. All I can think about is how I just want to die." She felt the tears streaming down her burning cheeks.

"Of course," he said. "You judge yourself a failure. You get angry at yourself. You hate yourself, and then all you think about is how you want to die. Then you can commit the ultimate act of self-hatred. Suicide. That's the story you keep holding on to. Like you're still guilty of some crime."

"I am."

"What are you guilty of?"

Her legs trembled as she settled onto her perfectly made bed. "So much. Not saving Linda from dying for starters." A bucket of tears threatened to break down the floodgates of her eyes.

"That's ridiculous," Henry said, simmering. "There was no way you could've saved Linda. You are getting stuck in an old story. It's ego-fiction! This is how your mind traps you again and again into believing you're a worthless loser. You take on the role of jailer. You're condemning that young girl called you from your past. This is a rerun. Reruns are boring. It's time to create a new episode and let go of the toxic guilt and self-judgment." Henry's warrior energy radiated.

Lori didn't back down; instead, for some reason, she zeroed in on his eyes, sparks of fire glowing in hers. "I know I couldn't have saved her, but I still feel guilty that I didn't get to her fast enough. I would always think that maybe I could have saved her. If I got to her sooner. If I called 9-1-1 right away. If I had known she had bought the bullets at the store we went to two weeks earlier." She turned her gaze to the floor. "If I prayed harder…" She closed her eyes. "I couldn't believe she didn't rise up."

Henry took aim. "Look at me." He waited until she did, and then he fired. "No one but you walked in on that suicide scene. Not your sisters, not your brother, not your mother, not your father, not your husband, no one in your family—but you.

You were the one who walked in and saw her brains splattered on the floor."

Lori started to rise up like an inflatable doll getting a pump of air. She moved to an open space, and then suddenly she lay down on the floor on her left side, bending her knees toward her head. She was recreating the suicide scene. She became Linda, dead on the ground. She opened her mouth halfway. "This is how she was," she sputtered out. "A pool of blood around her mouth and neck." She pointed to her brain, just above her right ear. "There was a piece missing right here."

Henry pulled in an extra dose of air. "Did anyone say, 'That must have been horrible for Lori, for her to see what she saw'? Did anyone say that?"

Lori pulled herself upright. "No!" Her eyes were aflame. "No one said that." She inhaled the words, then blew them out. "No one said, 'Your sister shot herself. Maybe something was wrong.' No. They didn't say anything like that. They said, 'It's the Lord's will.' And that was it. My twenty-first birthday was four days later. There was to be a celebration. It was scheduled in advance. Now we had to focus on that."

Henry tilted his head empathetically.

Lori winced as her whole body was stricken with pain. "Do you know they had the same food at my birthday they used at the funeral? They used leftovers because they didn't want to waste any food." Lori fought back tears again.

He scrunched his nose in disgust. That would kill an appetite, he thought.

"I used to believe I could never think about getting angry at Linda for committing suicide." Lori blew her nose. "I couldn't be angry at her. I felt so much sadness and compassion for her."

Henry listened like an owl in the dead of the night.

"But now I'm realizing," Lori continued, "she made it okay to kill yourself. She made it okay to commit suicide. I guess I learned from her it was okay to kill yourself if the pain was so great. I just didn't want anyone to have to walk into a room and see what I saw." Lori curled over on her knees and finally let the sobs roll through her.

Henry waited for her weeping to subside. He knew she'd have to let go of her self-judgment at being angry at Linda. He knew her anger, like pus in a wound, needed to be expressed in order to be released. He knew she wasn't quite ready to accept reassurances from him—they probably sounded like pity to her, but he tried anyway. "You don't have to feel guilty Lori, for feeling angry. It wasn't your fault that no one was there to protect you."

Lori peered at him through watery eyes. "I thought I killed Tom because I rubbed his shoulders where he had the Fentanyl patches on."

"Right." Henry paused, measuring his words carefully. "You feel guilt again. Emotions don't know the calendar. Just like with Linda. Doesn't mean you're guilty, just that you feel guilt. But your mind creates the same old story. Somehow, you failed. Guilt drives your perception and shapes your reality." He knew she didn't get it. "It wasn't your fault."

Lori tried to grasp what he meant. But her brain felt like a fog of overwhelming emotions. "Please, Dr. H," she whined, not able to see the truth of the matter. "You have to get me out of here."

Lori struggled to keep her composure as she sat limply on the center of her bed, bony buttocks lightly touching the white blanket, legs dangling downward, knees locked together, toes turned inward. Her mouth drooped downward in a curve of despair. She began to sob.

"Sorry, Lori, I'm not able to help you with that. I'm not Doctor Kevorkian. I can't let you go home to die." He tried focusing on his commitment to extending hope and possibility for people who were suffering, like her. But she was in so much agony. Would she be better off not suffering any longer?

"It's too hard being here," Lori moaned. Her eyes were half-slits staring far away, swollen with tears. "I have to leave!" she gurgled, wiping her nose with a soggy tissue and gasping for air.

Instead of frustration, Henry felt a wave of inspiration, got out a blank prescription from his pocket and took several minutes to compose a message. When he finished writing, he extended his hand to her, presenting the scrip.

Curiosity drew her attention out of her rainstorm of tears. Lori peered out from her gloom to see what he was now offering. She eyed the paper and clumsily slumped from the bed to the floor, using her hands to cushion the downward drop. She brushed a clump of hair away from her eyes, then shook away the several strands that fell out into her hand. She inched forward two or three feet, creeping like a paraplegic toward Dr. H's outstretched arm and beckoning eyes. Stopping at his feet, she reached up, grasped the prescription, and brought it to her eyes.

"What is this?" She sighed suspiciously, conserving her deathly low energy reserves. She brought her knees up to her chest, hugging her origami-like body with her arms and studying the small square-shaped piece of paper. She struggled to focus on the printed handwriting, straining to make sense out of the strange new words and sentences that appeared at the edge of her mental fog.

Henry watched hopefully as Lori read to herself slowly, mentally fingering the letters as if they were Braille:

1. ALL YOUR FEELINGS ARE IMPORTANT.
2. THERE IS NO "BAD" OR "WRONG" EMOTION.
3. YOU CAN HAVE ANGER AND NOT ASK FOR ANY FORGIVENESS.
4. THERE IS NO UNSAFE FEELING.
5. THERE IS NO UNSAFE FOOD.
6. ALL FOOD IS GUILT-FREE AND SHAME-FREE!

Lori shuffled her feet. *But I'm not supposed to have feelings, especially bad ones,* she thought. She couldn't even imagine what a good feeling was. People talked about being happy. But she wasn't sure what that really meant. She remembered laughing at Dr. H now and then, with his ridiculous grape-tossing show, but she couldn't imagine what she'd been thinking to act so inappropriately. And anyway, it was better to not risk letting feelings—any feelings—get in the way of behaving properly. She knew the risks. *Yesterday I was angry,* she thought, and winced as she recalled her verbal attack on Dr. H. It felt awful, and it was bad. Very bad. She looked at the words on the paper again. How could anger be important? She held her knees close to her chest, in front of her heart, puzzled by the threatening prospect of redemption.

"I…I don't understand," she said, turning her head toward Dr. H's feet as her tears began to well up again.

"What don't you understand, Lori?" He reached down and touched her forehead, perhaps to signal her to look up so that her world didn't have to seem so low.

"How can I have anger and not ask for forgiveness?" she asked, elevating her eyes. Her body was numb. All her life she had been trained to be meek, nice, polite, submissive, and conflict avoidant. Now it seemed that a lifetime of trapped emotions might spew like lava from every pore of her being. In her family, her home, her church, her community, you always had to repent for having bad emotions or thinking wrong thoughts or committing blasphemous behavior. Always. Trying to release a daunting layer of befuddlement, she lifted the wad of half-soaked tissues up to her nose and blew.

"Lori," Henry whispered softly. "You don't have to ask for forgiveness. You don't have to beat yourself up with anger, guilt, and shame."

She stared blankly at him, as if he were from outer space.

"You don't have to ask for forgiveness," he repeated again, knowing she was still struggling to grasp this simple concept in her emaciated state of body and mind. He loosened his tie and unbuttoned his collar.

"Lori, you can actually experience emotions without conditions."

Emotions without conditions? What planet does he come from? How does that work? Emotions always had conditions and consequences in Lori's solar system. *How can he teach such rubbish? He's not making any sense.* As she struggled to comprehend what he was saying, her mind spun out in a tailspin of doubt. *How can there be no unsafe food or no unsafe emotion?* Lori flipped the question over and over again, turning the unsolvable riddle-filled prescription up and down, left and right, inside and out, with no clue how to solve the mystery it posed.

There were all sorts of rules around food. Rules had to be obeyed, or there would be hell to pay. Didn't he understand? Food was terrifying. How could food be safe? Her body rocked with confusion. The prescription fell to the floor. She folded her arms around her waist, grasping at nothingness. She was dying to know what the prescription meant. To her it was a jumble of nonsense.

Clock time marched forward. Henry pushed down on his thighs through the silence and rose to leave, taking an extra amount of time to support Lori through her mental fogginess.

Still on the floor, Lori picked up the prescription and held on to it for dear life—as if it was a key to unlock one of the many gates of her inner prison. She fearfully glanced up at him as he quietly put a finger to his lips, silencing her noisy mind.

As he left quietly, he waved sweetly, and gently closed the door behind him.

18

The F***ing Rules

November 21, 1998

ONE DAY THE following week, Lori stood at the entrance of her room, rocking back and forth—one small step forward, one backward, one tiny step to the left, and one to the right. Her arms held tightly to her sides, she was getting nowhere, though her door was wide open.

"Dr. Kaplan, what in God's good name is Lori doing?" Carol, the charge nurse, asked.

Henry looked up from Lori's chart, on which he was writing a daily progress note. "Believe it or not," he said, "Lori is wondering if she can make it through the doorway. She perceives herself as too fat to pass through. In her reality, she weighs a ton and cannot see how extraordinarily thin she is. She keeps starving herself so she can just disappear, but she can never get thin enough."

Carol just shook her head.

On his way out, Henry stopped and walked back to where Lori stood rocking back and forth in the doorway. "Lori," he said. "Would you do me a favor and write down a list of your rules for eating?"

Lori stopped rocking. "Why do you want me to do that?" She had never thought about her rules for eating. There was no list. She had simply taken for granted her body's unique and special needs, which obviously justified her behavior.

Henry shrugged his shoulders. "I suppose we might learn something." He didn't want her to think too much about it.

The next day, she handed him not one list but two—crafted as if they were going to be meticulously scrutinized and graded. Henry eased himself into the chair in the corner of her room. The first thing he noticed was that she had one set of rules for when she was in the hospital and another set for when she was at home.

Lori fidgeted, too self-conscious to sit, choosing to stand as Dr. H examined her list. The rules, in her letter-perfect printing, read:

Rules (while in the hospital)
1. I deserve only shredded wheat (aka shredded shit).
2. It must look like mush.
3. It must not exceed 600 calories per day.
4. I must look down when I eat.
5. I must sit alone.
6. I can only put water on it.
7. If I break rule #6, it must be limited to only 3 drops of nonfat milk.
8. I cannot enjoy it.

Rules (at home)
1. I must only eat five foods per day.
2. It must be the same five foods.
3. I must wait until four to eat, no matter how hungry I am, no matter how much my stomach hurts, no matter how dizzy I get.
4. These five foods must not exceed a thousand calories per day.

5. They must be eaten in the same order and the exact same size portion. I must measure the portion to not make a mistake.
6. These foods can be cut up in very small portions, the same way each day, to make the foods last longer.
7. The feeding must be over in half an hour, or by four-thirty.
8. These foods cannot touch each other.
9. I must look down always when I eat.
10. I must sit alone.
11. I must wait twenty-four hours for the next feeding.
12. If I break any of the above rules—#1 through #11—I must fast for twenty-four hours. If I break rule #4 and exceed the calories limit (even by a few additional calories), I must fast for seventy-two hours.

*If I do not adhere to rules #1 through #12, I must commit suicide.

Folding the two pieces of paper together, he flicked them like a wobbly paper airplane onto the spare bed. He noticed a yellow plastic baseball bat standing in the corner of the room. One of the other patients had given it to Lori weeks earlier as a symbol for her to step up to the plate and hit a home run for her health.

Lori rocked back and forth by the head of her bed, a hand on her waist, her eyes riveted on the floor as if it might cave in right under her. Accustomed to hiding, she had dared to put words to her terrifying thoughts and behaviors and now felt incredibly naked.

Henry sprang up from his chair. Lori flinched and moved closer to her bed.

"Do you like these rules?" Henry asked. He tossed out the question like he was lobbing a softball for her to hit.

"No," she said meekly.

He felt like she had unconvincingly tapped the ball he'd tossed. "Say it like you mean it."

"No," she repeated, this time with an additional ounce or two of conviction.

Henry puffed out his chest and threw his shoulders back. This time it was a fast ball he fired at her, shouting, "I hate these fucking rules!"

Lori's jaw dropped. *He used the* F-*word.*

Seeing her reaction, Henry replayed his sentence with even more gusto, "I hate these fucking rules!" The veins on his temples bulged.

Lori shivered. Dr. H has broken a serious rule. That word was never allowed. But there he was, using it.

He quietly motioned toward the folded papers on the bed and implored once again, "Do you like these rules?"

"No!" Lori said, with more passion this time.

"Then say it. Say, 'I hate these fucking rules!'" He took a tiny step forward, inching his way into her fear.

"I can't," she whispered with conviction, moving back an equal amount.

"Why not?"

"I don't know." She shook her head hard. "I can't. I never said that word before."

"Never?" Henry acted incredulous. "What would happen if you did?"

She didn't answer. Maybe it wouldn't matter if she did say it. She was already living in hell. So what if she broke another rule? "Okay. I hate these fucking rules," Lori mumbled.

"Say it like you mean it."

"I hate these fucking rules," she said a little louder. She lifted her head and pulled her shoulders back, trying to force herself to meet his enthusiasm.

Henry grabbed the plastic baseball bat, raised it over the hand-written rules and brought it down with a decisive whack. "I hate these fucking rules!" he roared.

Lori stepped back several inches.

"Wow!" she cried out jubilantly. She opened her eyes wide, her cheeks flushed with excitement.

Henry pointed to the bat. "Now, you do it."

"No, no, I can't," muttered Lori, shrinking back, her hand inching involuntarily toward her ear.

"Why not?" Henry inquired relentlessly.

"I just can't." Her hand dropped back to her side.

"Okay then, let's do it together."

Lori hesitated. She felt trapped in a box with two uncomfortable choices—she could either join in the craziness or refuse Dr. H. Joining him felt less threatening. She placed her hands on the bat next to his. Lori eyed him, the bat, and their hands. She took a deep breath and held it. Dr. H raised the bat, four hands in the air, and they swung, bellowing in unison: "I hate these fucking rules!"

The bat snapped against the rules lying on the vinyl mattress. They rejoiced as Lori tapped her feet gleefully.

"Wow! That felt so good!"

Henry silently celebrated the girlish expression of joy on her face. He wrapped her hands around the bat once again.

Lori giggled and smiled wide-eyed as the vibration of the bat hitting the rules spread up through her arms.

"Now, you do it—alone," Henry urged, bolstered by her enthusiasm.

Suddenly she lost her confidence. She sank down on the edge of her bed, shaking her head. "I can't," she squeaked, dropping her chin to her chest.

"Go ahead," he said. "You can do it, Lori. I know you can."

She shot a glance at him, at the bat, and at the spare bed. She rose up tentatively and reached for the bat, lifting it up like it might hurt someone, and gently hit the bed, muttering, "I hate these fucking rules." To offset her own self-condemnation, she flashed her eyes at Dr. H for approval.

"Good!" He clapped vigorously. "Good, Lori. Now, do it harder, and say it louder, for Pete's sake."

She lifted the bat high up, pointing it to the ceiling, her arms steady. This time she brought it down with more force. It slammed into the paper and the mattress, sending an echo through the room.

"I hate these fucking rules!" she cried out. Her voice got stronger as she found her voice and her courage. "I hate these fucking rules!" She swung again. The bat came crashing down on the bed, harder and harder, carrying her anger with it. *It's okay to be angry! What a discovery!* "I hate these fucking rules!"

Henry watched like a proud father. He allowed himself to be cautiously optimistic. Maybe she was going to live through this after all.

19

Yes to Life

Thanksgiving 1998

TYPICALLY THIS TIME of year, Henry and Gabriella left town to visit his family, which meant he would not see Lori for five days. He knew that in her world five days would seem an eternity, since he was literally and figuratively her life support in the intensive care unit. He thought about telling her he was going to visit and comfort his mom, who was very much still in grief over the loss of his dad. But he knew that wouldn't be appropriate and could add more weight to her already emotionally obese state.

He tried to prepare Lori for his absence. They stood in the empty dining room of the hospital.

"Don't worry," he reassured her, knowing she couldn't help but worry. "I'll be back in no time. One of my colleagues will see you while I'm gone."

His words landed like a hollow pat on her aching back. She was used to him and felt safe with him. The other doctors who occasionally covered for him always made her feel like a bigger failure than ever. She was terrified. Five whole days he will be gone. Even though he was still standing right there in front of her, she already felt abandoned, as if she'd never ever see him again.

She paced around the empty tables, trying not to look at Dr. H as he stood nearby. Hours had passed since lunch, and dinner was still an hour away. She was safe from food for a little while. Despite her throbbing back pain, walking released a bit of her agitation.

Henry waited in respectful silence for her to go through her process. He recognized her pacing was a way for her to open up precious space in her constricted world.

As she rounded one of the tables, Lori stopped and stared at her pigeon-toed feet. In her mind she carried on an imaginary conversation with him. *What do you expect me to do?* She sat down in a chair and continued her silent, forbidden rant. *Well, here you're leaving and I have to stay behind in this rat hole of a mental-hell dungeon holding my disemboweled guts while you go on your little five-day family vacation in keep-the-location-secret-from-me-Thanksgivings-ville. What do I have to give thanks for? This living hell? Tell me!* She knew better than to speak such ruthless truths out loud. It was all she could do to manage the guilt of even thinking such awful thoughts. *My dear Lori, why is this such a big ordeal for you?* Dr. H replied in Lori's mental movie. *Don't you understand? When you're gone, there is so much pressure for me to perform. I have to look good and say the right things to please the other doctors. They don't understand me, nor do they care to. We both know my performances are always failures.*

Lori moved her gaze up from her feet and noticed that Dr. H seemed to be expecting her to say something. Minutes had passed since he had spoken. She squirmed in discomfort, her mind fighting to string together some words.

"Dr. H," she whispered timidly, risking a glance at his eyes.

"Yes, Lori?" He approached her table.

"Dr. H, you're not going away because you're sick of me? You're not leaving because you need a break from me?" She braced herself for the rejection she imagined was coming.

"Oh, no. No, Lori. This has nothing to do with you." He sat down in the chair next to her.

Lori was certain he couldn't understand the shame she felt at how pathetically inept she was.

He lightly touched her shoulder. "Dear Lori, I'm not trying to get rid of you. Don't you remember that I go to the east coast twice a year to visit my family? In the spring and in the fall." He placed his palm on his chest. "Please know in your heart, Lori, that even though it may feel personal, like I'm abandoning you, I'm not." He did his best to infuse every word with as much sincerity as he felt, but he doubted his words were getting through.

"I know it sounds funny," Lori said, "but it feels like you've had enough of me." Her face scrunched up with disgust at the idea that he was bolting.

"Lori, I will be back. I promise."

He must think I'm a baby.

After Dr. H departed, Lori felt a heightened sense of agitation. Her inner world was catapulting out of control. Everything inside her seemed to be moving so fast, yet she was going nowhere. Except down. She'd been barely eating before he left, and there was no way she could eat at all with him gone. The physical sensation of fear filled her body. Nothing matters. Nothing matters. Emaciated yet full, she began to fast.

Time slowed. She obsessively counted the seconds that made up each minute, and the minutes between the hours. Her mind seduced her into thinking that restricting food would make her feel safer and relieve the emotional weight that strapped her down. When even this didn't help to relieve the pain, she fell deeper into her crater of desolation.

Dr. H's colleagues stopped by to see her, but they couldn't begin to understand what it was like to be her. Nothing made anything better. She was a porcupine nobody could touch— not even herself.

* * *

Henry handed the airport shuttle driver a five-dollar bill and carried his suitcase up the driveway. Gabriella held the door for him, standing far enough aside to make sure they didn't touch as he passed into the front hallway. She followed him inside, picked up her blue cloth suitcase, and headed toward the stairs.

"Wait, Gabi, I'll take that for you," Henry said.

"It's okay. I've got it."

"I'm going to have a glass of wine. Do you want to join me?" Henry asked.

"Thanks, but no. I just want to go to sleep." She turned to look at him and started to say something more but didn't.

Henry watched as she walked across the landing into the guest room and closed the door. Then he took his coat off and headed to the kitchen.

As he opened the wine bottle, he reflected on how long it had been since he and Gabi had slept together. Despite seeing a marriage counselor, they seemed to be chasing the same old issues around and around again. Gabi was still trying to get him to fit into the traditional vision of manhood she had etched in her mind. The problem was, her vision bore little resemblance to the man he really was.

Henry had hoped their trip back east would be a chance to warm the chill between them. But that didn't happen. He and Gabi couldn't bridge nor hide the chasm that separated them. The trip had only brought their differences into stark contrast. He realized he just couldn't—nor did he want to—play the role of therapist in his own marriage.

He poured a glass from the freshly opened bottle, and let the calming scent of Pinot Noir quiet the restlessness in his mind.

* * *

Lori flitted around the nurses' station all morning. It seemed like Dr. H had been gone forever but he was supposedly returning. It was the Monday after Thanksgiving. "Have you heard when Dr. Kaplan is coming to see me?" she asked her assigned nurse. She dared not let anyone else know the secret name, Dr. H. She was the only one allowed to call him that.

"No, Lori, once again, we have not heard," said the nurse brusquely.

Lori retreated to her room, pacing nervously, her agitation overpowering her excruciating back pain. "When is he coming?" she said out loud, trying to keep her mind occupied. "He usually comes by noon," she said, answering her own question. But there was no confidence in her voice. She couldn't slow her pacing or her thinking or a flood of negative thoughts would break through. *He doesn't care about me. He's only seeing me because he gets paid.* The torment went on. *He is going to be quite angry. I've barely eaten a spoonful of shredded wheat all day. He'll know how terribly I've performed.*

She caught her fingers picking at her ears. She had not done that since the first time he put her on a high dose of Prozac. *I hope he doesn't see my ears.* It had started when he left, five days earlier. *I'll wear my hair over my ears.* Her skin felt like it was burning in all the old, raw places. All of a sudden, she heard three brisk knocks at her door.

She froze. Her heart caught in her throat. *He's here. Oh my gosh! Now what?* Panic set in. Tears followed. A hot flush filled her chest. She reached toward her bed for comfort and sat down, wishing she could hide under the covers. She had thought she'd be relieved to see him again, but she couldn't stop thinking he'd be mad at her.

He was.

He opened the door and trudged into the room, thinking about the nurses' disheartening reports of her decline over the past five days. As bad as he'd seen her in the past, he had never seen her quite like this. She was crying uncontrollably, slumped on her bed, her body curled tightly in a fetal position, her limbs pathetically gaunt and her skin ashen. Snot slithered from her nose.

Henry scanned the room, his jaw clenched. Piled on her desk were six unopened boxes of shredded wheat. Soggy tissues were scattered from her bed to the wastepaper basket under the desk several feet away. A white lily drooped atop her nightstand, dying from neglect.

She was a mess, and he was pissed. He ignored his urge to turn around and flee in disgust. The enormity of the situation was greater than his mounting fears of what would become of her if this continued.

"Lori, what do you need me to do?" The words rushed from his mouth uncontrolled. He could hardly believe it was his own voice. "Do you need me to be here three hours a day? Eight days a week?" He suddenly stopped, lowering his arms and getting control of his voice, reminding himself how important it was to appear confident and calm with his patients. "What is it you need me to do?" He stood close to the door, not really knowing what to do or say.

Lori rolled from her bed and fell to the floor gulping air and moaning. She couldn't talk. Her limbs seemed to scatter every which way. She didn't know, didn't care and couldn't have gathered herself together if she tried. Her body, mind, and spirit cried out in desperation and defeat. *I'm in so much agony!*

Her pain unexpectedly triggered something in Henry. He stepped forward and lowered himself to the floor, an arm's length from Lori's head. Crossing his legs, he sat in front of her crumpled shell of a body. He saw with absolute clarity how her whole being was drowning in pain. He saw how desperately she needed to be heard, how deeply she yearned to be understood, to be cared for, to be loved.

Like a bolt of lightning, her pain sparked a cloudburst of clarity. The heavens opened up. So did Henry's heart, raining streams of compassion around the storm of Lori's misery. All his judgment dissolved. Time stopped.

Without a word, he reached for her hands, hanging from the limp, lifeless appendages her arms seemed to have become. He gently grasped her trembling fingers and pulled her hands tenderly toward him.

Jarred by the physical contact, Lori managed to lift her head and turn toward Dr. H. She strained to focus through her flood of tears.

Henry peered intensely into the misty blue depths of her eyes. "You have a beautiful soul," he uttered softly.

The rhythm of her breathing slowed and calmed. "What?" she said.

He repeated what he'd said: "You have a beautiful soul."

She let out a deep wail. And then she seemed to be choking on her words.

"What is it?" Henry squeezed her hands to get her attention.

Lori tried once again to speak but all she could squeeze out was a stream of garbled sounds.

Henry took a deep breath.

"No one…ever…" Lori struggled to speak, her voice labored but growing ever so slightly stronger. "No one ever…told me that," she finally managed to say. A flood of tears washed away the painful debris of her past sorrow.

For a moment she felt a new sense of relief and freedom, something she had never felt before. The proverbial prison door of her past feelings of pain and shame and fear creaked open, if only just a crack.

"Say more," Henry whispered.

"I never," Lori gasped, "believed it was possible…"

"What was possible?"

Her eyes met his. *Me? A beautiful soul?* She teetered in a delicate balance between a descent into hell or a rise to grace. *With all my failures, disgust, and shame, could it really be true, as he just said, I have...a soul, a...beautiful soul?* She swallowed hard, considering this new yet dangerous idea. She tried to speak, drawing strength from the tenderness she saw in his eyes. Her voice was wobbly, but determined, hopeful. "I never imagined I could have a soul."

Like a fragile walkway across a wide gorge, a bridge of trust had formed that she only now dared to traverse. Perhaps she was willing at last to risk believing in herself, seeing how he unwaveringly kept still despite the ugly spill from the bottom of her pain barrel.

A warm light of hope flickered inside her—a beautiful light, an energizing light. *Maybe, just maybe, it's true...I do have a beautiful soul.*

She placed both of her hands over her heart, her whole being weeping in silent gratitude. Her mind rested for a few precious moments. *Maybe I'm going to make it after all,* she allowed herself to hope.

Later that day, Lori floated down the sunlit hallway toward the art therapy room.

For the first time since she had been on the ward, she felt drawn to join the other patients for what she'd always described in her own mind as *our daily, purportedly therapeutic, hands-on, art event.* Prior to her miraculous breakthrough session with Dr. H, when he said what he did about her soul, she believed doing artwork was silly and was only for patients who were truly losers. But that day Lori showed up on time, spotted some blue, green, and red paper, and asked to use the stencils. She politely sat herself down next to a younger woman emerging from a deep depression, and created a multicolored piece of artwork on a single sheet of green paper. She arranged nine beautiful letters into three profoundly simple words: YES TO

LIFE! Those three words were to become a driving force and a guiding compass on her evolving healing journey.

When she was done she examined her creation with awe and appreciation, like she was watching a butterfly open its delicate new wings. Ahh. More tension dissolved into a delicious flow.

YES TO LIFE spoke to her of possibility, as if her past were a dried-up creek bed that now had the possibility of becoming a rippling stream, a tributary of hope. For the very first time, in such an agonizingly long time, she felt a reason to live. YES TO LIFE. The words resonated with something deep in her heart.

That evening, she boldly added half of a banana to her box of shredded wheat. Even with her artwork concealed under her tray, she could feel the power of her three magnificent words.

20

The Healing Field

December 1998

DESPITE HER FRAILTY, Lori gained spiritual strength that day, and the next day, and in the days that followed. Her ear picking stopped spontaneously whenever she danced with the idea she had a soul. After nearly three months in the hospital, her will to live had emerged and was actually blossoming, nourished by her new sense of meaning and purpose.

"I have a beautiful soul," she hummed to herself as she walked the hallway, as she brushed her teeth, as she sat looking out the small window of her room. "I have a beautiful soul," she said out loud. YES TO LIFE sang out sweetly to her from atop the desk, where she proudly displayed her artistic manifesto. "I have a beautiful soul," she said, laughing, slapping her knees.

Lori's small but potent steps of progress were no longer negated by equivalent steps backward. Carried along by a new breath of hope, trips to the cafeteria were much less terrifying and her walk was less hurried.

One early December day, she and Dr. H headed outside for a stroll. "Lori," Henry said. "Let's do some exploring." They had just left the main entrance of the mental health unit, welcomed by a sun-streaked blue sky.

"What do you mean?" she said, expecting to take their customary circular walk around the hospital. Facing the brightness, she squinted at Dr. H, no longer needing to avert her eyes and avoid his gaze.

"Let's expand your comfort zone and stretch some boundaries. There's a field beyond the parking lot." He pointed to a grassy hill in the distance.

"Can we go up there?" she asked excitedly.

"Sure, come on." He motioned to her as he veered off the familiar path. They walked through rough, ankle-high brown grass until they reached the top of the rolling hill about a hundred yards from the hospital's main entrance.

"Wow!" Lori absorbed the full view of the spacious field, which boasted several palm and eucalyptus trees at its center. A row of dandelions danced in the breeze, patiently waiting for the next puff of wind to launch their seeds into flight.

"Follow me," Henry said, leading her to a tall eucalyptus tree. A flock of small birds took flight and darted into the deep green cover. A scattering of eclectic middle-class homes and one-story, cookie-cutter medical buildings lined the northern perimeter of the field. The hospital was now a matchbox-size dwelling in the distance.

"Let's have a seat," Henry suggested.

Lori sat down and stretched out her legs.

He sat across from her.

"Dr. H?" Her eyes were misty.

"Yes, Lori?"

"You know what?"

"What, Lori?"

"I don't feel so fat out here," she smiled as tears slid down her cheeks.

Henry's heart glowed. "That's nice to hear," he said. "Consider this the healing field."

"I love it," Lori moaned softly. "The healing field."

Out in the open field, she experienced a remarkable sense of freedom. There were no rules to adhere to, no hallways and doors to go through, no rooms or boxes to fit into. The profound worthlessness she felt on the hospital ward dissipated in the warm air like the floating dandelion seeds in the wind.

On the short trek back to the hospital, she paused by a pond where a duckling paddled to catch up to its mother, and watched as Henry continued toward the hospital parking lot. "Do you know how much I admire the way you walk?" she called to him.

"Huh?" He almost lost his footing.

"Well, it's the way you walk in the field, and the way you walk down the hall." She glanced at him to see if she should continue.

"What about it do you find admirable?" Henry searched her face for more clues.

"I mean, you look so comfortable in your space." She eyed the ducklings, now reunited. She was embarrassed by her forthrightness. Sometimes her mind wanted her to think he was showing off. Actually, though, she was jealous, and she wished she could experience such confidence.

"Thank you," he said. "Lori, how do you feel when you walk?"

She wiped her brow. "I've been having so much trouble planting my feet solidly on the floor when I'm in the hospital. And it's not because of my back pain." She rarely complained about her back, despite the fact that she took pain medication two or three times a day. "Sometimes I walk on the sides of my feet," she said with a cringe.

Then she sighed with relief that he didn't laugh or yell at her for being so ridiculous. She waved her hand over her shoulder in the direction they'd come from. "Out there in the field, it's easier."

"I see."

They turned and headed back toward the hospital.

"How come?" He wanted to encourage her to talk about this new awareness, to help her solidify it in her mind and perhaps supplant the dark memories that weighed her down.

"I feel so huge, especially in the hospital. I feel like I don't deserve to occupy so much space." A strong breeze came out of nowhere just as they reached the door.

"Lori, let your feet have the space they deserve." Henry opened the door and watched as she stopped at the desk to check back in.

"I'll see you tomorrow," Henry said.

The next day on their walk, Lori brought along a turquoise blue blanket from her room and spread it under the partial shade of the palm fronds. She knelt down and carefully swept her hands across the fabric to smooth out the stubble beneath it. She had also brought four bottles of water—just in case two were not enough—as her brain and body continuously broadcast the programmed unconscious belief: In lack we trust.

"Have a seat," she said, extending her arm proudly over the blanket she'd so carefully smoothed out in the grass.

"Nice job," Henry said, sitting down cross-legged on the blanket. Lori handed him a bottle of chilled water. Her face had an unusual softness, no longer strained by the mask of tension she typically wore.

"You know what?" he said, lifting the bottle to his mouth and letting a cool trickle of water slide down his throat. "I liked what you said yesterday."

Lori raised her eyebrows. "Really? What did I say?" Subconsciously mirroring him, she reached for her water but did not drink.

"I liked how you said you feel huge and that you feel you don't deserve to occupy space. You didn't say…" Henry jumped up. Deepening his voice for emphasis so he would sound like a villainous robot. "I am Lori. I am huge. This is who I am. I don't deserve to occupy so much space."

Lori laid back her head and laughed. "You're a riot."

Henry sat back down. "Maybe it's easier now for you to see more clearly how feelings drive perception and shape our reality."

She nodded, swaying back and forth, enjoying the movement.

"You see," he said, opening up his left hand as if to receive a gift. "On this hand are our feelings—the emotions that are present or that get triggered when we are in conflict or distress." Then he opened his right hand. "And on this hand are our beliefs—thoughts, judgments, conclusions—the stories we keep telling ourselves in our minds." He held his hands apart for a second and then suddenly locked them together tightly as if he were handcuffed. "Most of the time, feelings and beliefs are intertwined like this."

Lori's eyes stayed intensely focused on him. Somewhere deep inside she sensed impending danger, even though she knew there was none to be found out there on the blanket, talking to Dr. H. Still, something in the deep recesses of her brain told her to beware.

Henry saw the tension creeping into her body. An intuitive aperture opened, and the thought picture of a rope appeared in his mind. "Lori, can you imagine a rope, a large thick one with three strands?"

Lori's head bobbed up and down.

"Think of one strand as being our physical body."

"Uh-huh," she said.

"Another strand is our intellectual mind; that is, our thoughts, beliefs, judgments and conclusions. They can be conscious or subconscious."

"Okay." Lori put all of her energy into creating the images in her mind.

"And the third strand is our emotional mind; that is, our feelings or our emotions. Again, they may be conscious or subconscious."

She gripped her water bottle, her lips dry.

"Have a sip," he nodded to her bottle.

She brought the water up to her mouth and took a tiny sip.

"This rope with three strands," said Henry as he twisted an imaginary rope in the air with his hands, "gets real tight and twisted up—real quick." He grunted. "Your body and your thoughts and your feelings get tangled all up. Do you get it? Can you see the relationship?"

Lori furrowed her brow. Her chest tightened and her breath slowed. Unable to sort through these simple yet complex ideas, her body hardened like a statue. She felt stupid.

Out of the blue, Henry jumped up and began running around Lori in a circle, ten feet or so from her. "Is this how your mind acts? Does it run circles around you?"

Lori rose to her feet. "Yes," she cried out. "Yes! That's exactly what my mind does." *How does he know? He seems to know exactly how my mind works.* It amazed her. *He knows me so much better than I know myself. Does he also know how much I wish I could run, too?* Lori would give anything to be free from her back pain—for just a day, or even a few hours.

* * *

Prancing around the hospital's magical and spacious backyard, Lori experienced a profound sense of openness and freedom she had never felt before, as if she were a caged bird released after years of captivity. She forgot to hate her painful back.

One sunny afternoon, as she and Dr. H sat near the majestic eucalyptus tree, a hummingbird appeared, hovering in midair. Lori gasped in delight as she lifted her head high, entranced by nature's delicacy. She threw Dr. H a furtive glance, reassured that he too was enjoying this amazing spectacle. As swiftly as it had appeared, the hummingbird darted away, fading in the cover of a distant tree.

"Did you see that?" Lori pointed with wonder toward the foliage a dozen feet away.

"I sure did." He smiled enthusiastically, encouraging Lori's expanding expressiveness.

Emboldened, she turned back to him, straightened her short-sleeved yellow blouse, and blurted out, "Dr. H, will you fly me?"

Her father, who had owned several small private airplanes when Lori was a child, would take her and her siblings up high in the sky on special Sundays. She didn't mind that her brother always got the front seat—she loved to gaze down at tiny trees and houses, imagining a picturesque harmony found only in fairytale endings.

A bee whizzed by. "Fly you?" Henry muttered under his breath as little sparks of anxiety jumped in his chest. He squinted silently at the clear blue midafternoon sky.

"Will you fly me?" she repeated, her eyes widening. She stood above him like a stripped winter tree, casting a thin shadow onto the blanket.

Henry cleared his throat. "What do you mean?" His senses were on high alert.

"You know," Lori said. "When you were a kid, did your dad ever lie on his back and lift up his legs and let you jump on his feet so you'd fly in the air?"

Sure," he said. He had no idea where she was going with this, but her face radiated sunshine.

"Could you fly me?"

"You mean right here, right now, in the field?" Henry tugged on his earlobe, stalling to integrate this new information. What if someone saw him…flying Lori. He tried to imagine it, incredible as it sounded. It would definitely be a violation of protocol. In all his years of medical training, there were definitely no flying sessions with patients. He had never flown a patient in his life. They didn't give out flight manuals in medical school. He scoped the field for whistleblowers, like a centurion scouting for spies. No one else was around. Good. What to do? His conservatively conditioned mind made a strong suggestion: He should take flight himself. He should flee.

Lori's chin dropped dejectedly, her enthusiasm vanishing with Dr. H's hesitation. She felt stupid. And her body felt heavy again. "Maybe I'm too fat," she said, backing away from him as he sat on the grass atop the blanket, wondering what to do.

She wandered off several yards, shuffling back toward the hospital. Her mind began to unravel from rejection.

"No, no, no," Henry called. "Come back, Lori." He rose to his knees. "I'll fly you damn it."

Lori spun around hopefully. "Really?" Her eyes threatened to fly out of their sockets. "You'll fly me?"

"Yes. Come on."

He lay down flat on the blanket, surrendering to the heavens above. His mind flashed on a verse by Jelaluddin Rumi, the thirteenth-century Sufi poet:

Out beyond ideas of wrongdoing
and rightdoing, there is a field.
I'll meet you there.

The healing field. Come fly with me. No longer concerned if anyone caught him in this simple act of loving, compassionate care, Henry lay back, bent his knees and transformed himself into a human flying machine.

Lori leaned over Dr. H's welcoming size-eleven feet. She stretched out her arms like wings and filled her lungs with a breath of inspiration. Counting down silently she took a small leap and sprang into the air. Actually, it was a huge leap. She lifted off the unstable yet familiar ground of her rigidly controlling past into a present of uncertainty. She took a courageous leap of faith and trust. She took a quantum leap.

And so did Henry. No longer just a doctor or a man bent on fixing broken minds, he had become a healing partner and a human spirit who recognized another human spirit beyond the fragile yet stubborn ego shell. He reflected back to her a belief and a potential in herself that she had never imagined existed...until now. And not so strangely, she had a similar impact on him. Like two mirrors placed facing one another, the possibility for growth and expansion became infinite.

Lori's stomach landed squarely on Dr. H's feet. Her arms extended out from her frail trunk like a human cross suspended in air. A warm breeze lifted her spirit higher and higher.

"I'm flying!" she cried with delight. Her body radiated freedom and joy.

Tears streamed down her cheeks and fell like raindrops to the ground.

When the soul lies down on that grass,
the world is too full to talk about.

Her mouth opened softly. "Thank you," she whispered. "Thank you." Her spirit breathed new life as she sang out the words, "Yes to life!"

Out in the healing field, the feeling that something was missing, a feeling that had been there for such a long, long time, wasn't so strong any more.

The eucalyptus tree seemed to laugh joyfully.

The miracles were just beginning.

21

Knight Mare

December 1998

"**Y**OU DID WHAT to her?" Dr. Rosen's dilated pupils reflected alarm.

"I flew her." Henry instantly felt a pang of regret for confiding in Susan.

"You *flew* your patient? Do you have any idea what you're doing?" Susan was fuming. "What do you think you are, a knight in shining armor, for Christ's sake?"

Henry stared back at her with an equal and oppositional force. "I'm sorry I said anything to you."

"Listen to me," Susan grabbed Henry's shoulders. "Your judgment has become impaired. You're enmeshed in a sado-masochistic relationship you think you can fix by fulfilling a rescue fantasy." Susan's nostrils flared. "What are you trying to do? Give her the breast milk she didn't get as an infant?"

Henry brushed her hands away from his shoulders. "Don't give me your Freudian bullshit. She was going to die if I acted like a typical shrink and didn't give a rat's ass about her."

Susan's face turned bright red. "Oh, yeah? Is that right? Is that what you're going to say to the Medical Board of California? They're going to ask you where the hell you got your pilot's license, Doctor Kaplan, 'cause they sure as hell don't teach us to fly patients in Medical School."

Henry felt his temporal arteries pulsate. "Why don't you leave me alone?"

"I'm trying to help you stop your subconscious sabotage." Susan was panting. "You get loose in your boundaries with your patients, and then you know what's next?"

Henry couldn't suppress his agitation. He lunged at Susan, grabbed her cheeks and thrust his tongue deep in her throat. Susan fell to the ground. Henry collapsed on top of her.

Suddenly he sprang up in bed. A nightmare! Holy Shit. Henry gasped for air. Was Susan right? Had he gone too far? Did he kiss Susan? No. He questioned himself further. Was he violating Lori's boundaries or his oath as a doctor? No. She'd have been dead if he didn't dive deep in her pain, if he didn't care, if, as Jung said, he wasn't "affected." Was there a difference between violating boundaries and crossing them with carefully measured consideration? Surely there were times when the risks of crossing the boundaries were less dangerous than the risk of staying locked inside the box of professional protocol.

Henry replayed the events of that day in his mind. Of one thing he was certain; he had not done what he'd done naïvely, nor to satisfy his own selfish whim, nor had he been playing out his own fantasies of his relationship with his patient. Rather, he had sensed a moment when the trust he had carefully nurtured in their relationship was so solidly established that neither of them would mistake the other's intentions.

He recalled a line from a poem by Anais Nin: "And the day came when the risk it took to remain tight in the bud was more painful than the risk it took to blossom." Henry smiled inside.

22

Back Healing

January 1999

NEARLY FOUR MONTHS had passed since Lori entered the hospital. Other patients had long been discharged and new ones were coming in, but Lori still remained an inpatient. Therapy however, was no longer the energy-draining battle it had been for so long. Now when she breathed, she truly felt inspiration. Her mind clung to the yes to life affirmation, holding on with a determined but still slippery grip. And though her progress was real, she was still emaciated and emotionally fragile. Often she didn't shower or groom herself for days.

Henry noticed she wouldn't look at herself in the mirror. Ever. She avoided the mirror at all costs. All the years of stuffing dense feelings of guilt, shame, and self-hatred into her body continued to have the effect of deceiving and distorting what she saw.

Whenever Lori saw her reflection, she saw an enormous Pillsbury Doughboy, carnival-mirror hugeness that terrified her. She was still obese with shame. She couldn't yet shake the grip her weighty emotions had on her body.

One afternoon, Henry flashed back to a work-out session with Darla several years earlier. "Lori," Henry said. "Can you look in the mirror and say, 'I love you'?"

"No," she said, squirming in her chair. *Is he crazy? Of course I can't. If he saw what I saw, he wouldn't ask.* She wondered what he was up to. "There's no way I can do that," she said.

Henry led her to the bathroom in her hospital room, where there was a mirror above the sink.

She paused. It didn't feel safe.

"Come on in. It's okay," he said.

She entered cautiously and stood at his side, looking only at him, being very careful not to look in the direction of the mirror.

"Look in the mirror, Lori."

"No," she whispered. "I can't."

"Yes, you can, Lori. Look at me in the mirror."

Very cautiously and very slowly, she shifted her eyes to his reflection, taking care to not look at herself. Then, with a sigh, she looked straight at Dr. H. His eyes were on hers.

"Watch," he said.

She looked as he shifted his eyes and stared at his image.

"I love you," he said, gently. "I love you."

Her eyes widened. *Maybe if he can do it, maybe one day I'll be able to, too. But not now, no way.*

"Now it's your turn," he said.

She felt a huge tug of resistance. *I can't. It's not safe.*

Dr. H read her mind. It wasn't hard to do. "Okay, let's do it together."

Lori spoke to his reflection in the mirror. "Dr. H, I need help. Will you, would you hold my hand?"

He smiled inside and took her hand in his. Ever so gradually, she shifted her gaze from looking at his image to looking at her own. Amazingly, she didn't look so fat now. She wasn't grossed out. Still, this was scary. *How can I possibly say I love myself?*

He observed her trepidation as she continued to look at herself. She was barely breathing.

"I love you," he said. Then he repeated it.

The third time, Lori joined him. "I love you," they said in unison.

She quickly looked back at Dr. H. *This is exciting. I didn't think I could do it.* She wasn't terrified—at least not while she was holding his hand. *I did it! Well, with his help, anyway.* It was strangely exciting. She even felt a tiny bit proud of herself.

"Good job," he said.

Lori had an intuitive flash. "Dr. H, can you kiss yourself in the mirror?"

Henry hadn't ever thought about kissing himself in the mirror. "Sure," he replied. Inside, he applauded Lori's challenge. He let go of her hand, released his own self-judgment, then slowly stepped up to the mirror and kissed himself, matter-of-factly, on the lips.

Lori stood up on her tiptoes for a delightful second, then came right back down with a bounce.

Henry stepped back and looked at her. "Now let's do it together."

"Okay," she said, and took his hand.

They looked at themselves in the bathroom mirror and then, simultaneously, stepped up to it and kissed themselves.

He let go of her hand. "Now you do it yourself, Lori."

She looked at herself for a long moment, getting ready to take a huge step. Then, all by herself, all alone, she stepped to the mirror and kissed herself.

* * *

"Okay, great," Gabriella told the caller on her phone. "And you said his office is in La Jolla? Sounds good. As I said, I just think we've reached an impasse. The only thing I can think of is to make a switch. I'll give him a call first thing in the morning. Thanks, Francine…yeah, I'll see you Monday."

Henry closed the front door behind him, tossed his keys on the table, and followed the sound of his wife's voice. She sat cross-legged on the floor in front of the couch, the telephone directory in front of her and a legal pad on her lap. As he walked into the room, she scribbled some notes on the pad. Then she looked up with more enthusiasm than he'd seen in her face in a long time.

"Oh, good, you're here," she said, motioning him in.

He liked feeling welcomed by her, something that had become a bit of a rarity. "What's up?" he asked as he sat down next to her.

"I just got off the phone with Francine, my thesis advisor. She gave us a referral for a new therapist, Dr. Todd Mason. Francine went to school with him. They both went to Menninger's, so he's got really good credentials. It sounds like he'd be a good fit for us."

Henry cleared his throat. "But Gabi, what about Beverly? We've been seeing her all this time—someone *you* chose— and the issues we were facing when we started therapy haven't changed. We talked about that just last week. Why do you want to start over with someone new?"

Her face darkened. "I just think someone else might help us find a way to get back on the same page. Maybe working with a male therapist will help you understand what it is that I need from you."

Henry picked up his wife's hand and cradled it in both of his. "Hon, I understand what you need from me. The problem is, I can't be who you want me to be. If I tried to do that, it would be impossible for me to become all that I can be. Seeing a new therapist isn't going to change that."

Gabriella leaned over and pressed her head against his shoulder. He put his arm around her, pulling her close. He felt a deep, dull ache inside his chest.

After a few moments Gabriella pulled away, tears streaming down her cheeks. "So maybe…maybe this happily ever after of ours isn't going to work."

Henry felt the raw truth of the moment and it warmed him. "Maybe you're right," he said. He brushed his thumb lightly across her cheek, wiping away a tear. She reached up and wiped away one of his. Then they wrapped their arms around each other, and for the first time in a very long time there was no fear, no frustration, between them.

* * *

A few days later, Henry remembered the experience he'd had with Mariette, the intuitive healer Darla had referred him to. That became an impetus for an experiment with Lori.

"Do you mind if I try something on you?" he asked Lori. "Can you sit in the chair with your back to me? I'll be behind you."

No longer as tentative as she had once been with him, Lori agreed. She moved from the edge of her well-made bed to the chair near the pine desk.

Henry moved behind her. "Can I put my thumbs and fingers on your spine?"

What an odd request, Lori thought. But then she changed her mind. *I can be open. okay. What if love?* "Yes, Dr. H," she said. "Do whatever you need to do."

Henry slowly and carefully placed his thumbs and two fingers on her cervical vertebra at the top of her neck. He closed his eyes and took a breath.

Lori closed her eyes as well. Then her breath began to be in sync with his. Two breaths became one.

After several moments, Henry spoke. "Dear God, dear Creator, dear Spirit, dear Universal Being of Love." He drew in an expansive breath. "May the tension, the pain, and the stiffness be removed, released and cleared from Lori's spine." He took in another deep breath. "May the strength in Lori's spine be restored and reenergized to allow her to have more freedom, mobility and range of motion."

Yes, yes, yes. Lori whispered in her mind. *Yes, yes, yes.*

Henry gently moved his thumbs and fingers slowly down each of her vertebrae, from her cervical spine to her thoracic spine. As he stopped by each one of her vertebra, he delivered another version of the prayer, or affirmation, that came to him spontaneously.

Yes, yes, yes. Lori whispered in her mind, in her body, in her spirit. *Yes, yes, yes.*

Henry continued to guide his hands down her lumbar spine to her sacrum.

Lori didn't know what he was doing. She only knew the word *yes* flowed through her each time he touched one of her vertebral bones.

Henry didn't really know what he was doing, either. He knew only that he was acting from his heart with an intention of healing.

When he finished, Lori stood up with her arms outstretched. Neither of them said a word. There was nothing to say.

The next day, she was overflowing with excitement.

"Dr. H, look!" she exclaimed joyfully as she squatted up and down. Her arms were outstretched, as they had been twenty-four hours earlier, only this time she was bending and squatting, something she had not been able to do for years.

Henry stared in disbelief. Then he consciously released his expression and became poker faced.

Lori on the other hand, was laughing and weeping at the same time. "No more back pain," she cried, as she continued to bend, squat, and stand with ease. "No more back pain!"

He had never seen her demonstrate anything close to this level of flexibility in all the years he had known her.

"No more back pain. Can you believe it?" She began giggling. "After you left yesterday I stood up with my arms outstretched for about fifteen minutes. Like this." She demonstrated. "It felt like my whole body was electrified—in a wonderful way. Like there was a current going through it. And then when it stopped, there was no pain. And I could bend like this." She demonstrated again. And again. "It's a miracle."

Henry wondered what happened. The doctor and scientist in him wanted to know. Was this a cathartic reaction, a letting go of accumulated distress or pent-up emotions? Was this some kind of spontaneous remission? Was it the power of belief, or wishful thinking? Who could know? His mind drifted back to Mariette's healing story with Max. Max had been an instrument that saved her from the death grip of scleroderma. He recalled Mariette saying that each of us has the potential to access the god force. Was love, indeed, all we really need?

Henry celebrated with Lori, clapping his hands for real, in gratitude, in wonderment, and with joy. Though whatever just occurred was truly profound, he knew there was more work to be done.

* * *

Martin Luther King Day, 1999

As soon as Dr. H walked into Lori's room the next day, she opened her closet and bureau drawers. She had something to show him. Stuffed in each of the drawers and in the closet were hundreds of boxes of bite-size shredded wheat, all unopened. Hundreds. Lori had saved them all.

"Oh, my God!" Henry stood looking around the room in amazement. He knew she had stored many boxes of the cereal she hadn't eaten, but he had no idea that there were mountains of them. "How many are there?"

"Four hundred nineteen." She looked at him expectantly.

"You're kidding?" He knew she wasn't. "You're not kidding."

"What are we going to do with all these?" Henry shrugged his shoulders.

Lori scanned the enormous collection. "I thought, well, I was hoping you'd know what to do."

Henry pulled a box out of a drawer and threw it across the room toward the trash can. It almost appeared to be in slow motion as the package of shredded wheat tumbled into the trash can with a dull thud. He picked up another box and tossed it across the room. It too tumbled into the trash can. Whoosh! Another thud!

Lori's eyes grew wide.

Before she could say anything, Henry said, "Let's put all the boxes right here in the middle of the room."

They gathered up all the cereal boxes into a huge pile. Then he spotted her yellow plastic bat and motioned for her to get it.

"Lori, you be the batter," he said. "I'll be the pitcher." He tossed a small cereal box toward her.

She swung and missed.

"Try again," he said as he lobbed another box her way.

This time she swung and connected solidly. The shredded wheat box smacked against the opposite wall.

They laughed and tried again. Lori sent one cereal box after another flying across the room. They traded positions. After several hits, Henry put the bat down and jumped onto the pile in the middle of the room, crushing boxes under his feet. "No more shredded shit!"

Lori joyfully followed suit, and the two of them continued jumping and stomping on the boxes like children, exclaiming, "No more shredded shit!"

Fortunately or not, as far as they knew, no one was watching this unorthodox therapy through the glass window of the door of Room 173. Did it look silly? It didn't matter. What did matter was that it was healing. Energy was being released, and that was good. Lori knew she would never eat another bite of shredded wheat again.

She was finally ready to leave the hospital. So was Henry.

And what a great day to go.

Free at last. Free at last.

23

Flying Tiger

October 1999

A YEAR HAD passed since Lori was admitted for what had turned out to be her most extensive hospitalization: sixteen weeks. To celebrate the one-year anniversary of her freedom, Lori contacted an old family friend. Steve Rayburn was a pilot, and she asked him to fly her to a special location. They took off from the commuter airport in Carlsbad. The steady rumble of the engine excited her. So many years had passed since she'd been in a small plane like this one. As a child, her fondest memories were sitting in the back of their father's four-seat, single-engine Cessna Skyhawk, flying over fields and mountains where she felt so free.

At exactly five minutes past noon, Lori spotted what she was looking for. She shouted through her headset. "There it is, down there."

Steve adjusted his aviator sunglasses. Lori moved as close to the passenger window as she could and embraced the view below. A cluster of buildings occupied a plot of land the size of a city block.

Steve adjusted the throttle as he made a shallow turn, circling the scene below. "This is what you wanted to see?"

"Yes! Yes!" Lori cried delightedly. "Not so much the buildings but the grassy area beyond the parking lot. Do you see it?"

"Yup. I see it," Steve said. He pulled back the throttle, slow-ing down the plane. From the corner of his eye, he saw a tear fly from Lori's eye.

* * *

The following day, Lori planned to join Dr. H on the men-tal health unit for a prearranged continuing education meet-ing with the staff. He had solicited an enthusiastic Lori to join him for a lunchtime in-service presentation, something he volunteered to do several times a year. Never, however, had he taken a patient with him as part of the talk.

"Remember," Dr. H had told her in his office two days ear-lier. "Just tell them what you've learned since you were there. They only knew you as the severely mentally ill patient who almost died."

"Are you sure, Dr. H? Maybe I'm too fat."

Henry gave her a look as if to ask, are you crazy? "Lori, you told me last week you weighed a hundred and seventeen pounds. "That's still way too thin."

"I guess I'm feeling nervous, like I'm afraid I'll fail." She shrugged. "Do you really think I can do it?"

This was good. She was identifying feelings. "It's got noth-ing to do with weight. You know that."

Lori nodded in agreement. "But tell me the truth. Do you think I can do it?"

"Of course, Lori. I know you can. I have confidence in you. And I'm very proud of you." They walked in together. Neither of them had been back to the hospital since the day she was released. Henry couldn't help noticing her rapid breathing as she took in the old sights, sounds, and smells of the institution she had come to know so well.

Fifteen or sixteen staff members were already there. Lori spotted Roselyn, Carol, Sandy, Kathy, and several other nurses seated at the tables. She also recognized the director of the unit as well as the dietician, the occupational therapist, the art therapist, and other support staff. Wanda, the ward clerk, caught her eye and gave Lori a big grin.

Lori followed Dr. H to the front of the room by the wall-size blackboard. She noticed him taking a piece of chalk and drawing a picture on the blackboard. *Is that a house?* she wondered. *Now what is he doing? He's adding...a dog.* Henry drew a circle around the dog and the house, then drew a forty-five degree angle across the circle. Suddenly, Lori's face broke out into a smile of recognition. A doghouse. He had drawn a doghouse with a line through it.

Dr. H eyed Lori: "You're no longer in the Doghouse," he seemed to be saying. She beamed back at him with a huge smile of recognition.

Henry erased the drawing. He scanned those assembled. "Thank you all for coming here. We have a special guest. I think everyone here knows Lori, but what I don't think you know, and what I want Lori to share with you, is how she got to where she is today."

"Lori, you look great," Roselyn said from her seat a couple of tables from where Lori stood. Several other nurses nodded in agreement.

Lori smiled. Then she looked at Dr. H, who gave her a thumbs-up.

She began speaking from her heart. "I was admitted here last October, exactly one year ago. But instead of remembering how suicidal I was at that time and how much I wanted to die, today I choose to celebrate, because coming here saved my life."

Everyone in the room became still.

Lori continued. "Yesterday, I arranged a plane ride, and when I got to the airport, the pilot asked me where I wanted to go. To the desert, to the ocean—where? I told him, 'I wanted to go here, right here.'" She pointed toward the sky.

Henry quietly stepped back and listened.

"And I started crying, up in the sky, when I saw the healing field behind the hospital, and I directed my loving thoughts to all of you, for what you did for me. Because I've had such an incredible healing.

"Let me start by showing you the world of anorexia that I was living in. At eighty-six pounds, I was horrifically fat. My terror was that when I died, they'd do an autopsy, would weigh me, and even though I would no longer be alive, it would be unbearable for me to know that my weight was written down somewhere, because no number would be good enough or low enough."

Sandy, the graveyard shift nurse, put a hand to her mouth in disbelief.

"I was too embarrassed to walk through a door like that one." She pointed to the double-wide door they'd all come through. "I was so ashamed. I didn't know how to do it. I thought I was too fat. That's how far gone I was."

Carol, the daytime charge nurse, nodded at the memory of seeing Lori stuck in her doorway.

"Before I would walk down the hall, I would peek out the doorway of my room to see if anyone was coming, because I was too embarrassed to be seen. I felt so despicably fat and atrociously ugly. And if someone did see me, I would bow my head, and in my mind I would be walking under the carpet so nobody could see me. Because that's how worthless I felt." Lori took a sip of water. "One thing all of you did for me, which I'll never forget, is you didn't weigh me."

Henry shot Carol a glance. She smiled, graciously.

"I had been at two of the best eating disorder centers in the country," Lori said with apparent ease. "Most of the emphasis was on food—eating six times a day, counting calories, being watched like a hawk, keeping our elbows on the table so we wouldn't hide food, getting weighed every day."

Lori looked at Dr. H. "Did I ever tell you they made us back into the scale when we got weighed, like cows, so we couldn't see our numbers?"

Henry nodded. "Moo, moo," he said with a straight face.

Lori cracked up, joining the others for a moment of laughter.

"But it was terrifying." Lori winced at the painful memory. "So it really helped that here you didn't focus on weight. That allowed me to learn what Dr. H was teaching..." Lori blushed. "I mean, Dr. Kaplan. Well, I call him Dr. H."

Lori noticed a big grin on Wanda's rumpled face.

"Dr. H was teaching me how to change my thinking from 'I am fat' to 'I am feeling fat.' From there it progressed to 'I am feeling emotions.' I had no idea about emotions. I had no idea all these emotions were hiding. He used to call fat an acronym for fear, abuse, and trauma. He was showing me that I wasn't feeling full because I felt fat, I was feeling full because I was stuffed with emotions from long ago that were causing me to feel physically ill. Real sick. Emotional sludge, he would say. He was teaching me that it was safe to release emotions. Stuff that I had buried for years, ever since I was a child."

Henry glanced at Lori. He was impressed. He'd never seen her this amazingly articulate.

"We also called it JFS," Lori went on. "Judgment, failure, and shame. That's what I got stuck in. JFS. I didn't know what that was. The stuff had amassed in my body until I felt—physically—like this huge person. I still feel that way when I get overwhelmed."

A pager went off, and the director of the unit got up and left the room. No one said a word.

"All this time, Dr. H and I were playing this really stubborn game with each other. He was standing in for me as if by proxy saying, 'You're worth living.' I was saying, 'I am not and I'm going to prove it to you.' And we both got stubborn. And he would take me over to the cafeteria, always buying me breakfast. I would just sit there. I couldn't touch it. I was even afraid to touch anything greasy, because I thought that the oil, like from a French fry, would enter into my skin and get me fat. That's how foods terrified me. And one day, when we were at the cafeteria, he sat there, and instead of saying you need to eat, he said, 'You know what?' He looked me in the eye and said, 'You deserve to live. You deserve love. You deserve to eat.' And that's the first time I ever heard anything like that."

Lori wiped a tear from her eye. "I didn't know I was hungry for something else. I didn't understand until another day in the cafeteria, Dr. H asked me something that began to excite me." Lori looked over to him. "Do you remember?"

Henry smiled and nodded.

Lori shifted her focus back to the others. "What if love? That was the question. What if love? I had never imagined such a question before. What if love? It made me realize how I was seeing everything from a lens of fear and doom."

Henry's proud grin filled the room.

"What if love? That question allowed me to release the torture I had always felt being the last one to talk to my sister before she died. But you know, I would not have wanted to be anywhere else in the world than with her that morning. I got to smile at her. She told me I was pretty."

A couple of the nurses were quietly passing the box of tissues around.

Lori took another sip of water. "I grew up in a church where they preached hell, fire, and brimstone three days a week. They drilled it into you that you're going to hell if you don't repent. I had to repent each and every service, and it was, and has been, extremely difficult growing up believing I would go to hell if I didn't follow all the rules."

Lori looked at the clock and noticed the allotted hour was almost up. No one else seemed to pay attention except Dr. H, who whispered to her, "Go on."

Lori cleared her throat. "What if love?" She pointed to Dr. H. "That was the question that allowed me to accept this man when he dropped to the floor at my lowest-low, held my hand, looked deep into my eyes, and said, 'You have a beautiful soul.' That was my YES TO LIFE. It was the most loving thing anyone could ever say to me.

"And because he saved my life, because you all helped me save my life, I owe myself a life. I started to realize I didn't need somebody else to help me or to love. I needed myself." Tears welled up in Lori's eyes. "I'm crying, but it's because I'm so happy."

Lori looked at Dr. H, then at the rest of the group. "Can I read two sentences Dr. H wrote me in the cafeteria?"

The room filled with a chorus of yeses.

Lori fished in her pocket and pulled out a napkin. It was brown and wrinkled, though meticulously folded. Lori unwrapped it with exquisite care, and began to read:

> God equals love, total, pure, unconditional, nonjudgmental, compassionate, loving, warmth, white light, nurturing, soothing, comforting, cleansing, purifying, love. Energetically healing, breathtaking, inspiring, blissful and joyful love.

"That's what I felt from you all," Lori said, placing her palm and the napkin on her heart. "This journey has been a miracle, and sometimes I feel like maybe, just maybe, I am a miracle too."

Henry, Carol, Sandy, Kathy, Wanda, Roselyn, and then everyone else in the fluorescent-lit room, spontaneously rose to their feet, eyes glistening with tears, and began applauding.

EPILOGUE

Out Beyond the Field

September 2014

L ORI EXAMINED HERSELF in the mirror on the wall of the entranceway to her new home. Her lips were remarkably red. She forced a smile. Then she burst into laughter. *I love my new red rouge lipstick*, she thought. The thirty-something brunette at the outlet mall told her this particular shade of red was called "We've Got to Talk." It was the best selling gloss for "bold and empowered women," she added. Lori giggled. *Just the right color for today.*

Lori's smile faded. Her eyes became misty. *I would never have dared to look at myself or put makeup on for so many years*, she reflected. *I have to be strong today.* She pinched off the moisture in her eyes with her thumb and forefinger, then fumbled in her purse for her sunglasses.

Lori was meeting Dr. H at an eating disorder facility in San Diego. He had responded enthusiastically to her suggestion she could help young women by sharing the story of her battle with anorexia. Today she was to be the guest speaker.

* * *

"I'm just coming to support you," he told her at their last session. She was seeing him on an infrequent basis. For "tune-ups," they had agreed.

"I'm ready to come out," she said to him on many occasions. "But I get scared, you know. Do you think I can do it?"

Dr. H nodded in that special way he had that assured her he really did believe in her. "Just be who you are."

"Who's that?"

"You know."

"Tell me." She wanted to hear him say it.

"You are," he paused and looked deeply into her eyes, "someone who has battled with what most people would call a severe mental illness for many years. And you are not only alive to share with them your journey—"

"Our journey," she reminded him.

"Yes, our journey. And not only did you survive the hell you went through, but you are also learning to thrive."

"Go on." Lori's ears were on high alert.

"You've worked so hard," he said. "To free yourself from the prison of judgment, failure and shame."

"JFS," Lori said reflexively. "I'm still working on it." JFS, Lori's unholy trinity, had less power over her.

"Yes. And you've worked extremely hard to accept and understand your family's inability to deal with Linda's suicide and acknowledge her life. Their religious convictions didn't work for you. And in working through your painful past, you've found a purpose in your life. You've found your soul."

Lori nodded.

"You've found the grace to forgive them, and you're continuing to find the grace to forgive yourself."

"I work on it every day," Lori said.

"I've witnessed your spiritual and psychological growth and how you've been able to embrace a loving God."

"Yes." Lori leaned forward. "I think I have."

"I've seen you practicing a lifestyle of letting go of conditioned judgments and fear-based emotions. Look how you cultivated a loving relationship with your son, broke free from a marriage that wasn't working and boldly went forth and moved into an active retirement community. Now you volunteer and help others."

"I do love my new home and new life," Lori said. "And look how you've grown as well."

Dr. H paused. "What do you mean?"

"So many things. Like years ago when you took your wedding band off and told me you got a divorce?"

"Uh huh."

"Then you met this woman, you called her your sweetheart, and one day, years later, you had another ring on your finger." Lori smiled broadly.

Dr. H smiled back. "You got divorced and I got remarried. How funny is that? Comedy is tragedy plus time."

Lori looked at him softly. Their eyes locked. "We've both seen a lot of light shine through the darkness, haven't we?"

"Yes," he said without blinking. "We sure have."

* * *

Lori put her sunglasses on. *I can do this,* she reassured herself. She looked at the mirror once again. *The glasses are on straight.* She headed to the garage and got into her yellow Porsche, a gift she gave herself after her divorce finally settled. She turned the ignition on, and for an instant flashed back to the time she wanted to die from carbon monoxide poisoning. She clicked the thought off as she pressed the garage door opener and backed out of her driveway. She turned down the street towards the automatic gate for residents to exit. Her license plate told the story in three simple words, *YES to LIFE.*

Acknowledgments

If this were a meal, I'd serve Lori a heaping portion of gratitude and appreciation. She deserves every bite. The magnitude of her pain and depth of her despair inspired me to face my powerlessness, challenged me to cultivate compassion, and helped open in me a portal of intuition. A second helping of deep gratitude goes to all my patients, who courageously entrust me with their wounds and stories and inspire me to become a better doctor, human being, and partner in the healing field.

To my editors Jan Allegretti and Hal Zina Bennett, know that I deeply appreciate your homage to the power of words. Deborah Louise Brown's multi-talented fertilizing effects on The Healing Field have been invaluable. I'd like to thank my sweetheart for her unconditional love, beautiful heart and awesome partnering in the field; my parents for their consistent caring; and those family members, friends, and colleagues who've given me support and encouragement over the years. And to the mysterious nameless force that's helped me climb this alluring mountain of quicksand called authoring as well as the journey of life, I bestow my humble reverence.

About the Author

Integrative psychiatrist Howard E Richmond, MD is an inspirational teacher and coach who greets people where they are and guides them to create their best life ever. His lessons about releasing judgments and hidden emotions introduce a new language that fuels and stimulates personal growth. To rejuvenate himself with creativity and face his own fears, he frequently performs stand-up comedy as the "Comic Shrink."

The son of a State Department Foreign Service officer, Richmond grew up in Japan, Thailand, and Brazil. Now he lives with his wife and their two German shepherd rescues in San Diego, California where he is a daily practitioner of hot yoga. He is currently working on his second book, *The Story Beneath the Story: The Power of Emotions to Harm or Heal.*

Meet Me in The Healing Field

Thank you for joining Lori and me in *The Healing Field*. I hope it has been an enriching experience. Some of you have been so moved by the story and in particular, Lori's courage, you've asked how to write her. Please go to TheHealingFieldBook. com if you are interested, and look for "letters to Lori."

For more lessons from *The Healing Field*, please visit my website, **HowardRichmondMd.com**. You can also meet me in our loving Facebook community – **Facebook.com/thehealingfieldbook** or on **Twitter.com/HowardERichmond**.

Please watch for my next book, *The Story Beneath the Story: The Power of Emotions to Harm or Heal*. You can keep track of the book's progress on Facebook.

Namaste,
Howard E. Richmond, MD

Made in the USA
San Bernardino, CA
22 December 2018